"Lucifer?" Poppy said, her voice unnaturally high. "As in…"

"Old Scratch, Satan, the Devil," Langham finished for her.

He'd wondered what would shock the unflappable Miss Delamere. It would appear his great-grandfather's exploits had done the trick. "If it gives you any comfort, I suspect there was little actual glorification of the dark lord going on. From what I've learned it was more an excuse for licentious behavior in a novel locale."

When he glanced over, he noted the pink tinge in Poppy's cheeks and wished anything but his family's misdeeds had put it there.

"Didn't the people in the village object?" Poppy asked, stooping to slide beneath a particularly thorny branch he held out of her way. "I can't imagine they were happy to welcome such goings on…"

But just as she did so, she stepped on a root and lost her balance, falling against him with a gasp.

"Careful," Langham said, grasping Poppy's arms as he felt her hands press against his chest. In their current position, with her standing just above him on the hill path, they were at eye level, and his gaze went unerringly to her plump red lips. She smelled of roses and something else— something citrusy and clean.

When he glanced up, he saw her lashes lower…

…and without even thinking, he tilted his head as they moved closer together, in the timeless preamble to a kiss.

A Spinster's Guide to Danger and Dukes

"The mystery unfolds effortlessly, delivering a slew of suspects, tantalizing clues, and danger around every corner without ever overshadowing the love story. This sensual romance will have pages flying."

—*Publishers Weekly*

"Compelling, evenly paced, and delightfully fun."

—*Kirkus*

"Collins keeps the heat smoldering between the well-drawn main characters in this installment, and the mystery keeps the pace moving nicely…[for] fans of Julia Quinn and Evie Dunmore."

—*Library Journal*

An Heiress's Guide to Deception and Desire

"After delighting readers with *A Lady's Guide to Mischief and Mayhem*, Collins is back in fine fettle with another fetching mix of sprightly wit, nimble plotting, and engaging characters that is certain to endear her to fans of historical romances and cozier historical mysteries."

—*Booklist*

"The mystery drives the action while the romance provides the heartbeat of the story, and the two weave together to create a well-plotted, entertaining tale for fans of both genres. Expectations and prejudice based on class and gender are scrutinized throughout, while the leads are

witty, fierce, bighearted, and easy to love…A successful and thoroughly enjoyable mix of mystery and romance."
—*Kirkus*

A Lady's Guide to Mischief and Mayhem

"A delectable mystery that reads like Victorian *Moonlighting* (with a good heaping of Nancy Drew's gumption)…*A Lady's Guide to Mischief and Mayhem* is wickedly smart, so engrossing it'd be a crime not to read it immediately."
—*Entertainment Weekly*, A–

"This book is proof that a romance novel can only be made better by a murder mystery story."
—*Good Housekeeping*

"Smartly plotted, superbly executed, and splendidly witty."
—*Booklist*, Starred Review

"Both romance and mystery fans will find this a treat."
—*Publishers Weekly*

"Collins blends historical romance and mystery with characters who embody a modern sensibility…the protagonists and setting of this first in a promising new series are thoroughly enjoyable."
—*Library Journal*

"Utterly charming."
—PopSugar

"A fun and flirty historical rom-com with a mystery afoot!"
—SYFY WIRE

A Spinster's Guide to Danger and Dukes

Also by Manda Collins

A Spinster's Guide to Danger and Dukes

MANDA COLLINS

FOREVER
New York   Boston

Copyright © 2023 by Manda Collins

Cover design by Sarah Congdon. Cover photo by Lauren Rautenbach / Arcangel. Cover copyright © 2024 by Hachette Book Group, Inc.

Forever
Hachette Book Group
1290 Avenue of the Americas, New York, NY 10104
read-forever.com
@readforeverpub

Originally published in trade paperback and ebook by Forever in March 2023.

First Mass Market Edition: January 2024

Forever is an imprint of Grand Central Publishing. The Forever name and logo are trademarks of Hachette Book Group, Inc.

The Hachette Speakers Bureau provides a wide range of authors for speaking events. To find out more, go to www.hachettespeakersbureau.com or call (866) 376-6591.

Forever books may be purchased in bulk for business, educational, or promotional use. For information, please contact your local bookseller or the Hachette Book Group Special Markets Department at special.markets@hbgusa.com.

Library of Congress Cataloging-in-Publication Data
Names: Collins, Manda, author.
Title: A spinster's guide to danger and dukes / Manda Collins.
Description: First Edition. | New York ; Boston : Forever, 2023. |
   Series: Ladies most scandalous
Identifiers: LCCN 2022047932 | ISBN 9781538725573 (trade paperback) |
   ISBN 9781538725597 (ebook)
Classification: LCC PS3603.O45445 S65 2023 | DDC 813/.62—dc23
LC record available at https://lccn.loc.gov/2022047932

ISBNs: 9781538725580 (mass market), 9781538725597 (ebook)

Printed in the United States of America

OPM

10 9 8 7 6 5 4 3 2 1

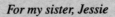
For my sister, Jessie

Content Guidance

This book, though primarily a romance, is also part murder mystery. As such, it contains off-the-page descriptions of violence and murder.

There is a very brief mention of attempted assault on the heroine, and one character is held captive for a time. The heroine's and her sister's mental abuse at the hands of their stepfather is mentioned at times. Some readers may find all of this disturbing.

The hero suffers from a mild form of claustrophobia but in keeping with the Victorian Era is undiagnosed and may refer to himself using ableist language at times.

All mistakes and unintentional insensitivities are my own.

A Spinster's Guide to Danger and Dukes

Chapter One

Paddington Station, London, 1867

Violence, regrettably, was out of the question.

Miss Poppy Delamere—or Flora Deaver as she'd called herself since arriving in London two years ago—had never been one to suffer fools gladly. And as she waited impatiently for the clerk manning the ticket window to finish chatting with the matron he was serving, she truly wished she could shove the older woman aside. Taking a deep breath, she tried to emulate her employer, the redoubtable Lady Katherine Eversham, who always managed to get her point across without resorting to rudeness.

At the thought of Lady Katherine, Poppy felt her gut clench with anxiety. What would the circle of friends she'd amassed during her time in London think when they learned she'd been hiding her true identity? She knew both Kate and her writing partner, Miss Caroline Hardcastle—no, she was Lady Wrackham as of this morning, Poppy reminded herself—championed the plight of downtrodden women, but how could they not be hurt by Poppy's deception?

She hated the idea of disappointing them, but it couldn't be helped. Nor could her flight from town now. Some things were more important even than friendship, and the bond between sisters was one of them. From the moment she'd read her sister Violet's name in *The London Gazette* that morning, Poppy had known she had to go to her.

"My Mary's family is from Dorset," the ticket agent said with excitement, while at the same time moving as slowly as humanly possible. "What a funny old world it is, innit?"

"What part, if you don't mind my asking?" the matron asked. "You must know Bournemouth, surely?"

Biting back a curse she'd once heard from a pressman at *The London Gazette*, Poppy clutched her valise tighter and waited.

The woman ahead of her was finally moving away from the window when Poppy felt someone lurch against her.

"Sorry, miss," the shabbily dressed man in a brown suit said, pulling his bowler hat down low as he hurried away. Poppy, intent on purchasing her ticket, didn't waste time replying.

"One for Little Kidding, Buckinghamshire," she told the agent, as she reached for the purse dangling at her wrist. But she realized even before her hand touched her arm that the cloth bag was no longer there. Oh no. Everything she'd saved, with the exception of a few pounds she'd put in the bank for safekeeping, had been in that bag.

"Miss?" the agent asked sharply.

Without bothering to explain, Poppy clutched her valise tight and took off running. "Stop! Thief!"

The station was busy with afternoon travelers and more than one person was thumped by her bag as she wended her way through the crowd, but she couldn't afford politeness at the moment. If she didn't get her money back, she wouldn't be able to afford anything for a good long while. Much less make it to Little Kidding to stop her sister from being hanged for murder.

And it was with Violet's plight in mind that she scanned the crowds for the familiar bowler hat and brown suit. Poppy was tall for a woman and was able to see above many of those in the crowd as she got closer and closer to the exit leading to Praed Street. If he managed to get outside, she'd never see her money again, nor would she make it to Violet in time to save her.

She'd just paused for breath when she spotted a brown serge–covered back disappearing behind a porter pushing a baggage-filled cart. Feeling a renewed burst of energy, Poppy set off at a near-run, shouting, "Stop! Thief! The man in brown stole my purse!"

For the barest moment, the man in the bowler looked back at her, and seeing she was gaining on him, he sprinted toward the doors leading to the street outside. Her quarry in her sights, but weighed down by her valise, Poppy called upon her every ounce of strength and threw herself forward. Her legs pumping until they burned, she could see he was slowed down ahead by an influx of travelers arriving at the station and felt a surge of triumph. She was going to catch him.

But her exultation was short lived.

One minute she was hurtling toward the man in the brown suit. The next she was brought to a sudden stop against a hard masculine chest. Cursing under her breath, Poppy would have disentangled herself and continued her pursuit if the man she'd run into, who was far taller and stronger than she, hadn't grasped her by the arms.

"I don't know where you're off to in such a hurry, my

dove," drawled a familiar baritone, "but I must insist you do so by going around and not thr— Oh! It's you, Miss Deaver."

Looking past the Duke of Langham, Poppy saw that the man she'd been chasing was long gone. On a sigh, she pulled back from the duke and scowled up at him. "Yes, it's me, Your Grace. And you've just cost me everything but the last few pounds to my name."

"Unless you were taking part in the world's most asinine foot race in order to win a wager," the duke said with a raised brow, "then I fail to see how that is possible."

"You would, wouldn't you?" Poppy demanded, noting not for the first time that it was one of life's great ironies that a man who looked so much like an angel should thrive on devilry. With his gold-gilded light brown hair, features that might have been copied from an Italian sculpture, and a body that owed much to his penchant for pugilism, he might well have made a bargain with the devil to obtain his good looks, though Poppy knew it was just cruel happenstance. "It would never occur to you that you might have your fortune stolen from you in one fell swoop. People like you have so much money, you very likely don't know how much. Well, not everyone is so gifted by fate, Your bloody Grace."

They were drawing a crowd, but honestly, Poppy didn't care. Langham, however, did care and was soon hustling Poppy out of the main area of the station and toward an antechamber where baggage was being collected. She wasn't surprised when he was able to send the clerk scurrying away with one pointed look. Men like the duke got what they wanted, even without speaking a word.

Once they were inside, she pulled away from him and collapsed onto a large trunk.

"I know you aren't particularly enamored of me, Miss Deaver," Langham said, his pale blue eyes narrow with puzzlement, "but that was a harsh outburst even for you. If I weren't so self-confident, you might have hurt my feelings."

"You'd have to have feelings in the first place for that to happen," Poppy groused, but it was half-hearted. She likely wouldn't have been able to catch up with the thief even without Langham's interruption.

Ignoring her barb, Langham pressed on, a lock of light brown hair falling upon his brow as he tilted his head with the question. "Now tell me. Who were you chasing after as if the hounds of hell were at your heels?"

The arrogance in his belief that she would answer him set her teeth on edge. And yet, if an answer would get her free of him she would gladly give it. "My purse was stolen. I was trying to get it back. And now if you'll excuse me..." Standing, she brushed off her gown and started to walk away.

"Not so fast, my girl." For the second time that day, Langham took her by the arm. "I have a few more questions."

She gave him a look that she hoped conveyed what she thought about his "more questions" and stared pointedly at his hand until he removed it.

"Now," he said, reaching into his coat and withdrawing his purse. "I presume you were here to catch a train. How much was the ticket?"

If it was possible, Poppy would have vibrated with indignation. "I don't need your money."

"I haven't offered you any yet," Langham said wryly. "But, if I did, how much would I offer you?"

"It doesn't matter because I won't take your money," Poppy said tightly. "Now, I really must be off. If you'll excuse me, Your Grace."

She heard the duke murmur what sounded like "pig-headed" as she stalked toward the door.

"I'm trying, Miss Deaver, to help out a friend if you'll simply look past your pride to see it."

That stopped Poppy in her tracks, and she turned to stare at him. "A friend? I don't believe a duke can ever be friends with an impecunious spinster, Your Grace." He'd made his opinion of her plain enough when they'd met earlier that week during Kate and Caro's investigation into the disappearance of a London actress.

To say he'd been dismissive might be overstating things, but his toplofty attitude and cutting remarks had made clear that he wasn't giving Poppy's theories—or Poppy—much thought.

As if she'd torn through the last of his patience, Langham cut a hand through the air dismissively. "Then let me pay your fare at least." When she opened her mouth to object, he continued, "You may not consider me a friend, but I consider both Lord and Lady Wrackham friends, as do you. So, while they aren't here to offer assistance, let me do so."

Then, to her astonishment, he spoke a word she suspected the Duke of Langham had never once in his adult life uttered before: "Please."

Joshua Fielding, Duke of Langham, wasn't used to making requests, and he'd certainly never considered himself a knight in shining armor. And yet, he felt an inexplicable need to come to Miss Deaver's rescue.

It was true she was lovely enough—assuming of course you looked past her unfashionable gown and abomination of a hat. Not to mention the way her fine features were downplayed by the way her guinea gold hair was bound at her nape in so tight a coil there was no possibility of a single strand escaping. Yet, despite her almost purposeful dowdiness, there was also a vulnerability in her slumped shoulders that tugged at some latent sense of chivalry within him. When they'd met he'd been pleasantly surprised by her lack of deference to his position. Indeed, her pointed remarks and quick wit had been refreshing. He disliked seeing her brought low by something as commonplace as a railway pickpocket. Especially when it was something he could so easily set to rights for her.

Still, it would not do to give her the wrong impression.

"Don't think this gallantry is part of a trend," he warned Miss Deaver. "I don't intend to make a habit of this kind of thing."

Her thickly lashed blue eyes rolled heavenward. "You mean acts of kindness? Never fear, Your Grace. I would never expect such a thing of you."

"Good," he said gruffly. "Now, come along with me and we'll get your ticket sorted. Where are you traveling to, anyway?"

Miss Deaver sighed but allowed him to steer her toward the door. "A small village in Buckinghamshire. You've probably never heard of it. Little Kidding."

Of course, that would be her destination. "I know it. As it happens, I'm going in the same direction. You'd better just ride in my private car with me. You'll be more comfortable, and there will be no danger you'll be accosted by a stranger." He hadn't missed the glances she'd received from the men passing by them in the station.

As he spoke, Langham reached down to take her valise and was rewarded with a scowl from Miss Deaver and predictable resistance to his gesture. "Who will save me from being accosted by *you*?" she demanded, clutching the bag to her chest.

He stopped, and they locked eyes for a moment. He tried to recall the last time he'd faced this much opposition from a woman, and failed. When she refused to blink first, he let go of the bag and tipped his hat. "Very well. If you don't want my help, then I will bid you good day."

He turned away from her and took a step toward the ticket counter. As he'd expected, she wasn't quite so stubborn as she made herself out to be.

"Wait," he heard her say from behind him. Turning back to her he raised a brow and gestured for her to continue.

"I don't mean to be churlish," she said, not meeting his gaze. "I simply am unaccustomed to accepting help from...well...from people like you."

He resisted the urge to pinch the bridge of his nose. "Dukes?"

"Men," she replied, raising those cornflower blue eyes to his, and revealing a vulnerability that he wasn't sure she'd meant to show him. "Not since I've come to London, at any rate. And not before that either, if truth be told. But I do appreciate your kindness."

As if it were a token of her apology, she held out her battered brown bag. He took it with a nod, and then they headed together toward the ticket agent.

Soon they were safely ensconced in the private train carriage he'd hired for his journey. It had been months since he'd been back to his family estate, and if he'd had his way he'd not be going there now. But it would not do to miss the dowager Duchess of Langham's annual birthday house party. He was quite fond of his grandmother, and though returning home to his country estate for the event would mean Grandmama would parade a half dozen or more eligible young ladies before him in the hopes he'd choose one for his duchess, he would endure it.

In truth, seeing how smitten his friend Val was with his new bride had roused an unusual sort of jealousy in Langham at their wedding yesterday. Not over Caro, who, while spirited and lovely enough, wasn't a temptation for him. No, it had been the connection between the newlyweds that left Langham feeling envious. Because he knew quite well that as appealing as Val and Caro's easy affection might seem, he was not made for that sort of easy intimacy. The realization had left him feeling wistful.

Which is why he'd determined to give Grandmama's bridal parade a closer look this year than he had in the past. He might not find the sort of happiness that his friends had, but perhaps a comfortable match would be possible. He only knew that the restlessness he'd been feeling of late was in need of a remedy and much as he disliked to admit it, he wasn't getting any younger. Much as he would prefer to put it off forever, he would like to marry before he was too old and decrepit to lift his children.

"Is this how you travel all the time?" Miss Deaver asked, interrupting his thoughts as she looked around the interior of the private car with wide-eyed shock. His luggage, which was a dashed sight more than one valise, had been stowed by his valet earlier, and the man himself was seated in the rear of the car, where he couldn't overhear them.

Langham frowned and tried to see his surroundings as she did, but couldn't understand her question. "It's much faster and more comfortable than going by horse and carriage."

"I don't mean by train," she said, her voice tinged with exasperation. "I mean, this." She gestured to the plush green velvet upholstery on the seats and the polished mahogany lining the interior ceiling and walls. "This sort of luxury."

"I'm a duke, darling," he said with feigned innocence, deciding to ignore the implied criticism of her words. "You can't very well expect me to ride in the cheap seats. That would be uncomfortable for everyone involved."

"It might teach you a little humility," she groused, frowning at the velvet seat as if it had personally wronged her. "Though you may have a point. I'd never considered that the other riders might find your presence upsetting."

"Upsetting" was putting it mildly. Langham knew from experience that his presence often made it impossible for even his fellow nobles to relax. Unless he was in the boxing ring, where all men were considered contenders, if not equals, then he was liable to set people on edge.

One of the reasons he was so amused by Miss Deaver, he realized, was that she didn't treat him like he pissed gold. She gave him a hard time of it, and it was refreshing.

"You may find it difficult to believe," he told her, "but inheriting a dukedom at a young age teaches one to be sensitive to the way your presence affects others." He'd found out soon enough when he returned to school after his father's funeral and discovered all his old alliances and friendships had shifted. Subtly in some cases, and drastically in others. But the change had happened, nonetheless. And his life had never been the same.

For the merest moment, he thought he saw sympathy in her eyes, but just as soon as it appeared it was gone. "I imagine it does," she said, glancing out the window, as if trying to evade whatever emotion his words had inspired in her.

Some imp of mischief prompted him to add, "This

is actually far more sedate than the usual fanfare that accompanies my travels to the country. I left earlier than scheduled, which means the customary battalion of footmen and various other servants who would have accompanied will follow tomorrow. What you see now is practically incognito by ducal standards."

Her eyes widened with shock. "But you are only one person. Surely it does not take so many servants to accompany a single man to his country house."

There was a hint of censure in her tone that set his back up. He hadn't been the one to invent the bloody aristocracy, for pity's sake. Sorry he'd brought it up, he changed the subject. "To whom are you traveling to visit in Little Kidding? Do you have family there?"

But even so innocuous a question did not pass muster with the contrary Miss Deaver. "I wouldn't have expected you to be the sort to pry," Miss Deaver said, pursing her lips.

"Do not fly up into the boughs. I'm merely attempting to take an interest in the life of my fellow man—well, woman, I suppose." Not that Langham could possibly forget she was a woman, and a deuced lovely one at that. She might be as prickly as a cocklebur, but his body didn't care about such niceties.

And when it wasn't her looks tempting him, it was the soft floral scent she wore, a blend of roses and just the barest hint of lemon that made him want to bury his face in her neck. It was a damned shame he couldn't do just that, but he only consorted with women who were willing.

He enjoyed his ballocks where they were, thank you very much.

Perhaps recognizing that she'd been harsh, she unbent a little. "My mother and sister are there," she said stiffly. "I hadn't made the connection with Langham Abbey, but it's near Little Kidding, isn't it?"

He didn't question how she knew the location of his primary estate. Anyone with a copy of Debrett's or a passing familiarity with the London gossip sheets would know.

"It is," he confirmed. "Though I don't recall a family by the name of Deaver in the neighborhood."

"That's because my mother remarried after my father's death." For a moment she stared down at her gloved hands, and Langham got the sense there was more to the story.

"I'm sorry for your loss," he said, thinking grief must have prompted her uncustomary reticence. "Were you very young?"

"I was three years old when my father died," she said, looking up at him, having regained her composure. "He was a vicar in a small village near Norwich. My mother remarried not long after and had my sister."

"And who is your stepfather?" he asked, sensing that there was no love lost between Miss Deaver and the man who'd married her mother.

Her laugh was bitter, and he was surprised by how much he disliked hearing that emotion from her.

"Lord Short," Miss Deaver said with a scowl. "If the truth be told, he's the primary reason I left home. And if I had my choice, I'd stay away. But my sister needs me. And however awful my stepfather has been to me, Mama and Violet did nothing wrong."

Try as he might, Langham couldn't recall anyone by the name Short in the *ton*. He was about to ask more about the fellow's title when Miss Deaver spoke again.

"You'll find out as soon as we arrive in Little Kidding, so I may as well tell you the truth. I daresay I won't be able to go back to my old life in London after this fracas, anyway." She paused, as if to strengthen her resolve. "Flora Deaver isn't my real name. I was born Poppy Delamere, and though I am the impoverished vicar's daughter I led Lady Katherine and Lady Wrackham and everyone else to believe, that's not the whole story. I left my family home two years ago to avoid an unwanted marriage, which my stepfather had insisted upon against my wishes."

Langham was stunned.

But even if he'd found the wherewithal to say something—anything—in response to her revelation, her next words would have robbed him of speech again.

"I'm not on my way to Little Kidding for a cheerful reunion with my family," she said with a tremor in her voice. "I'm going there to do what I can to ensure my sister doesn't hang for the murder of her husband. The black-guard my parents forced her to marry in my stead."

When she was finished, she sagged back against the velvet seat, as if making her confession had sapped her of strength. He felt an unaccountable impulse to gather her in his arms, but knew that would be met with about as much welcome as a head cold in summer.

"I'll say this for you, Miss Delamere," Langham said with a raised brow, "conversation with you is never dull."

Chapter Two

I'm so pleased my family travails amuse you, Your Grace," Poppy said tartly, though she was relieved he'd responded to her story with bemusement. If he'd offered sympathy, she wasn't sure she'd have been able to maintain her composure. "But then, for someone like you, such pedestrian matters as these must seem silly."

"Leave it to you, Miss Deav— ah, Miss Delamere," he said, correcting himself, "to refer to your sister's predicament as pedestrian. I hope no one is so used to hardship that they consider facing the hangman's noose beneath their notice."

Before she could retort, he continued, "And I was referring not to your sister's misfortune, but your own flight and change of identity. It was badly done of me, however, and I offer my apologies. No young woman should feel so unsafe in her family home that she feels the need to flee and go into hiding."

A frown twisted his generous mouth, and Poppy could

see sincerity in his blue eyes. Looking away before he could see how his words had affected her, she said softly, "Thank you, Your Grace."

It had been a long time since she'd trusted anyone aside from Kate and Caro—and she'd not even trusted them with this particular secret. That it was the Duke of Langham who'd been the one to whom she'd finally revealed all was a shock. But even more surprising was that he'd received the news with equanimity—even compassion.

"I am also sorry for the predicament in which your sister finds herself," the duke continued, looking serious for once. "I know the magistrate in the area quite well. Sir Geoffrey Stannings and I have been friends since childhood. I know he's a reasonable man. Perhaps I can say a word on your sister's behalf. If your sister was justified, or if there is any question of her innocence of the crime, I feel sure he will be persuaded."

At his words, Poppy blinked. "Your Grace, I wish I had the luxury of saying you needn't trouble yourself—and if it were just for me, I no doubt would—but this is for my sister, whom I know would not be in her present situation if it weren't for me, and I have no such luxury."

"You could certainly try, Miss Delamere," Langham said pointedly, "but you would not succeed in dissuading me. Little Kidding is my home village, and you will find once we arrive that I hold a great deal of sway there. I will have to learn more about the circumstances that led to her being accused of her husband's death, but if I find she has been wrongly accused, I will do what I may to correct the situation. Do you know if Scotland Yard has been called in? They usually are in cases as serious as this."

"I know little more than what was in the London papers

this morning," Poppy said, retrieving the folded copy of *The London Gazette* from her valise and handing it to him.

The article itself was brief, and by now Poppy had it repeating through her mind like a refrain.

> *A terrible murder happened in the village of Little Kidding, Bucks. yesterday when Mr. Alistair Lovell of Rothwell Grange was pushed to his death from the bell tower of the long abandoned St. Lucy's chapel. His body was discovered by Mr. Edward Jarvis, who happened upon the horrible sight while searching for a missing sheep. Suspicion rests upon the dead man's wife, Violet, who has been taken up by the local constable and awaits her fate with the magistrate.*

"Do you know this Mr. Jarvis?" Poppy asked when the duke had folded the newspaper and handed it back to her. "Could he have something to do with Lovell's murder? I know from working on Kate and Caro's column that very often the person who discovers the body is responsible for the murder."

"In this case, I very much doubt it, Miss Delamere," Langham said, though his frown suggested something about the article troubled him—aside from the fact of the murder, that was.

"But why?" she pressed him. "Is Jarvis elderly or infirm in some way? Has he such an even temper that you cannot fathom him ever behaving violently?"

Langham's blue eyes were not without sympathy, but he shook his head. "I know Jarvis cannot have had anything to do with your brother-in-law's death because I know the man as well as I know myself. He is my closest boyhood friend, a cousin in fact, who currently acts as steward on my estate. If he said he was in search of a lost sheep, then you may count on it that he was doing just that."

If Langham was mistaken about Mr. Jarvis, the fact that the man was the cousin of a duke would make Violet a far more palatable suspect for the authorities. Her face must have shown her dismay, because he leaned forward in his seat and took her hand.

"My dear Miss Delamere," he told her in a surprisingly gentle voice, "though I know you must be beside yourself with worry over your sister's predicament, it will do you no good to let every twist and turn play upon your emotions as if each development were a bow and you a violin. You will soon find yourself in no fit state for helping her."

She knew he was right, and the unexpected softness of his tone made her wish—even if only for a moment—that she could cling to him for comfort.

But then, her backbone reasserted itself and she pulled her hand away. Who was this man, with his title and wealth, who had very likely never endured a single hardship in his life, to tell her how she should react? Had a mere handful of kindnesses from him turned her into a quivering blancmange of gratitude? She had managed well enough on her own for the last two years, and she would manage well enough from now on without him.

Straightening her spine, she schooled her features into an expression she hoped conveyed hauteur. "I thank you for your advice, Your Grace, but I am quite capable of controlling my emotions well enough to give my sister the assistance she needs. There is no need for you to trouble yourself over me."

He blinked, at her sudden shift in mood, no doubt, but she made no apologies. She needed to remember not to fall prey to his overbearing ways. When he spoke, however, it was only to offer mildly, "But I thought we had agreed that I would speak with the authorities once we arrived. Or did I misunderstand our conversation just now?"

"No, you didn't," she replied, vowing to maintain her calm. "However, that was only as pertains to the authorities. When it comes to my person and my emotions, you may rest assured that I need no help."

A flicker of amusement in his gaze almost threatened to send her into a temper again. Really, what was it about this man that had her melting in appreciation one minute and boiling with rage the next?

"I sense, Miss Delamere," he drawled, "that when it comes to accepting assistance you have difficulty conceding gracefully. Especially when it comes to your . . . ah . . . person and emotions."

Something in his tone made her suspicious, but she nodded despite herself. She'd always had an independent streak—even as a child, when she'd resented even her nursemaid's attempts to help her perform daily tasks. "Perhaps," she said, and left it at that.

As if he hadn't noticed her reticence to discuss the matter further, he went on. "Then may I suggest that we enter into a barter of sorts? I will do my damnedest to help your sister out of her current situation, if you will be so good as to help me with a problem that has recently befallen me. I have need of a lady at the moment, you see, and—"

Poppy frowned. What possible problem might trouble the duke? Could it be that the rarified life of the Duke of Langham was not so perfect as it at first appeared?

Then, like a sting from a bee she hadn't even known was near, she felt a prick of understanding. Hadn't she read in the gossip pages that the duke and his mistress, one of the most celebrated actresses of the London stage, had recently parted ways? Was he suggesting that *she* take Nell Burgoyne's place in his bed in exchange for his help?

A bubble of outrage rose up in her and she hissed, "How dare you, sirrah?"

Rather than guilt, however, his expression betrayed... puzzlement? "I hardly think it's such an unreasonable suggestion. I have a problem that you can assist me with, and you have a problem I can assist you with. It's an elegant solution to both our problems."

If anything, she was even more livid. "An *elegant* solution? My sister is facing the gallows, you odious man, and you propose that I should trade my body for your assistance in the matter? I had no notion you were such a villain or I would never—"

Poppy was so overset that she lurched to her feet, though where she intended to go, she had no idea. It wasn't as if she could step out of a moving train carriage. But the car itself was large enough that she could at the very least attempt to put as much distance between herself and the duke as possible.

But as soon as she made to move away from him, the train took a turn and she found herself for the second time that day pressed against his hard chest. When the choice was between falling to the floor and remaining upright, her body chose the latter.

"For such a clever woman, Miss Delamere," Langham said as he gripped her upper arms, "you can be quite the hair wit."

Then, with a gentlemanly consideration she very much resented, he assisted her back into her seat. She stared at him as he resettled himself and looked back at her with what she guessed was a glare that matched her own.

"Explain yourself," she said curtly, though she was beginning to think she'd made an embarrassing mistake.

"I will generously agree to overlook your shocking assumption that I was angling to have you repay my help by pressing you into becoming my mistress," the duke said frostily. "But only because I suspect you are fatigued from worrying about your sister's plight. If you were a man I would, in all likelihood, have shown my displeasure at your assumption with my fists. I do not believe I have ever shown myself as to be the sort of man who would take advantage of a lady's vulnerability in such a manner."

She swallowed, feeling a surge of color rise in her cheeks. He was right on all counts. She was tired. She'd been up since the wee hours of the morning when she'd read the news of Lovell's murder, and it felt as if she hadn't stopped moving since. But what's more, he was right about his own character as he'd displayed it to her thus far.

Even in the descriptions of his exploits, which she'd read with shameful fascination in the gossip columns over the past few years, there'd never been even so much as a hint that he'd ever behaved in less than a gentlemanly manner.

"I...I am sorry, Your Grace," she said haltingly. "Truly, I cannot understand why I came to such a foolish conclusion. I suppose you are correct that I am exhausted from worrying over Violet, and my mind conjured a ridiculous notion. I hope you can forgive me."

She forced herself to look at him, though every muscle screamed against it. And to her surprise, she saw not the wrathful mien she expected, but one of dry amusement.

"Oh, do not don a hair shirt and flog yourself in remorse,

I beg you," he said blithely. "Though I must say ladies do not usually have such a strong negative reaction to the prospect of bedding me."

To her shame, for the barest fraction of a second, she allowed herself to consider what it might be like to be the focus of all that aristocratic intensity and felt a shiver dance down her spine. If the gossip sheets were to be believed, he was quite popular with the demimonde. Little doubt then that he was quite proficient at such things. Still, that was no excuse for assuming he had offered his assistance with the intention of taking liberties with her.

"I do apologize," she pressed. "Although our acquaintance is a new one, you have always behaved with propriety, and I should have known better than to think—"

He held up a staying hand. "If you insist upon it, then pray accept my forgiveness so that we may move past this awkwardness. There is not much longer until we arrive in Little Kidding, and I wish to make my plan known to you before our arrival."

Curious now as to what it was that he would require of her, she nodded for him to continue.

"When I arrive at Langham Abbey," the duke said with a frown, "my grandmother will have a number of eligible young ladies there waiting to pounce on the chance to become duchess. I have no intention of marrying any of them—my own tastes and my grandmother's diverging in all but the most superficial ways. It would save all concerned a great deal of difficulty if I were to arrive with a betrothed already on my arm."

Poppy's eyes widened. "You cannot mean me, surely? Why, you didn't even know my true identity before a short while ago. And though I am flattered, Your Grace—"

Perhaps realizing he should clarify, Langham interrupted. "Do not compose your rejection just yet, Miss Delamere. What I am proposing is a betrothal for the duration of this week's house party only. I will do what I may to assist your sister, and you will dance attendance on me during the week. Once we have managed to extricate ourselves from our contretemps, you will cry off and we will go our separate ways, neither of us the worse for wear. Indeed, you will have your sister back, it is to be hoped, and I will be free to live another year without a wife."

"Until your grandmother decides to try again next year, I would think," Poppy said with a tilt of her head.

"That will be for me to worry about. Now, what do you say, dear lady?" Langham's blue eyes were lit with a mix of amusement and sincerity. And Poppy had to admit that however difficult he might be at times, he was an appealing man. "Will you save me from Grandmama's ravening horde of prospective duchesses?"

If she were entirely honest with herself, her flight from London that morning, with no more than a brief note's notice to Kate and Caro, had been rash. She'd seen Violet's name in the paper and was compelled to go to her. She'd formulated no plan for where she would stay, or how she would go about attempting to clear her name. She didn't even have the most basic knowledge of Little Kidding and its environs.

The duke's offer was, in truth, a godsend.

What was one more week of playing another role, after all? She had done so for the past two years in London with no one the wiser. If it meant Langham would use his considerable influence to help Violet, Poppy would pretend to be his fiancée while wearing yellow cross-gartered stockings and dancing a jig.

Still, she could not help but warn him about the possible ramifications of their charade once it was over. "If the dowager is anything like the matchmaking ladies I've heard about, she will not simply give up once our supposed betrothal is at an end."

"Of course she won't," he said with a scowl, "but she's put me in a dashed difficult position. The very fact she's invited these ladies will have raised expectations in them. Not only will I have to act the host, but I will also have to try my damnedest to dampen their attentions without offending them. By agreeing to my proposal, you will save me a great deal of trouble. When we announce our betrothal, all will be disappointed at once, and I need not concern myself overmuch with their feelings."

"Ah yes, killing multiple birds with one stone," Poppy said dryly. It was a relief to know he hadn't metamorphosed into total selflessness all at once. "What a paragon of efficiency you are, Your Grace."

"If I were truly efficient, I'd have them ejected from the abbey as soon as we arrive," the duke retorted. "But I'm not quite *that* lost to good manners. Besides, I do not wish to embarrass them, or my grandmother. I simply don't intend to end up leg-shackled to one of them."

Perhaps reading skepticism in her expression, he continued, "Shocking though it may be, I do not go out of my way to be unkind to those in my orbit. But the truth of it is that I could insult everyone I encounter save the queen and they'd never make their displeasure known to me. What I think of them matters very little. It's what I can do for them that matters. Such is the double-edged sword of being a duke."

Something about his tone, the way he took it for granted that these ladies—indeed "most people," he'd said—cared more for his title than the man who held it, sent a pang of empathy through Poppy.

Was there anyone in Langham's life who cared about him without expecting something in return? Even his former mistress, Nell Burgoyne, whom she understood he'd cared about in his own way, had, if the rumors were true, profited handsomely from their arrangement.

All at once she knew what she would do. "I'll agree to your sham betrothal," she said with a suddenness that startled Langham from his casual pose.

"You will?" The smile he gave her was boyishly charming. "Never say it was that rot about the way I'm treated. I can assure you that while everything I said was true, the dukedom is no hardship. What's a little fawning when one has multiple estates and can have one's pick among the season's loveliest?"

"Do you want my assistance or not?" Poppy demanded, though she suspected he was only trying to amuse her.

Sitting up straighter and pulling at his cuffs, the duke sighed. "Yes, I want you to help me, Miss Delamere."

Grateful to have something to focus on other than her sister for the rest of the journey, Poppy straightened her spine as well. "Then we'd better get to work. If we're to convince your grandmother that we're betrothed, then we need to get our stories straight."

"How fortunate then, that we have the rest of the train ride to do so," he said blandly.

She glanced down at her plain gown and frowned. "My wardrobe is hardly the sort to endear me to the dowager Duchess of Langham. I'll be a pigeon among the fine feathers of the prospective brides she's invited to your estate."

But Langham waved off her concern. "It will reassure

her that ours is a love match. After all, what if not true love would make a man of refinement like myself look past that abomination of a dress to see the true beauty beyond it? Besides, my sisters will be there and have far too many gowns as it is. I'm sure they'll have something for you to borrow."

Poppy only just stopped herself from objecting to his characterization of her traveling ensemble. In part because he was right. It *was* an ugly dress. But it was also perfect for her role as the hardworking Miss Flora Deaver, secretary to Lady Katherine.

She'd had any number of fine gowns when she'd lived with her family. They'd been purchased in the hopes of helping her catch Alistair Lovell's eye. At the memory she felt a wave of anxiety wash over her. Violet had been forced to marry him in her absence, and now he was dead. This arrangement with the duke wasn't a game; it was a necessity for gaining her sister's freedom, and she would do well to remember it.

"I'm glad you see a way for my meager wardrobe to help our cause," she said aloud. "And I will remind you that I shall need to find where my sister is being held as soon as we arrive in Little Kidding. I realize you will wish to make for your estate straight away, but she's only eighteen and must be frightened out of her wits."

He looked at her with a puzzled expression. "I'm not entirely without feeling, Miss Delamere. Of course we will visit her first thing. It was my intention to do so whether you'd agreed to my proposal or not."

The casualness with which he made this declaration almost took her breath away, making Poppy feel even more churlish for her earlier misunderstanding of his motives.

She squeezed his arm, and said softly, "Thank you. I

don't know how I can ever repay you for your assistance in this matter. I was ready to fight for Violet on my own, but having your help has lifted a weight from my shoulders."

"Do not thank me yet," he warned her. "We have still to clear your sister's name. And there is also the matter of introducing you to my family. I'm not sure in the long run that you will find our arrangement to be an even trade."

Langham might be high-handed and arrogant, but he was not, it seemed, as unfeeling as she'd at first thought. She'd do well to remember that the next time she had the impulse to strangle him with his own neckcloth.

Chapter Three

The remainder of the journey to Little Kidding passed quickly—at least it did for Langham. He had known from their brief meeting in London, when she'd been acting in her role as Lady Katherine Eversham's assistant at *The London Gazette*, that the lovely Miss Poppy Delamere was intelligent and in possession of a quick wit. Further conversation with her did not disabuse him of the notion.

But it was also clear that despite having left her family behind for London, Miss Delamere was deuced loyal to her sister. As someone who, despite his at times fractious interactions with them, would lay down his life for his brother or sisters, Langham could understand Poppy's determination to come to her sister's aid.

"You've barely told me anything about your siblings," she said now, as if guessing the direction in which his thoughts had wandered. "I know you are the eldest, but where do the others fall? Will they be at the abbey this week?"

"I have two sisters, Charlotte and Eugenia, and one brother, Adrian," he said simply. "The order is just as I listed it. Charlotte is married to Viscount Felton—a bit of a stick to be honest—but they seem to hold one another in affection. And Genia is wed to the Earl of Bellwood. He's a bit livelier than Felton, and much better suited to Genia in that way. You'll meet them and their respective broods once we're settled in the abbey."

He had hoped she'd leave her questions there—he and his brother Adrian had yet to fully repair the quarrel they'd had over the younger man's decision to place himself in danger by working for the Foreign Office—but again with an unerring ability to sense just what he was thinking, Miss Delamere asked, "And what of Lord Adrian? Will he be in attendance this week?"

"I am unsure," he said brusquely. Then, recognizing that as his supposed future duchess she would need to be prepared in the event someone at the party pressed her on Adrian's absence, he continued, "Adrian is nearly a decade younger than I am, and we are not close. He was an infant when our parents died and I was away, first at Eton, and then at university, for much of his childhood."

In point of fact, they'd got along well enough until he'd made a misstep in forbidding his brother's choice of career. He should have known, given the family tendency toward stubbornness, that it was the wrong way to dissuade the younger man from embarking on a career that would take him to the other side of the world. In the end he'd relented and given Adrian his blessing, but the damage to their relationship was done. He'd tried to mend fences since then, but they were still not back on the easy footing they'd enjoyed before their rift.

But even given their false betrothal, he was hardly going

to divulge that to a lady he'd only ever really had a proper conversation with today. They were meant to be focusing upon her sister's plight, not his brother's continued coolness toward him.

Miss Delamere looked as if she wanted to press him further, but he'd not spent the greater part of a lifetime perfecting a forbidding demeanor to fail at it when he truly wished to be forbidding.

His decision to offer Miss Delamere the engagement in order to soothe her pride at accepting his help had seemed like a good idea when he'd proposed it, but as it was unfolding he was suffering all the discomfort of having an actual fiancée without any of the benefits.

"I suppose if Lord Adrian does attend then I can learn more about him when we are introduced," she said primly, though there was something about the downturn of her mouth that made him feel guilty for shutting her out.

This, he reminded himself, *is what comes of letting down your guard with people.*

The conversation moved on, and though they'd continued to discuss the household at the abbey, perhaps sensing his retreat, Miss Delamere did not press him about his brother again.

As they got closer to the tiny station in Little Kidding, she straightened her spine, and though she was shorter by several inches, he could have sworn she looked down her nose at him.

"You're certain you'll be able to remember all this?" she demanded, her lovely blue eyes narrowed with concentration. "It's not as easy to play a role as you think. It takes a great deal of energy and concentration to get it right."

Langham could have told her he was well aware of how difficult it could be, considering he'd been performing in one way or another since he was a boy. Instead he simply waved a dismissive hand at her, knowing it would annoy her and thus hopefully distract her from her own worries. "There is no need for such concern, Miss Delamere. I do intend to pull the wool over my grandmother's eyes, but it's hardly a matter of life and death. It's a fiction to save me from the annoyance of a betrothal I have no wish for, not an attempt to discover state secrets."

Her first reaction was to frown more deeply, then, perhaps realizing she'd taken the matter a tad too seriously, she sighed. "You are right. I suppose I've spent so much time over the past two years trying to keep my own identity from being discovered that I infused this situation with the same gravity. I apologize."

He could see from the slump of her shoulders that the day's emotional turmoil was beginning to wear on her. "No apologies necessary. Indeed, if I were planning to travel into enemy territory, there's no one I'd rather have coaching me on how to hide my true intentions."

"Thank you, I think?" she said with a shake of her head. "I have to admit, it never occurred to me as a child that I'd one day have garnered the skills necessary to spy for England."

The image of Poppy Delamere as a child, with golden pigtails and a propensity for asking questions, popped into his head, and Langham couldn't help but smile at the notion. He'd wager she'd been a handful.

Aloud he said, "I doubt any of us, as children, could correctly guess at what we'd become as adults."

She tilted her head in surprise. "I should have thought a duke would have his life mapped out for him in detail, even as an infant."

"Even dukes, Miss Delamere, have dreams of adventure

and lives beyond the ones they're given." He was annoyed to hear the note of wistfulness in his own voice, and as the whistle on the train blew, he continued in a more sober tone, "We'll go at once to see Stannings to find out where your sister is being held. He'll order her released into my custody, and you'll be able to learn more about the situation from her own lips."

"It is customary in cases involving a member of the upper or middle class for the magistrate to allow the suspect to remain at home while awaiting further investigation," Poppy said, worry etched on her brow. "Which means Violet is very likely with my mother and stepfather. I doubt they'll be willing to relinquish her to you."

"Surely your sister and Lovell will have had a home of their own where your sister could await the inquest," Langham said, frowning.

"Of course I have no notion of the situation since they've moved to Little Kidding," Poppy admitted, "but Violet's husband is, or was, my stepfather's private secretary. The fact that we would be expected to live in the same household with my mother and stepfather after our marriage was one of the many reasons I objected when Lord Short tried to force my own match with Mr. Lovell."

Since the private secretaries of noblemen were generally younger sons unable to get by on the meager allowance afforded them by their own fathers, it seemed odd that Short would wish either of his daughters to marry Lovell. That the baronet hadn't been more ambitious for either Poppy or Violet was suspicious in and of itself.

Before he could press Poppy further on the matter, however, she changed the subject. "The newspaper mentioned that Violet lives at Rothwell Grange, Your Grace. Do you know it?"

He was familiar with the grange, which had been inherited by old Squire Rothwell's nephew upon his death. As far as he knew, the nephew rented it out year after year. But something else that Miss Delamere said reminded him of a small annoyance he'd been meaning to repair. "If we're to make a convincing betrothed couple we should dispense with some of these formalities. No more 'Your Grace,' if you please. I will, with your permission, call you Poppy, and you will call me Langham. Or Joshua, if you prefer."

The train had by then come to a screeching halt, and they both rose. Langham offered her his arm. As they stepped toward the door of the private carriage, she took his arm but didn't look up as she said, "Very well, Your— Langham."

For some reason he wasn't willing to name, he felt a pang of disappointment that she hadn't chosen to address him as Joshua. Most of his intimates called him Langham, so it was hardly worth quibbling over, but some part of him wanted to hear her slightly husky voice use his Christian name.

That his imagination suggested that the most pleasing occasion for this utterance of his given name would be while they were naked in bed together was not something he was proud of, but he had never been one to ignore the erotic possibilities of a beautiful woman's proximity.

Any thoughts of bedsport with Poppy, or anyone else for that matter, were dashed almost as soon as they descended from the train carriage.

"Unca Josh! Unca Josh!" his niece Olivia cried as she broke away from a knot of what looked to be a mix of family and guests from Langham Abbey.

Marvelous.

His family had chosen, for the first time in his recollection, to meet him at the station. Beside him, he felt Poppy stiffen, as if bracing herself. A wave of protectiveness washed over him, and patting the hand she'd placed on his arm, he said in a low voice, "Don't lose courage now."

"I'm sorry, my lady," a harried woman who was clearly the child's nursemaid said as she rushed forward to waylay Olivia. "She was that pleased to see her uncle and broke away from me."

"It's all right, Maggie," said his sister Charlotte with a laugh. "She's very fond of her uncle, and I did promise her she could see him today."

After glancing over to assure himself that Poppy had regained her poise, Langham reached down and lifted his niece into his arms. "Hello, poppet. Whatever are you doing here?"

"We comed to see you, Unca Josh," Olivia said patting him on the cheek, as if assuring herself he was really there. "Me and the wadies 'n' gen'mens."

At her mention of ladies, he looked beyond where his sister and the nursemaid stood and noted that among the faces he recognized—his brother-in-law Lord Felton and a few cousins—were also some unfamiliar ones. They'd been greeted by a bloody welcome party from the house. This was Grandmama's doing, or he'd eat his hat.

Thinking of the way the walk from the station to the abbey would have gone if the dowager's plan had worked— no doubt with him fending off lures from more than one of the young ladies currently standing behind Charlotte— Langham gave silent thanks that rather than arriving here alone, he'd had Poppy by his side.

"What a lovely surprise," he said, reminding himself never to underestimate his grandmother again.

Glancing toward Poppy, he saw that she'd taken a few steps backward and stood off to the side, as if planning her escape before she was noticed.

That would never do. Gesturing to her with his free arm—the other occupied with Olivia, who hadn't stopped chattering since he'd lifted her up—he said, "Come, my dear, this wasn't how we'd planned things, but it's best we get the introductions out of the way."

Poppy's mouth was tight, but as he'd seen her do earlier, she steeled her shoulders and stepped forward to take his arm. "Of course, Langham," she said, a shy but adoring smile on her face. "I'm eager to meet your family."

The group from Langham Abbey were still talking among themselves as they shuffled forward to make their greetings to the duke, clearly not having heard his words to Poppy or hers to him. But Charlotte had heard them, and her eyes were as round as marbles. She clearly hadn't even noticed Poppy at first, and now that she had, she was not best pleased with what she saw. "Who is this person, Langham?"

Ignoring his sister, Langham cleared his throat loudly and called for the collected party's attention. "We hadn't expected to make the announcement on the train platform, but since Poppy's presence needs some explanation, I'm pleased to inform you that this lovely lady by my side, Miss Poppy Delamere, has done me the honor of agreeing to be the next Duchess of Langham."

For the barest moment, a silence the likes of which Langham had never encountered—especially not on a busy train platform—fell. Then a peal of laughter rang out which, like an infection, was soon spreading among the onlookers.

"You were ever a trickster, old fellow," Langham's

cousin Lord Leith crowed, wiping his streaming eyes with a pristine white handkerchief. "Imagine you betrothed to a woman like that. A good joke, jolly good joke."

"Badly done, Duke," said one of the ladies, a tall red-head whose nose proclaimed her to be the eldest daughter of the Duke of Gerson—clearly one of the guests who'd been invited by the dowager as a potential bride. "What a tease you are."

"You're incorrigible," Charlotte chided as she took Olivia from Langham's arms. "I daresay these ladies felt their hearts drop down to their very toes. I know mine did."

She turned to address Poppy, who still had her arm threaded through Langham's. "We mean no insult to you, miss. But it's clear from your attire that you couldn't possibly be betrothed to my brother. It's too bad of him to put you in such a position. I'll make sure he pays you handsomely for your role in his little charade."

Then, handing her daughter over to the nursemaid, she slipped her arm into his unoccupied one and made as if to lead him away.

When he failed to move, she looked up at him in pique. "What is it? We need to get back to the house in time for tea. The dowager is quite eager to see you."

It was then that she saw Poppy hadn't relinquished her hold on Langham's other arm. Charlotte's eyes widened, and she pulled away from her brother and raised a hand to cover her mouth. "No," she said in a horrified tone. "You didn't."

"I'm not sure where the lot of you learned your manners," Langham said, a cold fury running through him, "but you will apologize this instant to Miss Delamere. She has done nothing to earn this rudeness."

He wasn't sure what he'd expected from his revelation

that they were betrothed—sham though it may be—but it hadn't been the derisive laughter that had erupted no sooner than he'd got the words out. He glanced at Poppy to see that she held her head high, not wilting under the gathered crowd's scrutiny. But that only made him feel more outraged on her behalf.

He placed his hand over hers where it lay on his arm, thinking to give her some comfort despite her seeming imperviousness to the insults. To his chagrin, however, she glanced up at him in surprise. Did she think he'd simply let them sneer at her without giving them the dressing down they deserved?

Langham looked up to see Charlotte was staring at him as if he'd begun dancing a jig. At his glare she blinked, then, perhaps realizing this wasn't the time or place for the conversation she wished to have with him, she sighed.

"I do apologize, Miss Delamere," she said with what sounded like sincerity. "We meant no insult. It's just that Langham has a bit of a reputation as a jokester, and we all thought…what with your gown and…"

Poppy inclined her head, looking for all the world like a duchess. "Thank you, Lady Felton. And while we are being honest with one another, you may as well know that my sister is Violet Lovell."

Langham closed his eyes. In for a penny in for a pound, he supposed.

It took Charlotte a moment to connect the dots. When she did, the horror in her eyes was genuine. "The woman suspected of killing her husband?"

Several of the ladies in the background gasped, and Langham thought he heard his cousin Ralph mutter an aggrieved "I say."

But to her credit, Poppy didn't bat an eyelash.

"The very same," she said through clenched teeth. "So, unless you wish to insult some other aspect of my person— might I suggest my hair, which has no doubt slipped from its pins and was not styled terribly fashionably to begin with—we must go see about doing what we can to make her comfortable. I'm sure we'll see you all later at the abbey, by which time you will no doubt have conjured a longer list of my failings with which to berate me."

Torn between bemusement and amusement, Langham allowed Poppy to lead him away, leaving his sister and his grandmother's party guests to gawp after them.

Chapter Four

Once they'd got beyond earshot of the party from Langham Abbey, the duke gave Poppy a sidelong look. "I don't think I've ever seen my sister Charlotte speechless before. I must commend you on managing it. If this is what it will be like to have you as a fiancée—even a faux one—this arrangement of ours promises to bring me a great deal of amusement."

While His Grace, or Langham, she corrected herself in her head—made arrangements to have his valet take their bags to the house, Poppy stood to one side, fuming. She hadn't lost her temper in such a grand fashion in years. It was never a good idea to lose control of one's emotions. She'd learned that lesson not long after her mother had married Lord Short.

Langham, if his words were to be believed, hadn't minded her outburst, but she did. She was supposed to make a credible betrothed for Langham. Surely a lady who wanted to make a good impression would refrain from insulting her fiancé's sister? And had she really taken Langham's arm and steered him away from his welcome party? As if she were the one who made the decisions, and not the duke, who could probably have her transported to Australia if the notion took him?

She resolved to focus on convincing his family that theirs was a real engagement. And when a little voice in her head suggested that it might not be *that* difficult to pretend to be besotted with a man as handsome and kind as Langham, she told that voice to stubble it.

"We'll take my curricle to the grange," the duke said, interrupting her thoughts as he returned to her side and took her hand, leading her down the platform to the far end, where a highly polished sporting vehicle stood with a pair of matched bays harnessed to it. A young man handed the reins to Langham and neatly caught the coin the duke tossed to him. "Stevens will make our excuses for tea should we be unable to return to the house in time."

Once they were under way, Poppy pulled the jacket of her traveling ensemble closer as the cooler air of the country coupled with the moving carriage chilled her. Their route took them past sheep-dotted enclosures and farms nestled in the valleys of the glowing chalk hills.

"These roads were built under my great-grandfather's direction from chalk mined right here," Langham said with a nod in the direction of the Chilterns. "The harvest was poor for those several years, and the mining operation gave the people in the area much-needed work. Or so the story goes. I imagine, knowing my forebears, there was some ulterior motive there as well—I mean, beyond the profits that could be made from the mining operation."

"Are you always so cynical about your family?" Poppy asked dryly. She knew from experience that not all families—even aristocratic ones—were happy, but she'd somehow thought that someone like Langham would not dwell on the misdeeds of previous generations. After all, he was the duke now and could do as he pleased.

"About my great-grandfather I am," Langham said with a harsh laugh. "He was one of the most notorious rakes of his day. And I don't mean the sort of scapegrace scoundrel you ladies like to read about in sensation novels. The fourth duke was a seducer, an opium eater—honestly, it would save us time if I listed off the vices with which he was not acquainted. I wouldn't be surprised to learn the man was a murderer as well."

She wasn't sure what she'd expected him to say, but it hadn't been that.

"So," Langham continued, "you'd better know what sort of bloodline you're getting yourself mixed up in. Even if it is only for the space of a house party. Great-grandfather was even the leader of a secret society that devoted itself to every profane pleasure imaginable."

Poppy gave an astonished shake of her head. *I suppose that's one sin I cannot lay upon my stepfather's door.* Although his penchant for defrauding innocent people of their money ran a close second.

"You might well shake your head in disgust," Langham said with a glance her way. "He was a truly contemptible man. I'm only grateful he was long dead by the time I came along."

She nodded in agreement. "I think my stepfather and the fourth duke might have got along quite well with one another. Though Lord Short's misdeeds run more toward the financial than fleshly."

At that last word she felt herself coloring a little. What was it about Langham that made her feel like a green girl? There was no need for her to be maidenly when she was only speaking the truth. A lesson she'd only learned once she'd arrived in London and had the fortune to be hired by Kate to work at *The London Gazette*.

Unaware of her inner turmoil, Langham pressed her. "What do you mean? I thought you'd left your stepfather's home because he wished to force you into an unwanted marriage."

"I did," she said with a sigh as Langham directed the horses to the side of the road. "But that was not the extent of his misdeeds. We moved so often when I was a child, never staying more than a year or two in any village. I didn't realize until I was older that the reason we had to leave our home so often was that Lord Short was a confidence man, and he'd been grifting our neighbors."

She laughed bitterly. "I've often wondered how different my life would have been if my father, the vicar, had lived. He certainly would not have approved of my stepfather, that's certain. Lord Short was always very persuasive, and he used that skill to convince people in the community to entrust their money to him for the purpose of some scheme or another, which he swore to anyone who would listen was sure to give them an exponential return on their investment. Eventually, someone would catch on that there was no railroad in Argentina or diamond mine in America, and they'd alert the authorities. I don't know how, but Lord Short always managed to get us out of town before the constable or the bailiffs, or both, descended."

Poppy saw that the duke's jaw was clenched and his

blue eyes had grown stormy. "It can't have been easy to keep quiet about it. Did he threaten you?"

"I had learned by then what happened when I spoke out of turn," she said softly. "And Mama made sure to keep both Violet and me away from him as much as possible. She ensured that we received as much of an education as she could provide. And when Lord Short was doing well, he could be generous. There were always pretty gowns and even a governess for a few years when we were in Edinburgh."

If Langham had noticed she hadn't precisely answered his question, he didn't mention it. "And was Alistair Lovell involved in these schemes? Your stepfather's insistence on marrying him into the family suggests their relationship was more than one would expect from employer and employee."

At the mention of Violet and her marriage to Lovell, Poppy felt her chest constrict. *This is all my fault. If I hadn't left—*

Her emotions must have shown on her face, because Langham took her hand in his, the gesture sending a wave of warmth through her. "You did what you had to do to keep yourself safe. And you said yourself that you had no notion that Short would insist his own daughter marry Lovell."

And that was true. If Poppy had had any idea that Violet would be forced to take her place, she would never have left her sister behind. Still, it made her heart ache to know that while she was in London, finally able to surround herself with the sort of intellectual pursuits she'd always longed for and making herself useful at *The Gazette*, Violet had been enduring a marriage to Mr. Lovell.

"What do you know of Lovell?" Langham asked, taking

a different tack. She noted that his expression was patient now, as if he'd realized she was not quite so imperturbable as she attempted to seem.

Taking a deep breath, Poppy continued. "I don't really know where he came from or who his people were. He'd been with Lord Short for about five years at the time the betrothal was proposed to me. Before that I'd only had a handful of interactions with him. I certainly didn't harbor any girlish fantasies about him. He was unpleasant, even disrespectful. I can't imagine why Lord Short would want to tie him to the family. Especially since Mama's ideas on the matter were so very different. She imagined Violet and me married to a younger son at the very least."

"But your stepfather is a baronet," the duke argued. "Surely you and your sister could aim higher than that."

At this, Poppy made a moue of distaste. "If he were indeed a baronet, that might be true. However, one of the first things I did when I began working for Lady Katherine was to search out a copy of Debrett's in the newspaper's library. And as I suspected, my stepfather's title is as nonexistent as the diamond mine in America that he was touting to his investors."

Langham shook his head in disgust. "I believe you are correct, Miss Delamere," he said, giving her hand one last squeeze before he turned his attention back to the horses and got them under way again. "My great-grandfather and your stepfather would have got along famously. At the very least they could have lied to one another instead of the rest of the world and saved us all a great deal of trouble."

The drive leading to Rothwell Grange was tree lined, and when the tidy manor house built from local chalkstone came into view, it was just as Langham had remembered it.

Beside him, he could feel Poppy's anxiety like a palpable thing, despite her attempts to conceal it behind a rigid posture and neatly folded hands. He could hardly blame her.

"Do not forget to introduce me as your betrothed," he reminded her as the curricle neared the house. "This charade is intended to benefit us both. Your status as my fiancée will hold far more sway with the likes of your stepfather than your position as Violet's sister."

"I had no intention of neglecting that detail," Poppy said wryly. "It would hardly do you any good with your grandmother's horde of marriageable ladies if we told Mama and Lord Short the truth of things. Lord Short, at least, would have no qualms about informing the entire village the betrothal was a sham if given the chance."

"I didn't expect you to tell them the engagement is a charade," Langham assured her, "but having learned just what sort of man your stepfather is, I want it to be deuced clear to the fellow from the very start that you are no longer under his control. If he has any thoughts of bullying you, he'll have to go through me first."

He saw the flicker of surprise in Poppy's eyes at the fierceness in his tone.

"I mean it," he said firmly. Then, thinking to spare her pride once again, he added, "It will do my reputation no good if it gets out that I don't bother protecting my own fiancée."

"Very well," she said, nodding as if this last, at least, made sense to her.

Once the carriage came to a stop before the portico of the grange, a groom stepped forward to take the reins.

Before Langham could reach the other side of the curricle to lift Poppy down, she'd already jumped. "Headstrong," he said in an undertone as he pointedly tucked her arm into his as they ascended the short flight of steps to the door.

"Nervous," she retorted in an equally low voice, clinging to his arm like a passenger fallen overboard from a ship in the channel. Langham wished he could do more to calm her, but some feelings could not be taken on by others, no matter how one might wish to do so.

Before he could lift the knocker on the imposing door before them, it swung open to reveal a balding butler, whose expression revealed that he knew the duke, at least, by sight.

Not bothering to stand on ceremony, Langham told the man in his most ducal tone, "Langham and Miss Delamere to see Mrs. Lovell. And be quick about it."

At his words the butler frowned. "I do apologize, Your Grace, but I've been told Mrs. Lovell isn't seeing visitors."

Beside him, Langham heard Poppy make a sound of frustration. "Then show us to your master and mistress, man. My betrothed wishes to see her sister, and I'm here to ensure that happens one way or another." Bringing his quizzing glass to his eye, he examined the servant through it as if he were looking at a particularly puzzling form of insect. When the man stood mute, he said coolly, "Is there something about my request that was unclear to you, Mr.—?"

As if emerging from a trance, the butler shook himself and supplied, "Rogers, Your Grace."

"Well, Rogers," Langham said pointedly, "I wish you to show us to your best drawing room. Then you will go inform Lord and Lady Short that we are here to call upon them."

"Y-y-yes, Your Grace," Rogers said, his eyes wide. "At once, Your Grace. This way, Your Grace. Miss Delamere."

"I don't believe I've ever seen you in full ducal mode before," Poppy said with wonder as she took his arm again and they followed the butler down the handsomely furnished hallway. "It's quite impressive."

"I've had a few decades to perfect it," he said wryly. "I'm only pleased that I'm able to use my noble peevishness on your behalf. Usually it serves only to protect me from toadying strangers. And the occasional relation who wishes to borrow money."

As he'd hoped they would do, his words startled a soft laugh from Poppy, and he felt her relax a little beside him. Even so, she was still noticeably anxious. It was hard to believe she was the same woman who'd argued with him earlier on the train.

The drawing room Rogers ushered them into faced the back gardens of the house, where there was a pleasantly arranged parterre garden.

"I'll just go inform Lord and Lady Short that you've arrived, Your Grace," Rogers said, then he all but sprinted from the room.

"It is a handsome enough property and appears, at least here and in the entry hall, to be well furnished," Poppy said, running her hand along the back of the green velvet sofa near the fire. "But then, my stepfather always did like to put on a good showing when we first arrived in a new town. No one wants to hand over an investment to someone living in a hovel, after all."

Her tone was rueful, but Langham could hear the note of pain behind it. She clearly felt some degree of shame over what her stepfather had done—perhaps was still doing, he realized with a start. But Poppy wasn't to blame for Lord Short's crimes.

He was about to tell her so when he heard a deceptively pleasant male voice from the doorway behind them.

"Why am I not surprised, daughter, that you are filling His Grace's ears with lies even before we managed to greet him?"

Chapter Five

Langham turned to Lord Short and was startled by the very ordinariness of the man. Sir Sylvain Short was, like his name suggested, of small stature. His hair, which was slightly longer than fashionable, was the color of dishwater. His features were neither handsome nor ugly. Really, the fellow's only remarkable feature was his eyes, which were a muddled light blue, and so pale as to almost be colorless.

The effect was unsettling but hardly so outstanding to render the man himself memorable. If Langham were going to conjure the perfect disguise for a swindler or a criminal of any kind, really, he'd choose just this sort of fellow. Who could possibly recall enough about the man to describe him to a friend, much less to the authorities?

At the baronet's side, Lady Short remained silent, but something about her expression told Langham that Poppy's mother was under the sway of some strong emotion. Her eyes were bright with unshed tears, and he had a strong suspicion that if her husband wasn't there she'd have gone to her daughter as soon as she'd spied her on the other side of the room.

"Mama," Poppy said, pointedly ignoring her stepfather, and focusing her attention on her mother, "I'd like to introduce you to my fiancé, the Duke of Langham. Langham, may I present my mother, Thomasina, Lady Short."

"Fiancé?" Lord Short echoed in disbelief. "You? Betrothed to a duke? I don't believe it."

Then, as if he'd spoken before he could stop himself, Langham saw the man school his features into a mask of pleasant surprise and correct himself. "That is to say, what happy news. We are, of course, pleased to welcome you to our home, Your Grace. You could not have chosen a more suitable duchess than our dear Poppy. We must not let the sad news about our dear Violet's husband overshadow your joyous announcement. Life does go on, does it not? And here we thought you were destined to remain a spinster. What happy news you've brought us, daughter."

It was remarkable, Langham thought with something like awe, how quickly the man had gone from petulance to joy, and in the process entirely ignoring the fact that his own daughter was under suspicion for the murder of her husband. And the damnable thing of it was that Short's manner was so convincing—even to Langham, who'd seen the progression of emotions cross his face—that anyone who was unfamiliar with him would believe him to be sincere.

Lady Short, on the other hand, had flinched at the mention of Violet and the death of Lovell, and it was clear from her expression that she wished to speak to her elder daughter. But with Short beside her, that seemed unlikely to happen without Langham's intervention.

Cutting off Short, who had been asking about wedding

plans, midsentence, the duke addressed the older man. "Since only a few moments ago you called my intended bride a liar," Langham said coldly, making use of every inch of his superior height to tower over the other man, "I find your sudden change of heart questionable at best."

Short laughed as if there were some shared joke between them. "Oh, you mustn't pay any attention to that, Your Grace," he said with an easy smile. "Poppy knows I only spoke the words in jest. We were ever poking fun at one another. My wife and I are, of course, delighted to see our dear Poppy after so much time has passed and to learn that she has secured the hand of such an important personage as yourself, Your Grace. It is just the thing to bring us out of our doldrums."

Beside him, Langham heard Poppy gasp, and Lady Short raised a hand to cover her mouth.

But, unmoved by the ladies' reactions, Short kept smiling and offered his hand to Langham's to shake. "Welcome to the family, Your Grace."

But the duke simply stared at the proffered hand. The silence in the room loomed, but neither man broke it for several uncomfortable seconds.

Finally, without any sign that he'd taken offense, Short turned his attention to Poppy and stepped toward her as if he would envelop her in a hug. She physically recoiled, and Langham held up a hand to stop the other man from advancing any closer.

"My intended does not wish you to touch her, sir." Given the provocation, Langham would have shoved Short away, but Poppy's stepfather did not come any closer.

"Come daughter," Short said with a note of disappointment. "It's been nearly two years since you left us. You must know how much we've missed you."

"The last time I saw you, sir," Poppy said coldly, "was when you locked me in my bedchamber with a threat of a beating if I didn't accede to your wish that I marry Mr. Lovell. You'll forgive me if I don't wish to play at happy families with you. My sole reason for calling today is to see Violet and Mama. "

Lady Short, who had been standing mute through this exchange chose this moment to speak up. "You mustn't speak to your step-papa that way, Poppy," she said, though it was clear from her subdued tone that she was not entirely sincere. "He has been good to us, and if you'd only done as he wished, Mr. Lovell would still be alive and your poor sister would not be in her current predicament."

Poppy's face paled at her mother's implied accusation. "Mama, I know you feel you must come to his defense, but we both know that my stepfather is to blame for what befell Mr. Lovell. Not me, and certainly not Violet." Poppy managed to keep her voice level, though Langham could tell she was not as calm as she seemed from the way she gripped his arm.

"That's a lie," Short hissed. "How dare you accuse me of murder in my own house, you ungrateful wretch."

Again, he made to move toward Poppy, and this time Langham stepped in front of her. "I will not warn you again. As my betrothed, Miss Delamere is under my protection, and I do not take kindly to those who threaten what is mine."

Short glared up at him, all traces of his earlier false humor gone. Nodding, he stepped back. But his expression did not soften.

Taking Poppy's arm again, Langham said to Lady Short, "My betrothed is overset by this brangling. Perhaps you'd be so good as to bring her sister to us so that we may complete our business here."

Though his manner was gentler with Poppy's mother, Langham did not pose the request in the form of a question.

"My...my daughter is s-sleeping just now," Lady Short stammered, glancing nervously at her husband. "Perhaps you can return tomorrow. When she has had a chance to rest."

"Please may I see her, Mama?" Poppy asked, her voice softening.

Lady Short opened her mouth to reply, but her husband gripped her firmly by the arm and she shut it.

"Your poor mama is also weary," Short said to Poppy, slipping back into an air of husbandly solicitude. "You may leave us now."

And with that, the baronet escorted his wife from the drawing room, leaving Langham and Poppy to see themselves out.

"Why did you not press him?" Poppy demanded as soon as they were in the curricle and out of earshot of the house. "If Violet is resting, I'll eat my hat. She's likely been locked away in her bedchamber, just as he did to me when I refused to marry Lovell."

"Once they'd denied our request to see her," Langham said calmly, hoping to soothe her agitation through his own composure, "there was little hope of changing your stepfather's mind. And make no mistake, it was on his orders that your mother tried to fob us off with the excuse that your sister was sleeping. It was clear she did not wish to say the words, but she could hardly say anything else when he was right there beside her."

Poppy sighed, and the sound of defeat made Langham want to go back to the grange and throttle Lord Short.

"You're likely correct," she said, her earlier rigid posture now replaced with a slump. "His hold on her is much worse than it was when I left two years ago. I've never seen her so cowed before. Even when he was at his most cutting."

"She's endured much this week," he replied. "Your appearance on her doorstep after years away must have been an additional shock."

"A happy one, I'd have hoped," Poppy said bitterly.

"And I suspect it was," Langham said, glancing over at her. "But now she will fear for your safety as well as your sister's. We will need to find another way to see Violet, and then, hopefully, we will be able to arrange time alone for you with your mother as well."

"And by what miracle will you arrange that?" Poppy asked skeptically.

"We're going to see the magistrate and request that he change the location of your sister's confinement from Rothwell Grange to the abbey," he told her as he let the bays gain a little speed. "Even Lord Short cannot argue with that."

"Of course," Poppy gasped. "He won't dare step a foot wrong with the magistrate lest the man decide to look more closely at his business dealings. I don't know what scheme he is currently embroiled in, but I have no doubt there is one."

"Precisely," Langham agreed, thinking that Stannings would also have some idea if anyone in the area had complained about being taken in by Short. "It might not go amiss to contact Eversham about your stepfather's financial misdeeds, as well. If Short knows that Scotland Yard is looking into him, he will surely make himself more amenable to our demands."

At the mention of Eversham, however, Poppy's eyes

widened in alarm. "Do not contact Eversham just yet, please."

He frowned. "Why? I should think that your position with Lady Katherine would mean that—"

"I spent the past two years lying to Kate, Caro, and both their husbands about my true identity," she said, guilt shadowing her blue eyes. "I'm not ready to face their disappointment just yet."

"You had good reason for your deception, Poppy," he argued. "I feel sure that they would forgive you if you told them the circumstances."

But the tension emanating from her didn't diminish. "If it becomes necessary to contact Mr. Eversham in order to clear Violet's name, then I will agree to it, of course. But please give me a few days to get used to the idea. Because you know as well as I do that if he comes here, Kate and Caro will come with him."

Recalling the genuine affection he'd seen between the three women in London, Langham had a feeling that her friends would be much more forgiving than Poppy seemed to think, but it was clear she felt strongly about the matter, and he didn't wish to add to her upset. "Very well, but let me know as soon as you're ready for me to contact him."

She nodded, and her relief was clear. Then, as if remembering another concern, she twisted her lips into a pained expression. "Are you certain bringing Violet to the abbey is wise? I've already upset your sister with my mere presence, not to mention how I spoke to her. I haven't even met your grandmama yet, and she's sure to hate me. And now you're going to foist an accused murderess on them? It's hardly the sort of thing to endear any of your family to our betrothal—whether it's fictitious or not."

"You leave my family to me, my dear Miss Delamere,"

Langham assured her. "What good is it to be the Duke of Langham if I cannot simply do as I please?"

"You are the Duke of Langham! You cannot simply do as you please," the dowager all but shouted at her grandson as he and Poppy stood before her in her private suite of rooms in the abbey an hour later.

So much for the freedoms of being a duke, Poppy reflected dryly. She could feel his tension in the arm he'd offered her before they'd gone upstairs to answer the dowager's summons. It had never occurred to her that a man of his stature and status might feel anything but annoyance when called to the carpet by a female relation. But it was clear from the way he politely allowed his grandmother's tirade to continue unchecked that despite his intent to thwart her matrimonial plans for him, he disliked making her unhappy.

"You knew very well that I'd invited the crème de la crème of London's most eligible ladies, Langham!" the dowager continued, her face rosy with ire as she stroked the little dog in her lap in agitation. "You have a duty to this family to marry well, boy. You cannot simply elevate some nobody to the title of duchess without a by-your-leave, no matter how pretty she may be. She was *employed* for pity's sake. And lived *on her own* in London. Dukes do not marry ladies who work for a living, Langham. It's simply not done."

Finally, she stopped to draw breath, then said crossly, "And do sit down. Both of you. I will get an ache in my neck from looking up at you." Her blue eyes, so like her grandson's, were still narrowed with pique, but Poppy thought she seemed to have vented most of her spleen.

"As you wish," Langham said pleasantly, leading Poppy to a settee near the fire. It was still a little chilly for May, and she was grateful for the warmth. "The last thing Miss Delamere or I could want is for you to do yourself an injury. Isn't that right, my darling?"

Poppy gave the duke a sidelong glance at the endearment, sensing some devilry on his part, but the sweet smile he'd given her seemed so sincere, she almost believed he meant it. Unable to tell the difference, her heart constricted all the same.

The dowager huffed. "If you had a care for my comfort, you would not have brought this chit home with you in the first place. A fine thing to gift me on my birthday— unhappy guests and a betrothed so far beneath you even the servants will look askance at her."

Though she'd managed to change from the travel-soiled gown that Langham's sister had found so objectionable into a far more fashionable one she'd purchased ready-made from Kate's dressmaker, she now realized she could be wearing a custom-fitted Worth frock and the dowager would still have greeted her with the same enthusiasm as a snake in one's sewing box. The dowager had had plans, Poppy realized, and nobody liked to have their expectations thwarted. Especially not dowager duchesses accustomed to having their every whim satisfied.

Still, recalling the way Langham had come to her defense with Lord Short earlier, Poppy wanted dearly to repay the favor. "I fear you are being most unfair to the duke, Your Grace," she said, unable to hide her wince when the dowager turned her gimlet eye upon her. Still, Poppy pressed on. "Langham was very concerned over how our news would affect your party," she said truthfully. If his concern had been more about having to manage the disappointment of the prospective brides than worry over his grandmother's reception of their news, well, that was neither here nor there.

To her surprise, the dowager lifted a lorgnette to her eyes to examine Poppy more closely.

So that's where he learned to wield a quizzing glass. Poppy turned a speaking look upon the duke, but he shrugged, if a little sheepishly.

"Put that thing away, Grandmama," he said, making a show of patting Poppy on the hand. "You're making my poor fiancée nervous."

"I am no such th—" Poppy began.

But Langham interrupted her. "Though you have endeavored more than once to browbeat my duty into me, Grandmama, I have always managed somehow to forget those lessons when the need suits. The moment I asked my dearest Poppy to be my wife is perhaps the most felicitous. I had hoped you would have the good sense to wish us happy."

"Happy?" the dowager scoffed, dropping the lorgnette in disgust. "How can I wish you happy when I must go back down to the drawing room and pretend to welcome such a creature into our family. It is not to be borne."

Though she'd been trying to keep her temper, Poppy was growing weary of the dowager duchess's derision. But Langham's stillness beside her alerted her to the fact that he was more annoyed still.

His earlier good humor, she saw when she glanced over at him, had been replaced with a look remarkably similar to the one he'd directed at her stepfather.

"I was prepared for some degree of petulance on your part, Grandmama. But this denigration of my betrothed will end now. You will refer to her as Miss Delamere, or by her given name. And you will treat her with the respect that is due to her as the affianced bride of the Duke of Langham, madam, or we will begin your removal to one of the estates in Scotland this very day."

The sharpness of his tone made Poppy flinch, but the squeeze of his hand offered silent reassurance. She'd become so accustomed to fending for herself—first in Lord Short's household, and then in London—that she was nonplussed at his championing of her. She'd begun the day thinking him high-handed and a bit too accustomed to having his own way. And she hadn't exactly changed her mind on either point. But whatever her opinion of the man had been before, she now knew that he was more than just the arrogant aristocratic face he showed to the world.

Langham's words must have startled his grandmother as well, because she paled and blinked. Poppy could almost hear the calculations running through the older woman's mind as she tried to decide just how serious her grandson was about his threat.

"Try my patience if you don't believe me," he said, as if reading his grandmother's thoughts.

"Very well," the dowager conceded at last. "I am still put out with you, but I suppose you give me no choice but to do the pretty for her. No matter how unsuited she might be to serving as your duchess. Not to mention the bad business with the sister and her parents."

"I didn't hear an apology for Miss Delamere in that little speech," Langham said mildly.

"Langham, there's no need," Poppy protested, laying a hand on his arm. She'd been oddly moved by his defense of her, but she didn't wish to be the cause of a permanent rift between them. Especially given that their betrothal wasn't even real.

Not to mention that making an enemy of the dowager would only make her time at the abbey that much more uncomfortable.

"I don't need an apology." If she'd expected the duchess to be grateful for her demurral, however, Poppy was to be sorely disappointed.

"You see there? No backbone at all!" The dowager shook her head in disgust. "I suggest you learn to stand up for yourself, gel, or you will have every mushroom and hanger-on in society pulling you this way and that. A duchess must be sure of herself, above all. I have cultivated one of the most fearsome reputations in the *ton*. It wasn't through timidity, I can tell you."

Beside her, Poppy heard Langham give a snort of laughter. She turned to him with a frown. "What is so amusing?"

"Do not rip up at me, but I cannot help thinking that 'meek' is the last word I'd ever use to describe you," he said with a grin. And despite herself, Poppy grinned back.

"Timidity has never been what I'd consider one of my overriding characteristics," she conceded wryly.

"What are the two of you whispering about?" the dowager demanded. "It is quite rude, but not the sort of behavior from either one of you that should surprise me."

Before Langham could respond, Poppy took the opportunity to pat *him* on the arm. "Allow me," she told him in an undertone.

To the dowager she said in a louder voice, "Your Grace, I hope you will come to know me better. Indeed, it is my greatest wish that we become friends this week. But I must agree with the duke. I can stand up for myself when necessary, and in this instance, I was simply trying to keep Langham from being overly harsh with you. Clearly that was my mistake. If my concern for your feelings makes you believe that I have a propensity to let myself be trampled upon, then I will give him free rein to chide you as he sees fit from now on."

The dowager stared at her like a cat that had danced a jig for the barest moment before her scowl turned into a wide smile that was not unlike her grandson's.

"Well played, gel. Well played. I won't say that I'm any more sanguine about Langham's recklessness in choosing you, but I'm glad to see you don't bear any resemblance in personality to your pinch-faced mama. It will take all of my social standing to turn this misalliance into something resembling a good match, but make no mistake, I will do just that."

Ignoring the insult to her mother—that was an argument for another day—Poppy nodded in acknowledgment. "I thank you, Your Grace. I hope I will manage to make the task no more difficult than it has to be."

"The first thing we must do," the dowager returned baldly, "is to find a wardrobe for you that doesn't look fit for the rag bag. Am I correct in assuming the rest of the clothing you've brought is equally shabby?"

Before Poppy could reply, Langham spoke up. "I thought perhaps one of my sisters might have something she might wear until we're able to visit the shops in London."

"That will do for a few days," the dowager said with a frown, "but she can hardly be seen in your sisters' castoffs for the entire week. It's not fitting for the future Duchess of Langham. Of course, we'll have my modiste come up from London. In the meantime, I'll have Jacobs take her measurements to send with the messenger so Madame Roget can alter some gowns she's already working on."

"Oh, but there's no need—" This ruse had already left

Poppy far more indebted to the duke than she'd anticipated. She could never possibly repay him for gowns crafted by the sort of dressmaker patronized by the dowager duchess.

But Langham was already waving away her protest. "I'm afraid in this case Grandmama is correct. I hadn't considered the implications of your wearing my sisters' gowns for the rest of the week. I daresay they have several that they've never even worn, but servants gossip. And I cannot have it be put about that I'm a skinflint."

Poppy tried to convey her objection to the notion with her eyes, but Langham only raised his brows at her in an equally speaking look.

"Do not be stubborn," he said finally, his voice ringing with such finality that she knew she had lost this particular battle.

"Fine," she said grumpily. "I don't like it, but I suppose I have little choice in the matter."

"Every gel likes new dresses," the dowager corrected her. "And it's not as if Langham can't afford it. He's proved to be much better at managing the dukedom's fortunes than either his father or grandfather before him, bless them. My husband and son were dear men, but they didn't know the first thing about estate management."

It was the first nice thing the dowager had said to Langham since he and Poppy had entered her parlor. And to Poppy's surprise, rather than preen at the praise, he instead changed the subject.

"We'd better get back to your guests," he said pointedly to the dowager, standing and indicating that Poppy should also rise. "I daresay they have eaten all the sandwiches by now."

Could it be that the lofty Duke of Langham was uncomfortable with compliments? It was an odd notion, considering that he must find himself the object of all sorts of admiring comments. He was a duke, after all.

Then she recalled what he'd said about the fawning and flattery to which he was subjected and realized it might not be all that strange for someone who had reason to think praise was very often suspect to dismiss kind words. Even when they came from loved ones.

She would have reflected more on the paradox, but it was clearly time for them to go to the drawing room.

"I will ring for more sandwiches as soon as we go in," the duchess said, handing her sleeping Pekingese to a waiting maid. "I daresay Percy will wish for some as well. He is always peckish after a nap."

"You spoil that dog," Langham said with a roll of his eyes. "I daresay he eats better than some of the royal dukes."

"Now that you are betrothed," the dowager said with a speaking look, "perhaps I can expect to spoil a ducal heir soon."

To Poppy's amusement, twin flags of color appeared on Langham's cheeks.

But her own stifled laughter was cut short when the dowager said, "I hope your reason for marrying is not because you expect to do so sooner than is proper."

Poppy felt her own face heat and was about to utter a denial when Langham beat her to it.

"Grandmama, behave yourself," he said sharply. "You're embarrassing Miss Delamere."

"Given the haste of this betrothal, Langham," the older lady said without an iota of repentance, "and your reputation with the ladies, it is a reasonable question. Though in my day it would not make a difference one way or the other if you had anticipated your vows. My generation was far more practical about such matters than the current one. I blame the queen. Though given the number of children she has herself, one would suppose she's not quite so priggish as all that."

Poppy dared to look over at Langham and saw that he was just as uncomfortable by the dowager's frank talk as she was.

"What?" the dowager demanded looking from her grandson to Poppy and back. "You young people behave as if you were the ones to discover passion. Which is patently absurd, considering you would not be here to look so pained at my plain speaking if that were the case."

Poppy and Langham exchanged an amused look. The dowager did have a point, she supposed.

"Well," Langham said, after a cough that might have been covering up a laugh, "it is not something that we need be concerned about in this case."

When the dowager began to speak, he held up a stay-ing hand. "Pray, let us change the subject, Grandmama. I do not believe my heart can endure more of your plain speaking at the moment."

Looking amused despite her pursed lips, the dowager turned to Poppy. "Come, Miss Delamere. If we are to convince the young ladies I invited to parade before my grandson that I am happy he's chosen you, then we had better make a good show of it."

Feeling rather as if she were jumping from the frying pan into the fire, Poppy gave the duke a wide-eyed look that clearly asked for help. But he only gave her a cheeky wink and followed them into the hallway beyond.

Do not be such a mouse, she chided herself as she and the dowager neared the drawing room, where the sound of conversation could be heard even from outside the chamber.

But it had been such a long time since she had entered a social gathering as herself. Even if she was playing the role of Langham's betrothed, she hadn't been introduced to a crowd of guests as Poppy Delamere in two long years. She wasn't even sure she knew who that person was anymore.

As they neared the doorway, she felt Langham step up beside her and take her other arm. "Breathe," he said in a low voice only she could hear. "You aren't timid, remember?"

She felt the soft warmth of his breath on her neck and could just detect the sandalwood scent of his soap. And almost imperceptibly she felt herself relax.

"No, I am not," she said, although she wasn't sure if she was speaking to him or to herself. And then steeling her spine, she allowed the duke and his grandmother to lead her into the fray.

Chapter Six

Langham hadn't been apprehensive to enter a room since he'd been a schoolboy facing punishment at Eton.

So, it was a novel feeling to watch for signs of animus in the faces of his sister Charlotte—Genia must have been getting her children settled—and the other assembled guests in the drawing room. He didn't give a hang what they might think of him, but Poppy wasn't accustomed to this kind of scrutiny. And he was damned if he'd allow her to be insulted in his own house.

She might be just as adept as he was at hiding her true feelings, but he'd seen the way she'd reacted to Short's harsh words earlier. She was not, as she'd have him believe, impervious to insult. And if he could protect her from the harsher reactions of the assembled guests to the news of their betrothal, then he'd do so.

And it was clear from the way his grandmother surveyed the crowd that however much she might have objected to Poppy in private, she was now taking her under her wing.

"I know some of you have already been privy to the news," the dowager said after she had introduced Poppy to the assembled gathering, "but I am simply delighted to learn that my dear Langham has chosen a bride for himself at last. I should have known he would choose an original. He has always had a way of surprising us all, hasn't he?"

Langham watched in amusement as one of their neighbors, Mrs. Simkins, all but leapt bodily from her chair to offer it to the dowager, who inclined her head and indicated that Poppy should take the chair beside it, despite the fact that it was already occupied by Lady Adele Chambers.

The younger woman, who might have expected to retain her chair, given that she was the daughter of an earl, frowned, but relinquished her seat and moved to stand on the other side of the room.

"It certainly shocked me," Charlotte said with a raised brow and a glare in Langham's direction. Clearly, she was not over her annoyance from their encounter at the train station. He had hoped that realizing just how rude she'd been to Poppy would have given his sister some degree of shame over her actions, but stubbornness was a family trait.

"Especially," Charlotte continued, "given the fact that my brother and his betrothed cast proprieties to the wind and traveled together without benefit of even a maid to offer chaperonage."

A small gasp went up from the ladies in the room, and the duke fought the urge to roll his eyes. His grandmother was right. This insistence upon propriety above all else was foolish. Would it have been better for Poppy to ride in a crowded train compartment with a contingent of strangers?

He was about to say as much when Poppy spoke. "How kind of you to worry about my reputation, Lady Felton," she said, settling her teacup back onto its saucer. "But I'm afraid it could not be helped. My own maid became indisposed just as we were about to depart, and there was no time to find another. But His Grace's valet was there with us in the train carriage. It was all perfectly respectable, I assure you. Besides, we are betrothed, after all."

"Your maid *must* have been indisposed to let you out of the house in a gown like that," murmured Miss Louisa Beaconfield in a voice low enough not to be heard by the dowager. A few of the young ladies gathered around her tittered.

But Poppy responded to the barb as if it had been said in a voice that carried to all of them. "Oh, you musn't blame my maid for the fact that my gown is outdated. I'm afraid I've been unable to replenish my wardrobe during my time in London. I was away from my family, you see. And not everyone can be a wealthy heiress like you, Miss Beaconfield."

Miss Beaconfield looked as if she'd swallowed a spider.

"How did your father make his fortune again? I believe I read something in the papers about mining interests in Wales? What was it? Oh yes," Poppy said with a smile that didn't reach her eyes, "boys not even eleven years old were found to be working in those mines, weren't they? But I suppose a child's life is nothing when measured against the cost of a pretty gown, is it?"

"What is this vulgarity?" sniffed Lady Throckmorton, one of the dowager's cronies, whose eyes were gleeful rather than scandalized. "In my day we did not speak of such things in a genteel drawing room."

"But if no one ever speaks of such things, my lady," Poppy asked, unrattled, "then how are we to change such practices?"

Lady Alice Gerson gave a nervous giggle. "Next you'll be prosing on about the vote and how women should be allowed to go to university, Miss Delamere." But it was clear from the lady's tone that she thought both subjects to be beneath her notice.

A ripple of laughter traveled through the room. But Langham was impressed to note that Poppy didn't seem bothered by it.

"I do believe women should be able to vote and go to university," she said with a shrug. "The law affects women just as it affects men, after all. Why should not women be afforded the opportunity to choose who will make those laws? As for university, why shouldn't women who wish to be allowed to study there? Intellect is not a gift bestowed solely upon men."

"Your fiancée is a radical, Langham," said his cousin Viscount Carlyle from where he stood beside him. "I'm surprised you allow her to run on like this. If she were betrothed to anyone other than you, she would have ruined her chances with the *ton* with that little speech. As it is, she will likely find herself with few friends here."

But even as the words were spoken, one of the other young ladies whom Grandmama had invited—Miss Ingraham, whose father, Lord Hurst, had met and married her mother while a naval officer in the West Indies—said in a voice that gained strength as she went, "I agree with Miss Delamere on both counts. I have long wished to go to university to study mathematics. And I plan to do so just as soon as I convince Papa to agree to it."

A few of the other ladies nodded in agreement and began to say which field they would pursue at Oxford or Cambridge if given the chance. To Langham's amusement, the expression on Poppy's face was one of surprise. She most likely hadn't expected to receive this sort of response from this crowd.

Once the chatter had died down, Miss Beaconfield—of the father with the mines—spoke up again. "I now understand why you continue to wear such an outmoded gown, Miss Delamere." Her smirk was one of smug self-righteousness. "You are simply a bluestocking. I should be very surprised if you even have a maid at all." Dismissal rang in the lady's voice.

A muted gasp went up from the gathering. But Poppy wasn't cowed by the rudeness. "I daresay it is no longer in the first stare of fashion," she said, looking down at the light blue silk, which Langham thought looked rather fine with her eyes whether it was in the current style or not. "Though I beg you will not malign it too much. It is one of my favorites, and it has lasted me nearly a year and a half. Which outside the *ton* is counted a blessing rather than something of which to be ashamed."

Even if Poppy was as unbothered by the lack of respect the other lady continued to show her, Langham was not. He had invited her into this veritable den of vipers, and he would be the one to rescue her from it.

Stepping a foot in her direction, he asked thoughtfully, "Indeed, were you not wearing this particular confection on the day we met, my dear? I must admit, I will always have a fondness for it for that reason alone." She had been wearing no such thing, of course.

Never missing a beat, Poppy fixed a look of fond exasperation on him, and Langham almost believed it to be genuine. "My dear duke," she said with a laugh, "I was wearing an entirely different gown altogether that day. But I daresay you were distracted." The laugh that rose from the others this time was one of amused good humor. This was the sort of gentle teasing that they were all more comfortable with.

Her next words, however, had him stifling a groan. "He told me that day that I had the finest eyes he'd ever seen. Indeed, he's written several quite moving verses to them. Let me see if I can remember how the first one goes—"

"Now, now, my dear," he interrupted her before she could begin reciting what would no doubt be the sort of terrible poetry that would make him the laughingstock of London for decades to come. "There's no need to share my private writings with everyone here."

She was purposely mocking him, the minx.

Not *everyone*, thank tits, believed her faradiddle.

From her seat at the tea table, his sister Caroline stared at him as if he'd sprouted horns and a tail. "I've never known you to be the least bit poetic, Langham. In fact, did you not once say that poetry is the lowest form of art?"

"I believe I remember him saying that as well," Felton agreed with a frown. Then the man shook his head as if genuinely disappointed. "Never thought I'd see you fall to Cupid's arrow, old fellow. It's a deuced shame."

Langham reminded himself to refuse the man the next time he asked for a small loan.

"Do not be too hard on him," Poppy said, looking at him with the kind of expression usually bestowed by mothers upon their newly ambulatory offspring. "He can be quite eloquent when the mood strikes him."

The look he turned her way, he hoped, was telling her with great eloquence how much he wished to toss her—clothes and all—into the lake just beyond the abbey gardens.

Correctly reading his expression, no doubt, Poppy directed an unrepentant pout his way. "I'm so sorry, dearest.

I hadn't realized you weren't as proud of your poetry as I am. Do not be cross with me."

Deciding that her trial by dowager had probably warranted raking him over the coals a bit, Langham gave her the kind of fatuously indulgent smile he'd seen Wrackham give Caro often enough. Moving to stand beside her, he took her hand and brought it to his lips. "I could never stay cross with you, my darling. You are far too precious to me."

Poppy, he noted, was having some difficulty maintaining a straight face. Served her right, the mischief maker.

Grandmama, who had been watching their interplay sharply, narrowed her eyes. Poppy must have noticed, because she squeezed Langham's hand and then let it go. "We are just teasing one another, Your Grace," she said to the dowager. "You know well enough that your grandson is not one for such effusiveness. Especially not in public. I was twitting him because I'd asked him not to come to my rescue if there were any trouble, but he couldn't help himself and did so anyway."

Realizing she'd hit on the perfect way to deflect Grandmama's suspicions, Langham marveled at how skillfully Poppy had averted potential disaster. He, of course, had taken the show of affection too far, and had almost sunk their scheme when it was barely afloat. But he should have known that two years of living as someone else would have given her an ability to feint as deftly as any prizefighter.

"I couldn't tell you what she was wearing at our first meeting if you threatened to lock me in the tower," Langham admitted, deciding it would be better if he confessed to his small lie to add credibility to Poppy's story.

"I don't understand," Charlotte said, looking from him

to Poppy and back again. "Do you mean you haven't written reams of poetry to her? I was hoping to hold this over your head for decades to come, Langham."

"Not a one," he said with a laugh. "Though I stand by the compliment to Miss Delamere's fine eyes."

He did not dare look toward Grandmama until she gave a bark of laughter.

"It serves you right, Langham," she said, dabbing at her eyes with the lace edge of her handkerchief. "This gel of yours is more than up to the task of withstanding a little drawing room conversation. The next time you'll think twice before intruding on ladies' business."

No one except his grandmother would dare speak to him that way, Langham reflected ruefully. His grandmother and Poppy, he amended.

"I certainly will," he said, exchanging a look with his fiancée. "Now, I will wander back over there to converse with the gentlemen and leave you to your ladies' business. My betrothed, it would seem, is more than capable of defending herself."

He'd just settled his shoulder against one of the decorative columns in the expansive drawing room when he heard an amused voice from just behind him.

"She's held her own among these cats."

Langham turned to see Sir Geoffrey Stannings, the very man he'd wanted to speak to regarding Poppy's sister. They had known one another since they were in short coats, and though there was a liberal amount of silver threaded through his old friend's dark hair, life as a country squire appeared to agree with him.

"Stannings," Langham greeted his friend. He decided to wait to broach the topic of Violet until they had more privacy. "I'm surprised to see you here."

It was the sort of gathering both men would have avoided like the pox in their salad days.

"I'm not so secure in my standing in the neighborhood that I can blithely ignore an invitation from the dowager, my good fellow," the magistrate said with a raised brow. "Besides, my wife would have had my guts for garters if I didn't attend."

Since Mrs. Stannings was as mild-mannered a lady as Langham had ever met, he took this last assertion with a grain of salt.

"Speaking of wives," Stannings said, "or rather betrotheds, why on earth would you spring yours on this crowd without at least buying her a new gown for the occasion? It doesn't reflect favorably on you or the title for your prospective bride to be forced to compete with them."

"I know you're an upstanding man in the county now, but when did you become such a snob about fashion?" Langham said in a voice only the two of them could hear.

But Stannings didn't take insult at the question. "It doesn't make me a snob to see that her shabby appearance gave the other young ladies here—most of whom expected to compete for your favors—the idea that she is beneath them."

Since the observation wasn't entirely wrong, Langham let the criticism pass. "If you must know, my intended happens to be one of the most stubborn creatures I've ever encountered. I daresay the queen herself wouldn't have persuaded her to accept a new dress from me for the occasion. And besides that, we left London in something of a hurry, considering the circumstances."

Stannings frowned. "I don't follow. What circumstances?" Then, as if considering a possible explanation, he said in a low whisper, "If you've got the chit with child—"

Before the other man could finish, Langham shot him a quelling look. "Keep your damned voice down. It would be a pity to have to kill you, given that you're the local magistrate, but do not doubt that I will if you create more trouble for Poppy. She's dealing with enough just now."

Raising his hands in a defensive gesture, Stannings said hastily, "No disrespect intended. My apologies, of course."

Somewhat mollified, Langham tried to shake off the surge of protective fury. He'd offered this false betrothal as a way for Poppy to salvage her pride, but if any of the assembled guests had overheard his friend's whisper, honor would dictate he offer for her in truth.

Knowing Poppy, she would turn him down flat and go on with her business. If he had to wed, however—and one day he would—he was convinced that at least with Poppy he wouldn't have to worry about false flattery or simpering. He could trust her to tell him the truth.

"Perhaps you aren't aware of it," Langham continued in a hushed tone, "but Miss Delamere is the half sister of Violet Lovell."

"No!" Stannings said, in a voice that immediately drew the attention of everyone in the room.

The duke glared at the man before turning to the others with a laugh. "You must excuse Sir Geoffrey's outburst. I just informed him that I bested Gentleman Jim Hyde in the ring earlier this week. But I can assure you it's the truth. Hyde gave me quite a bout, but I managed to overcome him in the end."

"A barbaric sport," Charlotte said with disgust. "I have never approved of your lowering yourself to dabble in it, Langham. I cannot imagine what Papa or even Grandpapa would say about such a stain on the title."

"Since your grandpapa frequented Jackson's Boxing Salon and was quite the pugilist in his day, my gel," said the dowager, "then I think he, for one, would have only praise for your brother. As for your father, though, I cannot say whether he practiced the sport. If he were here, then your brother would not be the duke and your point would be moot."

The guests, wisely noting that the dowager had put an end to the conversing across the room, turned back to their respective huddles, and Langham nodded at the magistrate to continue.

"I didn't realize there was another daughter in the Short household," Stannings explained. "Not that it surprises me that Short, at least, would leave out information. His wife seems to be a rather timid sort, but Short himself is..." He paused, as if searching for the right word. "Wily, I suppose. He's friendly enough, and never has an ill word to say. But I always get the impression he's talking out of both sides of his mouth."

"I had the displeasure of meeting him earlier today, and that was also my impression," Langham agreed. "Poppy fled from her stepfather's household two years ago— before they moved to Little Kidding. He'd tried to force her into a marriage with Lovell, who was Short's personal secretary at the time. And when neither man would take no for an answer, she ran away to London."

The magistrate frowned. "I would think a baronet would try to get someone higher for his daughters than a mere secretary, though it's an honorable enough position. I'd say he might have arranged the match for Poppy because she wasn't his child by blood, but the fact that he then gave his own daughter to the man belies that notion. Perhaps he simply wished to keep the young ladies close to home. A less than advantageous match is perhaps unwise, but it's hardly illegal."

"Not illegal, no." Langham replied. "But the fact that Poppy was forced to flee, coupled with the way Short then immediately changed course and arranged Violet's marriage to Lovell, seems questionable at best. Then there's the fact that Lovell is, indeed, dead. I'd like to know more about the circumstances of the death, Stannings. And why you think Violet might be responsible for it."

Stannings scanned the room. "Let us talk about this in a more discreet location. As you have already pointed out, it would be easy to be overheard here. And seeing as how you're betrothed is the accused's sister, it would not look particularly proper for me to be seen discussing the finer details of the matter with you."

Langham opened his mouth to object, but the other man raised a staying hand. "I didn't say I would not discuss it with you, Langham," he said in a low voice. "Only that we should do so more discreetly."

Satisfied with the other man's answer, Langham nodded. "Once this tea is finished, we can retire to my study. I cannot go before Poppy has been introduced to everyone, and besides that, I wish for her to come with us so that she has a chance to speak with you as well. She has questions about her sister's situation, and I did promise her that I would do what I could to smooth the way for her to ask them."

"I am more than happy to speak with her," Stannings said with a frown. "But I can hardly get into the ugly business of the actual murder with her. You know as well as I do that ladies are constitutionally unable to listen to such dark realities, whatever your Miss Delamere might say about suffrage or women attending university. I have heard my own physician speak about the ways in which that kind of knowledge can cause hysteria and in some cases sterility. I would hate to be responsible for your inability to get an heir on her."

Langham had heard such theories regarding the supposed fragility of the female constitution, of course, but he'd long since come to believe that such notions were hogwash. One only had to look to the queen and her nine offspring to realize that serious subjects didn't damage a woman's ability to conceive. But he could hardly say that to Stannings's face when he was asking the fellow for a favor.

Instead, he simply made an ambiguous sound that he hoped the magistrate would take as agreement.

At that moment, the dowager rose from her chair with the aid of her crystal-topped walking stick and spoke to the room at large. "It has been an eventful afternoon. I shall see you all again at dinner."

Langham watched as Poppy rose as well and offered the dowager her arm, but the older woman batted it away. "I'm not in my dotage yet, gel. Go find that grandson of mine. I feel sure there are more introductions to be made before the evening falls upon us."

Their hostess having gone, the rest of the guests began to disperse as well. Some followed the dowager upstairs to their rooms to nap, while a few of the men planned to meet in the billiard room for a game.

When Poppy appeared at Langham's side, he slipped his arm through hers. "Well, my dear, you have survived your first afternoon tea with my family. How do you feel?"

"It wasn't your family who proved difficult," Poppy returned with an arched brow. "But even those young ladies who were less than cordial will come round eventually, I imagine. Or I hope, rather."

"My dear Miss Delamere," Stannings said before Langham could reply. "You have managed to snare the most eligible bachelor in all of England. Dukes below the age of forty with all their teeth are thin upon the ground. You must expect that there will be a few aristocratic noses put out of joint by your triumph."

"All the triumph is mine, Stannings," Langham said before Poppy could respond. To Poppy he said, "My dear, you must allow me to introduce Sir Geoffrey Stannings. He is the local magistrate and has kindly agreed to speak with us about your sister's situation in my study."

At the mention of the other man's name, Langham saw Poppy's eyes widen, and he didn't miss the glint of gratitude in them as she looked from Stannings back to him. Something about that left him feeling cold. He didn't want her to be grateful to him, damn it. He was simply fulfilling his part of the bargain, just as she was fulfilling hers.

"I am delighted to meet you, Miss Delamere," Stannings said, bowing deeply over Poppy's hand. "Leave it to you, Langham, to snare the loveliest lady in London before the rest of us even had a chance to meet her."

"Need I remind you that you already have a wife?" the duke drawled, fighting the urge to drape his coat over Poppy to hide her from the other man's too-intent gaze. Clearly, he needed to get a hold of himself. He was not, as a rule, a jealous sort, but there was something about Poppy that raised his blood. It must be the fact that this betrothal, no matter how false it may be, had placed her under his protection.

Keep telling yourself that, said the impertinent voice in his head.

"I do, indeed," said Stannings mildly. "But last I checked she does not object to my being introduced to other ladies,

Langham. *Ton* entertainments would be overrun with wall-flowers if married men were not allowed to make the acquaintance of ladies other than their wives."

But Poppy had taken no notice of the interplay between the two men. Her eyes revealed her desperation to speak with the magistrate about her sister. "Sir Geoffrey, I am so pleased to meet you."

"Let's retire to the study," Langham said slipping an arm around her waist and leading her toward the hallway, leaving Stannings to follow.

Once they'd arrived in the book-lined room and all three had been settled into chairs with stronger spirits than the tea they'd imbibed in the drawing room, Poppy turned her expectant gaze on Stannings and waited.

"I'll be happy to assist you in whatever way I can, Miss Delamere," Viscount Stannings said with a nod. "Though I must warn you that there are certain things I may not discuss because of the ongoing investigation."

"Of course," Poppy said with a nod, her voice strong and unflinching. "And given that you can only answer a limited number of questions, I'll ask the most pertinent one first. I'd like to know what you intend to do about the fact that my sister is innocent of her husband's murder."

Chapter Seven

Poppy watched as the magistrate tried to formulate a response to her question.

It was, of course, no surprise that the man would not believe her at first. He probably had family members of accused criminals approaching him with claims of innocence all the time. But in this case, her claim was true.

"I know you must be unwilling to think your sister capable of such a thing, Miss Delamere," Sir Geoffrey began finally, after a pained look in Langham's direction, "but I can assure you that we have investigated the matter fully. Now, please, do not overtax yourself with thoughts of such a macabre nature. What your sister needs from you now is—"

"I know she is innocent, Sir Geoffrey," Poppy interrupted him, doing her best to keep a hold on her patience, "because Violet has a fear of heights. There is no possible way she would have voluntarily climbed the bell tower of St. Lucy's. To murder her husband or to do anything else."

Really, why did so many men assume that a lady couldn't possibly know something that they did not?

The magistrate lifted a hand as if to dismiss her. "Fear of heights is hardly proof of innocence, Miss Delamere. It's entirely possible she was taken there against her will and pushed him off while defending herself. Either way she would still be responsible for his death."

Before Poppy could object, Langham spoke up. "At this point, her presence with her husband at the top of the bell tower seems to be only conjecture on your part, Stannings. What is the evidence that she was even there?"

The viscount looked uncomfortable. "There are some details I simply cannot share with you, Langham. No matter how I might wish to."

Turning to Poppy, he said with a sterner attitude, "I really wish that you would leave this matter in the hands of your fiancé and your stepfather, Miss Delamere. It is not the sort of thing a lady should—"

Poppy had had enough. "Sir Geoffrey, I am quite capable of talking about the guilt or innocence of a beloved sister without dissolving like a blancmange left in the rain. The duke has no objections to my hearing your report. Therefore, your own objections are immaterial. Now, please answer my question. What evidence do you have that my sister is guilty of this crime?"

The magistrate's eyes flashed at her forceful tone, and Poppy was afraid for a moment that she'd gone too far. But she had come to Little Kidding to find out how she might help her sister, and if this man refused to give her even the most basic facts about the case against Violet, then she was sunk before she'd even begun to investigate.

Finally, after a baleful look in Langham's direction, which the duke returned with merely a raised brow,

Stannings said to her, "It was well known among those living in the Short household that Mr. and Mrs. Lovell's marriage was not a happy one. Indeed, Lord Short himself told the constable that as soon as he learned Mr. Lovell had been found dead, he feared that Violet had finally taken matters into her own hands. He even said that he saw her following Lovell on foot that evening and heard her return later that night. Alone."

Poppy's fists clenched. She might have known her stepfather would be behind the accusation against Violet. She wouldn't be surprised if Lord Short himself was the one responsible for his secretary's death. Though she had no proof, of course. Not beyond her own distrust of the man.

"Thus far," Stannings continued, his voice a little calmer now, "your sister has refused to offer any explanation for her husband's death at all. All we have to go on is your stepfather's accusation. And as he has an unblemished reputation in the neighborhood, I have no reason to doubt his account of the matter."

At the description of Lord Short as upstanding, Poppy couldn't hold back a bitter laugh. It would seem that he'd managed to fool the denizens of Little Kidding in the same way he'd done in so many communities before.

Misinterpreting her reaction, Stannings said with a little stiffness, "I understand you have been estranged from your family, Miss Delamere. Your father said you'd left them without a word a year or so before they moved to Little Kidding. I hope you will not allow an old wound to prevent you from seeing the truth about your sister. It will do her no good for you to offer false hope if she is indeed guilty of her husband's murder."

It was only the warm press of Langham's hand on her shoulder—he'd come to stand behind her, clearly noting that she was nearing the end of her tether with Stannings's condescension—that kept her from telling the magistrate just what she thought of his advice. He was not the first to be taken in by her stepfather's smooth manners and congenial attitude. But it was crushing to see that the man who held her sister's fate in his hands had failed to see Lord Short's true nature.

"Stepfather," Langham corrected the other man tersely. Poppy could hear the steel in his voice and drew such comfort from the fact that he was on her side that she could barely breathe. Without him, she'd never have been able to speak to Stannings at all, much less alone in the company of a man who had the power to make the magistrate listen. "And I would take what Lord Short says with a grain of salt. It is not my story to tell, but the man is not what he seems."

She felt her gut clench at Langham's hint about Lord Short's scheming, but she was grateful that he hadn't gone into detail. She needed to ensure that her sister and mother had somewhere safe to go before Lord Short was brought to justice and they were cast out upon the streets.

"But Miss Delamere has been away from her family for years," Stannings argued. "Isn't it possible her sister wanted to marry Lovell and wasn't forced into it at all? Long separations can mean changes in personality. After all, Miss Delamere, wasn't your sister only sixteen when you left? She might have become another person entirely while you were gone."

"I admit that I may not know her as well as I once did," Poppy said sharply, "but I can tell you this—there is no way that my sister, then or now, would have willingly married a man twice her age. Especially not Mr. Lovell. She dreamt of a match with a handsome young man with, oh, a castle and an estate with rolling hills and a fine carriage. What she did not envision was marriage to a man who took every opportunity to ogle us and was rude to the servants. He was an unpleasant man, and I cannot imagine he changed overly much in the time since I'd left."

"That's just girlish notions," Stannings protested. "I met the man on several occasions, and though he did seem a bit brusque, he was perfectly polite. Certainly, he didn't deserve to be murdered."

"She didn't say he deserved to be murdered," Langham snapped. "She said he was rude and couldn't keep his eyes to himself. I will thank you to have more respect for my betrothed. I told her she could trust you, but it seems you are determined to prove me wrong."

Sir Geoffrey blanched, and Poppy once again felt a rush of relief that Langham was on her side.

"I am sorry, Miss Delamere, Langham is correct. I didn't mean to imply you wished Lovell dead."

It had been a decade or more since Langham had spent more than a few minutes in Stannings's company, and he couldn't say that the man's treatment of Poppy had made him regret it. As a boy, Geoffrey Stannings had been a good-natured, at times mischievous, friend. But as an adult he was a pompous bore.

Just because the magistrate had never witnessed Lovell behaving badly, that didn't mean it had never happened. Langham knew damned well that some men showed one face to their peers and another to those they considered beneath them. And he had little doubt that Stannings knew it, too.

With a sigh, the magistrate took off his spectacles and began cleaning the lenses with his handkerchief. "I must tell you, however, Miss Delamere, that right now you are the only one who has come forward to speak in your sister's defense. Although I am sure when I speak with her, she will have a story of her own to tell."

"Of course I'm the only one who has come forward to defend her," Poppy said, rising from her chair in agitation. When the magistrate made to stand as well, she waved him back down with a shake of her head. She didn't care about the proprieties at the moment. "My mother is far too cowed by my stepfather to be an effective champion, and if my stepfather has behaved in Little Kidding as he always has done, then he has prevented Violet from forming attachments with anyone in the village, lest she somehow reveal too much about his own machinations. I doubt she has a single friend here, much less one with enough bravado to defend her against a murder charge."

Coming to a stop before the fire, Poppy stared down into it with a scowl. Langham wished there was something more he could do to help her. It was clear that her sister's ordeal was weighing on her. If only they'd been able to—

Something Stannings had just said struck him. "Are you saying that you haven't spoken at all to Mrs. Lovell about the events on the night of the murder?"

At Langham's question, Poppy turned to stare at the magistrate. "Is this true?"

Stannings raised his hands in a staying gesture. "I can assure you it's not unusual at this point for only the constable to have interviewed the accused. I did attempt to speak with your sister this morning, Miss Delamere, but when I called at the grange, she was resting."

At the other man's words, Poppy raised her gaze to Langham, but she didn't address the news. Only nodded.

While there was nothing overtly suspicious about the fact that visitors for Violet had twice been turned away, Langham had a bad feeling about it. He and Poppy would need to return to the grange and try to determine what was going on.

Perhaps deeming the issue resolved, Stannings said, "You've both alluded more than once to some misdeeds on your stepfather's part, Miss Delamere. I wonder if you might be a bit more explicit about his wrongdoings?"

One glance at Poppy's face revealed that this was a difficult subject for her. He stepped forward to take her hand in his. "You don't need to tell him anything you don't wish to," he said in a voice that only she could hear. "Though I imagine hearing the truth from you will go a long way toward explaining why Lord Short might not be the most credible of witnesses when it comes to casting blame for Mr. Lovell's murder."

Her blue eyes were troubled, and he guessed what might be bothering her. "If it's your mother's safety, I will make sure she's protected. She can come here if need be."

Langham was frankly more worried about what Poppy's stepfather would do to Poppy if he learned that she'd revealed what she knew about his past crimes. But, unwilling to disquiet her further, he kept that concern to himself.

At his assurances, something in the set of Poppy's shoulders relaxed a bit, and he knew he'd said the right thing.

"Thank you," she said in a low voice.

Moving to stand at the other end of the mantelpiece, he gave a nod to Stannings, who had been watching them with undisguised curiosity.

"Lord Short is a confidence man, Sir Geoffrey," Poppy said, conviction strong in her voice. "From the time that he married my mama when I was four years old, he has made a living by cheating people out of their wealth."

Stannings glanced from Poppy to Langham then back again. He didn't bother trying to hide his skepticism. "I understand that you have no fondness for your stepfather, Miss Delamere, but this is a serious accusation. I don't suppose you have any proof?"

Langham stared at the magistrate in disbelief. Clearly, his warning earlier hadn't been strong enough.

"Are you calling my betrothed a liar, Stannings?" he asked silkily. "Because if you are—"

The words hung in the air for a moment, like the sound of a rapier being unsheathed.

Stannings must have noted the underlying menace in Langham's voice, because his denial was immediate and not a little alarmed. "Of course not," he said hastily. "It's just that children can often misinterpret their elders' actions. And it's possible that Miss Delamere's dislike for Lord Short colored the way she interpreted his business dealings. And without proof, all we have is her words. Which, while damning, are not enough to convict the fellow in a court of law."

What Stannings said made some sense. Even so, Langham wasn't entirely convinced. He was about to say so when Poppy stepped closer and rested a hand on his arm. "You forget I have experience in such things. I understand very well what Mr. Stannings is saying."

Searching her face for some sign of anxiety, Langham saw there was none. Of course she'd be familiar with the workings of the law and the scrutiny with which witnesses were examined. Her work at *The Gazette* had made it imperative she understand them. With a nod, he indicated that he'd stay quiet.

Poppy turned back to Stannings and pulled her shawl closer around her. "While I have no documents with which to prove my claim, I did overhear, before I fled for London, a conversation between my stepfather and Mr. Lovell that may shed more light on the situation."

Poppy hadn't given him an account of her flight from Lord Short's household. Langham was more than a little curious to hear it, though he suspected he would only become more irate than ever at the stepfather who'd brought so much chaos into her life.

"In the weeks before I ran," Poppy said, "my stepfather's anger at my refusal to agree to Lovell's proposal grew more and more intense. Over my mother's objections, he ordered that I would be locked in my bedchamber, and for all my meals to be restricted to the plainest and most unappetizing fare. I was allowed no visitors—not even my sister and mother—save two, himself and Mr. Lovell."

She must have seen the thunder in Langham's expression, because Poppy's next words were for him. "They did not harm me physically. For all his faults, my stepfather drew the line at violence. I suppose I should be grateful for it. It was one of the reasons I was able to leave my mother and sister in his care with some degree of . . . if not comfort, then without fear, I suppose."

The duke wondered, given how timid Lady Short had been earlier today, if that had changed since Poppy had run away. But he kept that thought to himself.

"One evening," Poppy continued, "whether by mistake or on purpose—the servants were not overly fond of Lord Short, and though they never voiced their objections to his treatment of me aloud, I could tell they were uncomfortable with being turned into de facto jailers—the maid failed to secure the locks on my bedchamber door after she removed my dinner tray. I had managed to pack a valise earlier in the week, and seeing my chance for freedom, I took it. I slipped from the room and made my way toward the servants' stairs."

"He had no one standing guard at the door?" Stannings asked, once more looking skeptical.

"If he had before," Poppy said, "there was no one there that night. As I reached the landing on the second floor— where the drawing room, parlor, and Lord Short's study were located—I saw that the door leading into that hallway was ajar, and I could hear voices. It was my stepfather and Mr. Lovell, and they were arguing."

Her fists were clenched, and Langham could only imagine how terrified she must have been at the prospect of being found out. It only made him admire her courage even more.

"The gist of their quarrel was this: Mr. Lovell was convinced that their scheme was on the verge of being uncovered by one of the more suspicious members of the investment circle, Lord Twombley. His lordship had written to a friend in the Foreign Office and inquired about the viability of a railway line in the part of South America where Lord Short claimed he would construct it. Lovell was adamant that they should flee to another, larger city so that they could avoid being caught. Especially since the government was now involved."

"What was your stepfather's response?" Langham asked with a frown.

"He thought Mr. Lovell's fears were unfounded. South America was far larger than Lovell realized, he argued, and the odds were against the diplomat having traveled anywhere near the location they'd spoken of." Poppy shook her head in disgust. "As for Lord Twombley, my stepfather was certain he could handle the man in the event that the fellow from the Foreign Office made him doubt the scheme."

"How did they leave it?" Stannings asked.

"I do not know," Poppy said with a frown. "They moved farther down the hall toward my stepfather's study, and I was able to continue along the servants' stairs and out the door before anyone saw me."

"Surely that is enough to convince you, Stannings," Langham said to the other man. "It isn't hard evidence, of course, but my brother, Adrian—who, as you know, is in the Foreign Office—may be able to confirm the viability— or lack thereof—of a railway. Or he may be able to recall an inquiry about it around the time that Poppy overheard the argument between her stepfather and Lovell."

"Since Twombley is now dead, and you don't know the name of the man he brought his concerns to at the Foreign Office, I'm afraid this *isn't* enough," Stannings protested.

"Dead?" Poppy's voice had risen an octave, and Langham watched as disappointment washed over her. "Since when?"

"A couple of years ago," Stannings said, not without sympathy for Poppy's reaction. "I believe it was a climbing accident near his estate in the Lake District."

The duke swore. "That's a bit of coincidence, don't you think? Two men in the orbit of Lord Short fall to their deaths from great heights?"

"We don't know that Twombley fell," Stannings protested. "He might have met with all manner of mishaps in the Cumbrian Mountains. Besides that, we don't even know that Miss Delamere's family was still living in the area when Twombley died. It's all conjecture at this point."

But when Langham made a sound of impatience, Stannings raised a placating hand. "Very well. I can speak with Lord Short again and see what he will tell me about his previous business dealings. I'll tell him I am interested in making an investment and that I'd heard he is savvy with financial innovations. But I won't accuse the man of anything related to Twombley."

"Thank you, Sir Geoffrey," Poppy said, her shoulders relaxing a little. But Langham knew she wouldn't be truly calm until her sister was no longer under suspicion.

With that in mind, he addressed his old friend again. "You will also consider the notion that Short is purposely trying to throw suspicion from himself to his daughter, will you not?" Langham demanded. "The question of Twombley aside, if Short was responsible for Lovell's demise, it would hardly be the first time a disagreement between partners in crime led to murder."

"Of course I will consider it," Sir Geoffrey said with a hint of impatience. "But I can only go where the evidence leads me."

To Poppy he said, with a little less heat, "I know you are afraid for your sister, Miss Delamere, but I do wish you would leave this matter in your fiancé's capable hands. Much as you would like to disagree with me, this is not a matter for a lady's delicate sensibilities. And I cannot help but think it would be better for you to forget your hardships in Lord Short's household and focus on your future as the Duchess of Langham."

Rising, Stannings promised to keep them apprised should he learn anything new, then took his leave.

Once they were alone again, Poppy turned to Langham

and gave a huff of indignation. "Delicate sensibilities, indeed. I should like to show him just how delicate my boot against his shin can be."

Despite the seriousness of the situation, Langham bit back a laugh.

"I do not recall Stannings being such a prig when we were children," he said aloud, still somewhat puzzled at his friend's transformation. "But aside from the local constable, Mr. Rhodes, he is our best hope of ensuring your sister is freed."

Poppy sighed. "I know. And I cannot tell you how much that troubles me."

Chapter Eight

It bothered Langham more than he cared to admit that the conversation with Stannings had not gone to plan. If he was being entirely honest, he'd assumed—wrongly it turned out—that his status would ensure Poppy's sister would be, if not cleared, then at least lifted out from under the cloud of suspicion that currently hung over her.

So, the troubled furrow of Poppy's brow now felt like a sign of his own failure. And he wanted to make it disappear.

Thinking to lighten her mood a bit, he turned the subject to the far more frivolous topic of the house party. "You did well with the other ladies this afternoon. I believe even Charlotte was impressed with your quick wit."

Sighing, Poppy moved to sit in one of the armchairs near his desk. "I'm glad you think so. I must admit, after two years of living the life of a secretary, I've forgotten how to interact with genteel company."

"I don't understand. You seemed comfortable enough

with Kate and Caro. Indeed, it looked to me as if they considered you their equal despite your role as Kate's employee." When he'd conceived of the idea to have her pose as his fiancée, it hadn't occurred to him that Poppy would have difficulty maneuvering among his grandmother's guests.

"Kate and Caro never excluded me, or ever treated me as if I wasn't worthy of being listened to," Poppy said, her hand plucking at the fabric of her skirt, "it was more that I was so afraid of giving myself away that I spent most of my time with them carefully regulating my every action."

Langham hadn't considered what it would be like to live in constant fear of discovery. And what had he done but put her in another situation where she was doing the same thing?

Well done.

"I apologize for placing you in a similar circumstance, my dear," he said, feeling like the veriest clodpate. "But truly, I have never doubted that you were of gentle birth. When we first met, I assumed you were simply in straitened circumstances."

To his surprise, she laughed. "I suppose I should be grateful for the governesses Lord Short hired for Violet and me. Though I have dispensed with any number of the rules required by polite society—really, why on earth should I be required to take a maid with me wherever I go simply because I am unmarried?—most of the teachings were so deeply ingrained they are like second nature."

He disagreed with her about the necessity of having a maid—if only because young ladies were more prone to being preyed upon by the unscrupulous. "However uncertain you might have felt today," he said, "it was never evident to anyone looking on. Indeed, if I didn't already know how you'd spent the past few years, I would have thought you were fresh from the most exclusive entertainments of the London season."

"Now that," she said with a raised brow that was belied by the color in her cheeks, "is a bouncer if I've ever heard one."

"You acquit yourself admirably," he said, moving to sit behind his desk and busy himself with a stack of invitations simply to give him an excuse to look away from the delectable dimple that had appeared when she quirked her lips. "You must trust in your own abilities. I certainly do."

A silence fell, then, and when he looked up he saw that she was biting her lip, and if he wasn't mistaken her eyes were suspiciously bright.

"What is it?" he asked, frowning. "Have I said something to overset you? If so—"

"No, of course not," she interrupted, shaking her head. "It's just that I've never been able to speak frankly about my self-doubts regarding my, well, my performance. I hadn't realized how much I needed to hear someone tell me I am successful in my endeavors."

In the early days after he'd reached his majority, when he'd fully taken up the reins of the dukedom, Langham would have given his eyeteeth to be able to confide his doubts in someone. But by the very nature of his role, he had no one he could speak freely to about such things. He had no father or grandfather living, and he'd lost trust in the uncles who'd served as his guardians years ago.

Swallowing against his own unexpected emotions, he gave her a curt nod. "I'm delighted, then, to be at your service."

Perhaps because she too was feeling the awkwardness of the moment, now it was Poppy's turn to change the subject. And he wasn't surprised that she went back to the topic of her sister.

"Since you seem to be pleased with my performance as your betrothed," Poppy said, lifting her chin in that familiar way she had, "then I have a request regarding our investigation into my sister's troubles."

"You say that as if I am keeping a ledger and will only mete out my help if you do your own bit in turn." His words were meant to be teasing but instead sounded sharp even to his own ears. But dash it all, here he was thinking they were kindred spirits of a sort, and she was thinking of him as some sort of earthbound St. Peter, keeping track of her good works before he'd let her into heaven.

"Not at all," she said with a frown. "But I do not wish to take advantage of your generosity."

Before he could object to that bit of nonsense, she continued, "Even so, I would like to visit the site where Lovell's body was found tomorrow. As well as paying another call at Rothwell Grange so that I might speak with Violet."

"That should be easy enough to arrange," he said. "I am unsure of what Grandmama has planned for the guests tomorrow, but if we leave early, we should be able to visit both St. Lucy's and the grange before luncheon."

The smile she gave him lit up her entire face, and he was reminded that despite the way she liked to talk about herself as a spinster, she was, in fact, barely twenty-five years old.

"Thank you, Your Grace," she said, rising from her chair. "I believe I will go lie down for a while before dinner. Even if I gave a credible showing at tea time, I wish to be well rested and ready to resume my role."

Following her to the door, he said, "I meant what I said.

You might feel out of practice in polite society, but you conducted yourself like exactly what you are: a lady."

She looked as if she wanted to argue, but in the end she just gave him a half smile and shut the study door behind her.

Poppy felt a headache brewing in her temples as she made her way to her room, but any notion she might have had of lying down was dashed when she entered the sitting room attached to her bedchamber to find unexpected visitors had taken up residence there.

"Ah, there you are Miss Delamere," said Lady Charlotte Felton, making Poppy wonder how long they'd been lying in wait for her. "We've come to deliver some gowns for you at the request of Grandmama. Heaven knows we both have far more than we can ever wear in this lifetime, or the next, for that matter."

The other occupant of the chaise rose and hurried toward Poppy with a broad smile. It was clear from the shade of her eyes and the shape of her face that she must be a relation of Charlotte's and therefore Langham's. "Miss Delamere, what a delight it is to finally meet you," the lady, whose hair was just a shade lighter than Langham's dark blond, said as she took Poppy's hands. "I do apologize that I wasn't at tea when you were introduced to the rest of the party."

Before Poppy could respond, Charlotte made a distinctly unladylike noise that sounded remarkably like a snort. "This rag-mannered creature, Miss Delamere, is my sister, Eugenia, Lady Bellwood. Really, Genia, you have the most appalling habit of rushing into conversation without conveying the pertinent information."

Seeing that Poppy stood staring, Charlotte continued, having the grace to look chastened, "I realize that I was less than welcoming to you both at the train station and at tea earlier. I have a tendency to be a bit quick tempered and will confess to being surprised by my brother's news. But Genia soon put me in my place. I can only apologize and hope that you will forgive me."

This day was growing odder and odder, Poppy thought as she listened to the other woman. Still, she knew it wasn't easy to beg forgiveness and the fact that Langham's eldest sister was willing to do so raised Poppy's opinion of her considerably. "Of course, you're forgiven, Lady Felton. Langham and I knew our betrothal would come as a surprise to his family so I was expecting there would be some difficulty. I thank you for reconsidering."

"Please sit," Lady Felton said gesturing to a comfortable looking chintz armchair and Poppy needed no further prodding.

"I regret to inform you, Miss Delamere," Lady Bellwood said with a warm smile, "that you will soon find this family can be, well, trying. But I hope you will not hold our fractiousness against Joshua. He is my favorite brother, and so deserves to be happy."

Poppy blinked. Langham had mentioned he wasn't close to his younger brother, but was Lady Bellwood implying there was something more than an age gap between the siblings? Before she could ponder the notion further, Lady Bellwood continued.

"Oh, I don't mean to imply Adrian isn't wonderful as well." She smiled, and Poppy could tell Lady Bellwood's affection for her brother was genuine. "But he's the baby, and so delightful in an entirely different way than Joshua. Although they're really very alike. Which is what makes it even more distressing that they don't get along. At least not since Adrian's decision to join the Foreign Office against Joshua's wishes."

The mention of the Foreign Office reminded Poppy of Langham's suggestion that his brother might be able to assist them with details on the viability of the Amazon railway scheme.

"Will Lord Adrian be coming this week to celebrate your grandmother's birthday, Lady Bellwood?" she asked aloud, thinking that it would save time waiting for correspondence to travel from here to London and back again if he were.

"Oh, my dear, let us dispense with the formalities. You are to be our sister, after all," said Lady Bellwood. "We must be Genia and Charlotte from now on. And we will call you Poppy, if we may?"

A glance in Charlotte's direction revealed that lady to be sanguine with the idea, and so Poppy nodded. "Yes, of course."

It occurred to her that aside from when she was with Langham earlier that day, this was the first instance when she was hearing her given name since her flight from her family two years ago. It was both a relief and unsettling in a way she hadn't been able to identify earlier. But now, she recognized it for what it was—a conflict within herself between the Poppy she was when she left for London and the Poppy she was now.

In London she'd experienced the excitement of using her natural curiosity and intellect in a way she'd never have been able to in her old life. It was a freedom she hadn't anticipated, and one she was loath to abandon.

Before she could refine upon the matter, she realized Lady Bellwood—or Genia, rather—was speaking again.

"To answer your question, Poppy, yes Adrian will arrive tomorrow. He is quite fond of Grandmama, as are we all, so would not miss her birthday. Especially since this is the first time he's been in England for it in several years."

"In that case, the dowager must be overjoyed to have him join her this year," Poppy said, although clearly the same couldn't be said for Langham.

"I'm surprised no one mentioned him at tea," Genia continued with a frown. "He's a favorite with the young ladies whenever he's in residence. Though I suppose everyone was focused on the news of your betrothal. I daresay the prospective brides Grandmama invited were put out by your presence."

"That is putting it mildly, sister," Charlotte said before Poppy could respond. "Poppy was forced to give a set down to Louisa Beaconfield, who was positively dreadful. I once counted her a friend, but I'm afraid I may have to cut her acquaintance after this party. She has shown herself to be quite ill-mannered."

Poppy felt a little as if she'd been caught up in a whirlwind. She'd still been offered no explanation for why Langham's sisters were in her bedchamber, and from the various tangents their conversation was taking, it seemed as if she wouldn't be getting one soon.

At her sister's mention of Miss Beaconfield, Genia's blue eyes grew round. "Oh! I am sorry I missed it. I've never been overfond of Miss Beaconfield. But my dear little Sibyl was feeling unwell, and I couldn't help but make sure she was able to fall asleep. The nurseries at the abbey are so much larger than ours at home, and she always has difficulty settling in on our first day here."

"Manners," Charlotte said to one of the maids, who had, Poppy realized, been sorting through clothes in the attached dressing room the entire time, "you'd better ring for some tea before you get started on fitting Miss Delamere for those gowns. She looks a bit pale. And I believe Genia could use a cup as well, since she missed tea with the rest of us."

"Oh, are you feeling unwell, Poppy?" Genia asked, looking alarmed. "I hope you aren't coming down with something?

"I am not unwell," Poppy protested even as she pressed her forehead with her fingers. "I merely feel a bit of a headache coming on. It's been a busy day."

"Of course you have a headache," Charlotte said tartly. "Your sister is accused of murdering her husband and you've been thrust into the midst of the dowager's house party and subjected to some of her less than appealing guests. Not to mention I was at my most unfriendly to you earlier."

Poppy's expression must have shown her surprise, because the other woman continued. "Oh, I know when I'm being a fright, make no mistake. My only excuse is that I dislike being thwarted, and I had thought I'd be able to convince my brother to marry one of Grandmama's guests. The fact that he arrived with a fiancée in tow, and one I'd never heard of before, rather took the wind out of my sails. I am not one to apologize, but in this case, I must. Please forgive me for my earlier ill manners."

Charlotte's apology spoke well of her character, Poppy thought. But her own conscience pricked at the knowledge she was guilty of perpetrating a fraud on Langham's sisters. At least Charlotte's sharp words had come from a place of sincere irritation. Poppy had spent the entirety of their acquaintance lying. It made her feel underhanded and dirty, as if she were no better than her stepfather.

But she had agreed to do this for Langham. "Pray, think nothing of it," she assured the other woman. "I realize we sprang the news of our betrothal upon you without warning. You must have been unpleasantly surprised."

"Not least because I was so rude to you before I knew who you were," Charlotte said with a rueful smile that made her look very like her elder brother.

"She told me everything that was said," Genia said with a shake of her head. "What a dreadful way to welcome you to the family, Poppy. I am sorry I wasn't there to smooth things over."

"Let us put it behind us," Poppy hastened to say, not wanting to dwell on the unpleasantness. Especially not in light of how betrayed they would feel once they learned the truth about their brother's betrothal. Just the thought of it made her chest tighten—though a small part of her questioned whether it was the thought of hurting the ladies before her or, more alarming, the notion of never seeing Langham again that was causing her the most pain.

She was saved from dwelling on this dangerous thought any further by Genia's next words.

"I will not press the subject if it is an uncomfortable one, my dear," she said gently, "but I am so sorry about the trouble with your own sister. I must admit I'd not heard much about your brother-in-law's murder beyond the fact that our cousin Ned, that is, Mr. Jarvis, who serves as Langham's steward, was the one who found his body. Charlotte tells me that your sister has been accused of killing Mr. Lovell? That must be perfectly dreadful for you."

"Of course it is," Charlotte said to her sister with an impatient sound. "Especially given, as I understand it, that it's been some time since Poppy has seen her sister. Isn't that right, Poppy?"

"It has been just over two years, yes."

At that moment, one of the housemaids arrived with a heavily laden tea tray, and Poppy was grateful for the distraction. Before she could protest, Charlotte was pouring her a cup of tea and Genia was piling a plate with sandwiches and biscuits for her. Seeing that it would be useless to argue, she took the plate and then the cup and saucer. The tea, at least, was comforting, and perhaps her headache was the result of having eaten so little in the drawing room earlier.

Poppy was biting into a watercress sandwich when Charlotte continued where they'd left off. "Given that you've been away from society for such a long time, perhaps we can guide you in determining who at the party you might wish to cultivate as a friend. It would not hurt for you to have a few allies besides Genia and myself as the week progresses. I should say you've already endeared yourself to Miss Ingraham if her response to your little proclamation in the drawing room is anything to go by."

Before Poppy could reply, Genia spoke up, "It might be even more helpful, sister, if we tell her who is most particularly upset at having missed their chance at becoming the next Duchess of Langham. One of the generals Bellwood is always quoting—Sun something or other—said 'keep your friends close but your enemies closer,' and I cannot think of a more pertinent sentiment for Poppy just now."

Charlotte nodded. "A good point. I'd say you've definitely made an enemy of Lady Alice Gerson, as well as Miss Beaconfield. But truly, I've never cared for either of them. Lady Alice has always been far too puffed up with her own importance, if you ask me."

"I would have counseled Grandmama against inviting her at all," Genia said with a nod, "but Gerson and

Grandpapa were cronies, so I suppose she felt obliged. Miss Beaconfield was a surprise, however. I thought she had better sense than to be so badly behaved in front of Langham. Though I suppose she believes her father is wealthy enough to make her poor manners irrelevant."

Poppy looked from one sister to the other and back again, trying to focus on the fact that they were trying to help her rather than on the way all the doubts she'd confessed to Langham came rushing back in the face of their advice.

Her appetite gone, she put the sandwich down and set her cup and saucer on the low table. "If Manners is ready, I should like to get the fittings under way, if that's all right. That way I can have a gown ready for the morning at least."

Genia shook her head. "Oh, Manners is a genius with a needle. She'll have one ready for dinner tonight, if I don't miss my guess. As well as a few for tomorrow. And of course, we'll send your measurements to our dressmaker in London—we heard that Grandmama intended to have someone from her own modiste come here and, well…"

"Oh, spit it out, Genia," said Charlotte impatiently. "What my dear sister means to tell you is that Grandmama's modiste is as old as Methuselah and has the fashion sense to prove it. We cannot, of course, pop over to Paris to have Worth create a new wardrobe for you, but with the train making things so much faster now, we can have you outfitted for the rest of the week in a day or two."

Their generosity, and the way they had decided to take her under their wings, was enough to make Poppy's eyes sting. It was suddenly too much and she had to turn away.

"If you'll excuse me for a moment, I just need to refresh my face."

"We have overwhelmed you, Poppy. I do apologize." She felt Charlotte touch her lightly on the shoulder. "We will go and let you rest before dinner. Unless you'd prefer to have a tray in your room. Whatever you wish, my dear. You have had an exceedingly trying day."

But cowering away in her room wasn't Poppy's way.

Turning back to Langham's sisters, she said, "Thank you both for your generosity. If Manners is able to complete one of the gowns in time, I shall see you at dinner."

An hour later, Poppy stood before the floor-length glass in her dressing room and marveled at how much a life could change within the span of a few hours.

While she had meant what she'd said when defending the blue dress she'd been wearing at tea—it was indeed one of her favorites—there was no comparison between it and the sartorial confection she now wore. With a peony-pink silk bodice and underskirt, and overlaid with intricately woven black silk netting, this gown was far and away the most sumptuous item of clothing she'd ever worn.

Unless, that was, one counted the new silk underthings that Manners had brought along with the dinner gown after she'd completed the minor alterations needed for it to fit Poppy.

There had been a time when silk gowns and fine linen petticoats had been the rule rather than the exception in her life, when the absence of such finery would mean true feelings of privation. She felt some shame about the ways in which, despite her disapproval of the way her stepfather brought money into the household, she had nonetheless reaped the rewards from it. The guilt had made it easier for her to adjust to life as Miss Flora Deaver, country vicar's daughter and working woman, who would never have known the feel of fine fabrics against her skin.

But now, answering once more to Poppy and clothed in a manner that was closer to the way she'd once dressed as a matter of course, she wondered which of these women was the genuine article.

The chiming of the pretty Sevres clock in the bedchamber reminded her that there was no time for woolgathering now. With one last glance in the mirror, she took a deep breath and moved to make her way to the drawing room.

She had promised Langham a fiancée, and a fiancée he would have.

Chapter Nine

Having taken the time to bathe, shave, and dress for dinner, Langham joined his guests in the drawing room, where they were discussing the latest bills up for debate in the Lords. He wasn't particularly political, but he took his responsibility in Parliament seriously and tried to keep abreast of the more pressing of the issues that arose in the government.

The prospective brides, he was pleased to note, seemed happy to leave him to his conversation, and thanks, he supposed, to the performance he and Poppy had put on during afternoon tea, they made no attempts to attract his attention. He could not help but be pleased.

He was listening to Bellwood's rather verbose explanation of some parliamentary act or other relating to the Canadian territories when a hush fell over the room. Bellwood continued to speak, but when Langham saw Poppy standing in the entryway of the room, he stopped listening.

As if pulled by an invisible thread, he crossed the chamber toward her—all but unaware of the way his family and guests watched him.

She was so changed as to be almost unrecognizable.

It wasn't just the gown, which was, admittedly, lovely and shaped her curves in ways he would find it difficult not to think about later in the cold solitude of his bedchamber.

It was the way her very manner of being seemed to have... softened. And there was a vulnerability about her that made him want to sweep her into his arms and promise that all would be well.

Her hair, striking before in its guinea gold luster, was no longer wound tightly around her head in an uncompromising coil. Instead, it was now dressed in a loosely gathered knot atop her head with a single shining coil draped over her collarbone. The style was meant to make a man think of replacing that curl with his lips, and Langham was no proof against its allure.

He shook his head as if that could clear the image forming in his mind. He was not supposed to be lusting after her, for pity's sake. He was meant to use her as a shield against the marriage-minded misses who were no doubt watching them with avid interest now.

Swallowing the lavish compliments that hovered on the end of his tongue, he instead tried for cool appraisal. "My sister's maid was able to work a miracle, it seems. It is a lovely gown and suits you," he said, though his voice sounded hoarse to his own ears.

Her eyes flashed with something that looked like hurt for the barest moment before she resumed her customary poise. With something like relief, he bowed and then lifted her hand to his lips for appearances' sake. After that, he avoided her eye, and when he placed her hand on his arm, he was almost able to ignore the lemon and roses scent of her as they crossed to where his sisters were standing with the dowager.

"I believe there is a saying about silk purses and sow's ears," Poppy said evenly as they walked, and she sounded so convincing that he was almost assured he'd misread her momentary discomfort a moment ago. "But you are correct, Your Grace. Manners is a genius with a needle and thread, and I'm grateful to Lady Felton for the loan of the gown. It was very kind of her to come to my aid."

"Nonsense," said Charlotte, who had been watching their approach with an acuity that made Langham wish he'd been gifted with duller siblings. "The gown looks far better on you than it would have done on me. Don't you agree, brother?"

He could see from the glint in her eye that Charlotte had got some bee in her bonnet over Poppy. *Wonderful.*

Aloud he said, "I do agree that it is a most fetching gown. On the matter of how it might have looked on you as opposed to Poppy, however, I will hold my tongue. It is never wise to compare two ladies in company."

"I am just grateful you were able to come down after all," Genia said to Poppy with a warm smile. "I always hate to remain in my rooms when there is sure to be spirited conversation in some other part of the house. One is always afraid of missing out."

"It has been so long since I've attended a gathering like this," Poppy said ruefully, "I'm afraid I'd almost forgot that feeling. But I do understand what you mean."

"And of course you must be thinking about your poor sister," Charlotte said, surprising Langham with her show of empathy, and also reminding him just why Poppy was at Langham Abbey in the first place.

He was about to say something that might reassure her that he hadn't forgotten her sister's plight when the dinner bell sounded.

Cursing the protocol that required he escort the highest-ranking lady into the dining room, rather than his betrothed, he gave Poppy a nod of reassurance, then moved toward the Duchess of Gerson so that they could lead the way.

Throughout the meal, he kept a watchful eye on the other end of the table, where Poppy, to his relief, seemed to be managing her dinner partners with aplomb. Though he shouldn't be surprised, given the deft manner in which she'd handled his grandmother and sisters, not to mention the other guests at tea.

She looked up at him just then, and the sight of the smile she gave him made his heart give a terrifying lurch in his chest. She was playing a role, he chided himself, willing his fool heart to return to its natural rhythm. The look she'd given him was no less practiced and no more genuine than the laughter she used to deflect the flirtations of Lord Toby Dalrymple on one side, or her attempts to charm the irascible Sir Hugo Ballantine, one of his grandfather's cronies, who sat scowling across from her.

"It's clear you're fond of her," said the Duchess of Gerson from where she was seated beside him, smiling indulgently. "You cannot seem to take your eyes off of her. I would not have been content to accept Alice's defeat for anything less."

She said the words in a joking manner, but Langham suspected she was all too serious. Of course, given his lack of interest in the chit, Lady Alice was not, and never had been, in the running to be his duchess. But he wouldn't tell her mother that. "She is a remarkable lady," he said instead, and meant it. He had never met anyone like Poppy before.

"She has certainly managed to endear herself to the dowager," the duchess said with a nod toward the other end of the table, where his grandmother was smiling at something Poppy had said to Lord Toby. "Though I daresay your grandmother would adore anyone you chose to be your bride at this point."

"I'm not sure that's—" He was saved from saying something that would later earn him a scold from his grandmother by raised voices toward the center of the table.

"Miss Delamere," said Lady Carlyle, raising her hand to get the attention of the table, "you must settle a little matter between Miss Beaconfield and myself."

He knew from the lady's tone that she intended some mischief, and to his credit, his cousin Pierce did his best to rein in his wife.

"I'm sure this is something that can be better discussed once the gentlemen have been left to their port, my dear," Carlyle said pointedly to his wife.

But Lady Carlyle was unmoved by her husband's warning. "I was certain this afternoon when you arrived that I'd seen you somewhere before. I know you said you'd been away in London for some time, but I'd never seen you at any entertainments in town. Indeed, I'd never heard your name before at all. Then, it hit me! On a lark, a dear friend and I decided to go to a lecture of sorts."

Langham knew what was coming, but with Lady Carlyle so far into her story, it was impossible to stop her.

"Perhaps the rest of you have heard of Lady Katherine Eversham and Miss Caroline Hardcastle, who write the 'A Lady's Guide to Mischief and Mayhem' column for *The London Gazette*? Well, they host a lecture series of sorts where they discuss popular novels that center on crime—most particularly those crimes that affect women. The lecture itself was rather dull, if I'm being honest. Far too much chatter about the lower classes for my taste. But what I remember most was a young lady who appeared to be assisting them with organizing the meeting."

The meandering way in which Lady Carlyle told her tale only served to keep the rest of the table on tenterhooks—no doubt, Langham thought grimly, waiting for the cat's claw to swipe.

"The thing of it is," Lady Carlyle continued, "Miss Beaconfield and I both agree—she attended the same lecture, you see—that the young lady we saw, who was clearly employed by Lady Katherine, was you."

Langham would have thought given the way his fellow peers were marrying into the middle classes—where hard work was considered to be a virtue rather than something of which to be ashamed—would have put paid to this snobbish insistence that it was beyond the pale for a gently bred lady to accept employment. And yet, he would have been wrong.

A few of the ladies gasped, and more than one gentleman cleared their throats, as if wishing to give some show of their surprise without actually saying anything that might insult the duke.

"That is quite enough, Serena. You must apologize to Miss Delamere at once," Carlyle snapped.

"I mean no insult, dearest," Lady Carlyle said with false surprise. "It's commendable that Miss Delamere should have taken employment with Lady Katherine rather than stoop to some other, less respectable, means of keeping herself from the poorhouse. I simply wished to know if my suspicion was correct. After all, it's possible the young woman we saw was another person altogether."

"I should have hoped you would know better, Serena,"

the dowager began, giving Lady Carlyle a scowl across the table.

But before she could finish, Poppy, her posture straight and her expression one of unconcern, spoke up. "It's all right, Your Grace. I am not ashamed of my time working for Lady Katherine and Miss Hardcastle—well, Lady Wrackham now. You are perfectly correct, Lady Carlyle, Miss Beaconfield. It was very likely me whom you saw attending them at the lecture. I took a position with Lady Katherine not long after I arrived in London and worked for both ladies as amanuensis, fact-checker, and personal secretary at various times over the past two years. It was a position I enjoyed a great deal, and I do not regret it for an instant."

"I don't really see much difference between what Miss Delamere describes and the work of a teacher or governess," Charlotte said with a shake of her head. "Really, Serena, dear, you are making far more over the lady's work than is warranted."

"Indeed," said Langham, putting his quizzing glass to his eye and surveying first Lady Carlyle and then Miss Beaconfield through it. "Miss Delamere and I became acquainted through her position with Lady Katherine and Lady Wrackham, if you must know. There was nothing improper or unladylike about the work. It was perfectly respectable, as I am happy to tell anyone who wishes to take up the matter with me."

Under his withering gaze, Lady Carlyle had the good grace to look chastened. "Of course, Your Grace, I did not intend to imply—that is to say, I meant no—"

But the rest of the table, having heard the duke's family come to Poppy's defense, had decided there was no scandal and the conversation turned to other topics. Indeed, many of the ladies professed themselves to be regular readers of the "Lady's Guide" column and began to pepper her with questions.

"She is handling these attempts to put her in her place with remarkable poise," the Duchess of Gerson said once Langham had turned back to her. "I know from experience how jealous some ladies of the *ton* can be when faced with a fresh face. And I do believe your Miss Delamere will have little trouble holding her own."

Thinking back to his earlier conversation with Poppy, Langham was increasingly convinced that the duchess was right. She might have doubted whether she was convincing in her role as a duke's betrothed, but once again she'd proved herself equal to a societal obstacle thrown in her path.

The more time she spent playing this role, he thought later as he went up to bed, the more he regretted the fact that it was just that: a role.

Because the truth of the matter was, Miss Poppy Delamere would make a damned fine duchess.

Chapter Ten

The next morning, having indulged in a brisk morning ride to clear his head, Langham made his way to the section of the house designated for estate business.

Before he and Poppy visited St. Lucy's, he wanted to hear Ned Jarvis's account of finding Lovell's body. He found his cousin poring over the estate books in the steward's office, which was tucked away on the ground floor with a view of the stables and the kitchen garden.

"You are supposed to be napping with your feet up on the desk so that I may catch you out," Langham groused, scanning the neatly arranged room, where it seemed everything had its place. He'd known when he'd offered the job to his cousin that Ned would excel at it. In the ten years since Jarvis had been running the estate, Langham hadn't once regretted his decision, and the farms had never been more thriving or profitable. "Now I have nothing to dress you down about."

"Langham," his cousin said with a grin. "I'd heard

you'd arrived, but I was waiting to be summoned. I know how you enjoy wielding your ducal power."

The two men embraced, each giving the other a hearty slap on the back for good measure.

"What troubles you?" Ned asked, his ability to read Langham's mood as keen as it had been when they were boys. "A newly betrothed man shouldn't look so Friday faced. Especially if your fiancée is as pretty as servants' gossip says she is."

"Do you still keep a decanter of my best Scotch whisky in here?" Langham asked, once they'd exchanged greetings. "It is early, I know. But I'm not ashamed to admit I could use a wee dram, as our neighbors to the north call it."

"Betrothed life is treating you that well, is it?" Jarvis asked wryly. But he indicated that Langham should be seated as he turned to take a decanter and two glasses from the cabinet on the far wall.

When they both had drinks in hand, Langham took a sip and appreciated the alcohol's smooth warmth. "It's not the betrothal that's the problem," he said at last. "It's her sister's situation."

"Ah yes," Jarvis said gravely. "The servants might have mentioned that as well. It seems it was her husband's body I found at the foot of St. Lucy's bell tower." Jarvis shook his head, and then cleared his throat before continuing. "I suppose you have good reason to be grim. It's a bad business."

Accepting his cousin's sympathy didn't sit well with Langham, knowing that he was keeping to himself the fact that the betrothal was a false one. He'd had no qualms about hiding the truth from his sisters and grandmother; it served them right for all their scheming to marry him off. But Ned hadn't done anything to deserve his lies.

Still, it would not do to tell him the truth. At least not before the end of this house party. Besides, there had been times yesterday—particularly when Poppy had walked into the drawing room before dinner last night looking like a goddess come down to earth—when he'd had to remind himself that the betrothal wasn't real. Surely that was enough to assuage his conscience for the moment.

"It is indeed," he said now, putting his other concerns aside for the moment. "And Poppy is beside herself with worry over her sister. I want to do what I can to ensure that her sister is treated fairly."

"It's a love match, then?" Ned's voice didn't hide his disbelief. Which was hardly surprising given Langham's declarations over the years that he had no intention of ever falling in love.

"Not as such," Langham said with a shake of his head. "But I do hold her in affection, and I can hardly ignore the fact that her beloved sister is suspected of murder."

"Ah, that makes sense," Ned said. "Well, I wish I could give you some information that would put your Miss Delamere's mind at ease, but I have none. I did find Lovell's body, it's true, but I'm hardly an expert when it comes to investigating murder. If it hadn't been for the knife wound in the man's chest, I'd have assumed he'd taken his own life."

This brought Langham up short. "What do you mean, 'knife wound'? There was no mention of a knife in the newspapers."

"Well…" Ned said with a shrug. "I wasn't supposed to mention it. Constable Rhodes wants to keep that bit confidential until the inquest, but I can hardly keep the information from you, can I?"

Grateful for his cousin's loyalty, Langham gave a

grateful nod. "If he gives you any trouble for it, just tell him that I demanded you tell me everything."

"You can be a damned intimidating fellow when you wish to be," Ned agreed. "I'm sure he won't give me any trouble."

But Langham wasn't really interested in the constable. "Tell me about the chapel itself. Is the path up the rise as difficult to navigate as it used to be?"

"Worse," Ned said with a scowl. "The brush has taken over. I daresay that's why Dolly wandered up there."

"Who the devil is Dolly?" Langham asked.

"The sheep I was searching for that day," Ned said dryly. "Daft thing got herself up there but then couldn't find her way down. I was near the edge of the woods when I heard her bleating like her heart would break from up near the chapel. It took me a bit to get to her, and as soon as I got to the clearing, I saw the fellow at once. There was no question he was dead, of course. His neck was obviously broken."

"How familiar were you with the fellow?" Langham had no doubt that Ned knew most everyone in the area, including Lovell.

"We'd met a few times in the village," Ned said with a shrug. "But he didn't have much time for a mere land steward, however impressive the Langham Abbey holdings might be. I thought he was a deuced odd fish if you must know. How he'd managed to snare a wife like Mrs. Lovell was a mystery to me and several others in Little Kidding."

"So, you've met her as well?" Langham asked, his curiosity piqued by Ned's words. It wasn't like his cousin to gossip, so if enough people were talking about the mismatch between Violet and Lovell, then it must have been a common topic of conversation. "What is she like?"

Ned closed his eyes, as if that made it easier to envision her. "She's pleasant enough. And pretty. Like her sister, I'd imagine. But I don't know her well enough to say whether she'd have killed her husband. But then, I'm not the first man to find the workings of the female mind impossible to understand."

Though his cousin looked calm enough, there was something about his manner that gave Langham pause. Perhaps he was still unsettled from finding Lovell's body? Though somehow the duke didn't think that was the issue.

With what seemed to Langham an obvious desire to change the subject, Ned sat up straight in his chair and set down his glass. "Now, Yer Grace," he said in a mock country accent, "I must be getting back to these ledgers. You may not have met him, but my employer can be quite demanding."

His cousin's tone was jovial, but Langham noticed Ned had begun tapping the edge of his desk. The rhythm was familiar, and Langham suddenly recalled it was a song Ned used to hum when they were boys; specifically when he was lying. Could it be possible his cousin wasn't as pleased with his role at the abbey as he'd assumed?

"Thank you for telling me about Lovell," Langham said, after he'd shook Ned's hand and made his way to the door. "And you have my trust. I won't reveal that I learned of the knife wound from you."

If there was a chance that Ned wasn't happy in his position, Langham certainly didn't want to do anything to upset him more before he could try to remedy the situation.

Ned nodded. "I'm obliged. I can't imagine Rhodes would do anything about it, but I'd just as soon not find out."

Langham bid him goodbye and headed up the back stairs toward his rooms.

Ned Jarvis was definitely hiding something, and Langham meant to find out what. He might love the other man like a brother, but he'd promised to help Poppy clear her sister's name.

And for now, keeping his vow to her was the only thing that mattered.

Despite her fatigue, Poppy found it difficult to sleep after the unsettling events of the day. Whenever she closed her eyes, the reunion with her mother and Lord Short, the at times fractious conversation with the other guests, and even the mostly pleasant chat with Langham's sisters would push to the forefront of her mind and keep her awake.

And then there were the snatches of remembered conversation with Langham himself, and the many small kindnesses he'd offered her throughout the day. And the even more unsettling reminders of how his perfectly tailored coat had showed his broad shoulders to such advantage. Or the way the corners of his eyes fanned with fine lines when he laughed. The heady sandalwood and citrus scent of his shaving soap.

She'd done her utmost to ignore how attractive he was as they'd gone about the day, but as she reached for sleep, her mind had betrayed her. As a result, she arose far too early the next morning, feeling only marginally more rested than when she'd lain down.

Manners had filled the wardrobe in her dressing room last night with a larger selection of gowns than she could possibly wear in a week, and a cheerful housemaid named Jenny was currently settling her into a pale blue morning gown trimmed in darker blue ribbon. Poppy hated accepting more charity from Langham, but she had to admit that having someone see to her hair and clothing was a luxury she had missed.

After thanking Jenny for her assistance, Poppy set out to search for the breakfast room, which was empty when she arrived. No doubt the partygoers were accustomed to sleeping half the morning away.

Thanks to the respite, Poppy was able to eat her eggs and toast without more needling from Lady Carlyle or Miss Beaconfield—a circumstance for which she was grateful.

When she'd finished her meal, and Langham hadn't yet come downstairs to break his own fast, she made a quick trip upstairs to retrieve the straw bonnet meant to be worn with her gown and then found her way to the doors leading from a prettily decorated parlor out onto a terraced garden.

It was a crisp morning, with enough sun to keep it from true chilliness, and she took a moment to breathe in the fresh country air. She enjoyed the bustle and energy of London, but there were days when the fog and soot of the city made her long for just this sort of day.

From this vantage point it was possible to see across the gently sloping landscape and out across the lake beyond where she noted the presence of a temple folly. Farther out, there was a steep incline and atop it, obscured by an overgrowth of vegetation, a bell tower.

Poppy's heart leapt. Was that the chapel that was mentioned in the newspaper article about Lovell's death? She needed to see it. She reminded herself to mention it to Langham when she saw him later.

Turning her attention back to the vista before her—in the hopes of calming her mind before visiting the grange again—she focused on the parts of the grounds that were not associated with murder. It was a breathtaking view, and combined with the elegant décor of the house itself, Poppy wasn't surprised Langham had so many young ladies clamoring to be his bride. Even she was not immune to the lure of imaging herself the mistress of all this, however much she might recognize just how absurd the very notion was.

"Oh, I do apologize. I hadn't realized anyone else was out here."

The female voice came from the other side of the terrace, and when Poppy looked over she saw a young woman of about twenty, whose plain gray gown and severely dressed dark hair proclaimed her to be some sort of upper servant.

"There is no need to apologize," Poppy said to her, grateful for the interruption. "I daresay there is room enough for both of us in this extraordinary space."

"How kind you are," the lady said with a wide smile. "I don't believe we've met. I'm Miss Halliwell, governess to Lord and Lady Carlyle's daughters."

Poppy made sure not to show it, but hearing that the poor lady was employed by Lady Carlyle made her inwardly shudder. What a dreadful position that would be.

"I am Miss Delamere," she said aloud.

"Oh," Miss Halliwell said, her dark eyes wide, and Poppy knew her notoriety—at least in this household—had preceded her.

"How dreadfully rude of me," Miss Halliwell said, her cheeks reddening. "It's just that... well, you must know you're rather famous among the upper servants. You've put quite a number of their mistresses' noses out of joint, to be perfectly frank."

Poppy was grateful for Miss Halliwell's candor. "I am well aware of that," she said dryly. "They have made their pique known to me in no uncertain terms."

The governess winced in sympathy. "How dreadful it must be for you," she said, and Poppy could detect no hint of irony in her tone.

"I daresay I would be annoyed if I journeyed to a country house party with the aim of enticing a duke, only to learn shortly after my arrival that he's already betrothed." Poppy shrugged. "It must have been quite a shock to them. Not to mention how their mamas must have felt. There are very few eligible dukes who have all their teeth, much less as handsome as Langham."

"Ah, my dear, are you extolling my fine looks again? What have I told you about bragging about your conquest? It's most unbecoming to gloat."

To Poppy's horror, the man himself stepped from a door farther down the terrace. She felt her face heat and cursed her fair complexion, which made it impossible for her to hide either ire or embarrassment. And unfortunately, the present moment made her feel both.

Before she could explain herself—and really, what was there to explain?—he stepped up beside her and brought her hand to his lips. His eyes were merry when they met hers, and she felt her stomach flood with butterflies.

"I was merely paying you a compliment, Langham," she retorted with as much dignity as she could muster. "Perhaps you should take your own advice and refrain from gloating yourself."

"Your Grace," Miss Halliwell said, dropping into a curtsy. "I'll leave you both to your privacy."

"Do not go yet, Miss Halliwell," Poppy implored. "I assure you, the duke is not nearly as fearsome as you've been led to believe. Langham, show her how unthreatening you can be."

"No, I really must go," said Miss Halliwell with a smile. "My charges will have finished breakfast by now. It was a pleasure to meet you, Miss Delamere. I hope the rest of the party is more pleasant for you."

To Langham, she gave another curtsy, and said, "Your Grace."

And before Poppy could protest further, the governess hurried back into the house.

"And who is this Miss Halliwell?" Langham asked turning to face her with a raised brow. "I wouldn't have thought you would confide in a stranger about your difficulties with the other ladies at the party."

"She's not a stranger," Poppy said, giving him a pointed look to let him know she knew that by "stranger" he meant "servant." "Well not exactly. She is governess for Lord and Lady Carlyle."

"That's an unfortunate position for your new friend," he said with a grimace, and suddenly Poppy wondered if she'd judged him too harshly moments ago. "Carlyle is pleasant enough, but as you now well know, his wife is, well, not."

"Exactly what I thought," Poppy agreed. And not for the first time, she was grateful at having been employed by someone like Kate, who treated her with respect and had become a friend. "The poor girl must have a wretched existence in that household."

They were quiet for a moment, and as Poppy's mind wandered, without meaning to, she allowed her gaze to take in Langham's appearance more fully. He was dressed for riding, in boots and breeches—the picture of a country gentleman. And though there was no denying he seemed comfortable with himself no matter what he wore, she couldn't help but note that here in the country he was far more relaxed.

"Do I pass your inspection, then?" he asked, his voice lower than normal. Despite her resolve to remain indifferent to him, she felt a tickle of awareness skip down her spine.

"Don't be absurd," she said primly. "I was just thinking you'll need to change before we depart for Rothwell Grange."

He looked skeptical but didn't argue. "I'll only be a few moments. I've already asked the curricle to be brought round."

At her look of surprise, his expression turned stern. "I haven't forgot the reason you're here," he said. "We may be under constant attack from thwarted matchmaking mamas, but that has hardly obliterated your sister's plight from my consciousness."

She was about to protest that she had thought no such thing, but before she could gather her thoughts he had turned away and disappeared inside the parlor, leaving her to stare after him in frustration.

Poppy had been quite happy to think of him as an arrogant aristocrat, and perhaps too often quick to paint him with that brush. In fact, he was proving himself to be far more decent than she'd first thought with every passing moment.

Unfortunately, as it turned out, she found decency more attractive than all the ducal coronets in England.

Chapter Eleven

Once they were in the curricle and driving down the tree-lined lane away from the abbey, Langham had informed Poppy of his conversation with Ned.

She was not pleased.

"What a vexing creature you are," she said, not bothering to hide her exasperation. "I would have liked to be present for the interview. Especially as he was the first person to see Lovell's body. Why did you not ask me to come with you?"

"Because I know my cousin," he said, grateful for the need to keep his eyes on the road, because he knew by now that her ire gave her cheeks a lovely flush that made him want to kiss her. "He would not have been comfortable describing the unpleasant details of your brother-in-law's demise to a lady."

As it was, Langham was convinced that there was more to the story than Ned had let on. And if it was, as he suspected, something to do with Mrs. Lovell, then Poppy's presence would hardly have made him more forthcoming.

She made a noise of disgust. "You do realize for whom I was employed in London, do you not? Caro even has a dollhouse furnished with famous death scenes, for heaven's sake."

Langham had not known that last bit and wondered for a moment how Val had reacted to that. But recalling the besotted way his friend had looked at his bride, he was confident Val didn't give a damn.

Realizing that Poppy required a response, he turned his attention back to her. "Of course I know who you worked for, but my cousin does not. And it would not have made a difference to him at any rate. This is the country, you must recall. And there is not as much tolerance for the sort of ideas espoused by Kate and Caro here as there is in London."

A glance at Poppy told him she would have liked to argue, but she must have decided against it, for her next words were resigned. "What did he tell you, then?"

Quickly, he explained what Ned had said about the knife wound in Lovell's chest, as well as the instruction that they must not let the authorities know where they'd learned of the injury.

"I cannot imagine Violet choosing to climb up the bell tower," Poppy said thoughtfully once Langham was finished relating his conversation with Ned. "Especially not at night. She is uncomfortable enough with heights during the daylight hours."

"It certainly wouldn't be my preference," Langham agreed.

Poppy was silent for a moment, and when she spoke up again, it was in a determined tone. "I should like to go to St. Lucy's now, if you are agreeable."

He was grateful for his ability to keep his voice even.

"But I thought you wished to see your sister at once?" There was no reason to tell her that St. Lucy's was the last place he wished to go, this morning or any other.

"I do," she said emphatically. "Of course I do. But it is early yet, and it occurs to me that there might be some clue to the identity of Lovell's killer there. And if we can show it to Violet, she may recognize it and point us in the right direction."

Langham bit back a sigh. The devil of it was that her idea made sense.

"Of course," she went on, this time with anger, "it isn't as if my stepfather is going to let her out of his sight. If we do find something potentially connected to the murder, we'll have to devise a distraction for Lord Short so I may discuss it with Violet outside his hearing. The last thing we need is for him to think he needs to ramp up his efforts to falsely incriminate her."

"We don't know that he's lying. It's possible he truly believes she is guilty." But Langham's argument sounded weak even to his own ears.

"If that were the case, then why is he keeping her away from the magistrate?" A glance in Poppy's direction revealed that her gloved hands were tightly fisted in her lap. "It makes no sense."

"Fine," he conceded. "It's unlikely he'd let her remain in his home if he believed her truly guilty. But are you sure you wish to climb the hill now?" he asked. "In that gown?"

"What's wrong with my gown?" Poppy glanced down at the delicate blue fabric of her skirts with a frown.

"Nothing is wrong with it," he said, wishing he'd kept his mouth shut. The truth of it was, the gown was just as becoming on her as the one she'd worn at dinner the night before. Maybe more so because the color brought out the blue of her eyes in a way the other had not. "It just seems impractical for a traipse through the woods."

"If I were able to wear breeches," she said, oblivious to the way that mental image affected him, "then it might be a sensible claim. But as I cannot, then whatever gown I choose to wear will make no difference."

Resisting the urge to pinch the bridge of his nose in frustration, Langham tried one last time to dissuade her. "It looks as if it might rain. Perhaps it would be better if we go another day."

She glanced up at the sky, then back at him, as if she suspected him of being on the brink of a brain fever. "There is not a cloud in the heavens, Langham. Why on earth are you so determined to keep me from examining the scene of Lovell's murder? Surely you are not of the opinion, as your cousin is, that it is an unfit topic for a lady to contemplate. Because if that is the reason, then I can tell you right now that—"

He cut her off with a shake of his head. "Of course not. Don't be absurd."

"Then what?" she persisted.

Realizing that she would continue her interrogations until he bared his soul on the matter, he sighed. "If you must know, I was accidentally locked in the tower when I was a youth, and ever since I have been made…uncomfortable by enclosed spaces."

Langham clicked the reins and kept his eyes trained on the road ahead. He'd never been gladder to have a reason not to meet someone's eye.

"Oh," she said with the air of someone having unraveled a great mystery.

"Yes," he said hating the fact he had to speak of this at all. *"Oh."*

"There's no need to be embarrassed," she said with her usual practicality. "I told you about my sister's fear of heights. It happens to a great many people."

"But she is—"

"You are not going to say that she is a lady," Poppy said, steel in her voice, "for if you do, I will lose a great deal of respect for your intelligence."

He was about to say just that, so he said nothing at all.

"As much as you men—and especially aristocratic men—think you are meant to be immune from the sorts of weaknesses and foibles that affect the rest of the human race, I am here to tell you that you most certainly are not."

"I know that," he said sullenly. "I simply do not like admitting to such a thing. Especially not to you."

"Why not me?" she asked, sounding curious now instead of cross.

There was no way in the devil he would tell her the truth—that she seemed to be invulnerable herself, and he didn't wish to appear weak by comparison. So instead he said, "Because a man doesn't wish to seem vulnerable to a lady he finds attractive."

The words were out of his mouth before he realized this might have been a worse admission than the one he was trying to avoid.

"It's nothing to concern yourself with," he said hastily. "You must have seen yourself in the glass. You know you are beautiful."

And to think, he is considered by most to have a silver tongue when it comes to women.

"I'm hardly going to agree with such a statement," she said on a strangled laugh.

He was pleased to note, when he chanced a quick

glance, that the elusive dimple in her right cheek had re-
appeared. And her blush this time seemed to have nothing
to do with ire. Interesting.

"But I thank you for the compliment, I think," she
continued, unaware of the direction of his thoughts.

"Of course," he said with a brisk nod. "Now, getting
back to the subject of the tower. If you really wish to
go, then I will take you. I haven't been there in decades,
so it's possible I will no longer be affected in the same
way now."

"Or, if you are," she said, "then I can go up there myself. You can remain on the ground level while I search for
signs of what might have happened."

He disliked the idea of her going up the bell tower alone
almost as much as the idea of accompanying her up the
narrow, winding stone staircase to the top. But he decided
he'd had enough of negotiating over the matter. "Let us
simply go to the chapel and make the attempt. I daresay it
will no longer be an issue."

At least he hoped like hell that would be the case.

Poppy was still contemplating both of Langham's con-
fessions as they drove along the road that led into Little
Kidding.

His anxiety over visiting St. Lucy's again was entirely
understandable, considering his explanation of what had
occurred there when he was a youth. He hadn't said so,
but she guessed it had also been dark as well as narrow.
The very thought of it made her shiver with sympathetic
dread.

The admission that he was drawn to her was not quite

so easy to interpret her feelings about. Given that she was not unaware of his own good looks, she could hardly be put out by his revelation. Indeed, his words had given her a warm glow of pleasure—though she'd never admit as much to him. Their false betrothal had already brought them far too close to the brink of emotional entanglement. It hadn't even been two full days since they'd embarked on this charade, and already she felt as close to him as she did to Kate and Caro.

If he'd proved to be the man she thought he was at the outset of their journey there would be no question of her succumbing to his charms. But instead of the outrageously arrogant nobleman he'd been at their first meeting, he'd instead revealed himself to be good humored, kind, and determined to do whatever he could to help her when it came to her sister's plight.

A man like that she could find herself falling in love with.

And even if she had any desire to be a duchess—which she most assuredly did not—there was also the fact that she wasn't even certain she wanted to marry at all. She'd become so accustomed to thinking of herself as a spinster— in a way that made her feel independent and strong, rather than a failure left on the shelf—that it was difficult to imagine a future that included a husband and children.

She certainly wasn't able to contemplate such a thing now. Not with Violet's life hanging in the balance.

Her ruminations were interrupted by Langham as they neared a clearing. "Over there," he said, pointing toward a lane bisecting what looked to be two fields of sheep, "is the drive leading to Stannings Hall. He and I used to run back and forth between our two estates so often when we were boys that if I couldn't be found at the abbey, the dowager would send a footman to look for me there."

His reminiscence about his boyhood escapades with Stannings reminded her of what his sisters had revealed last night. "Did you not share such boyhood adventures with your brother, Lord Adrian?"

At the mention of Adrian, the duke sighed. "I told you last night that we are not close. There is a decade between us. When Stannings and I were running wild in the hills, Adrian was in the nursery. My parents were killed in a carriage accident not long after his birth."

"How dreadful," she said, thinking of not only the infant who had lost his parents before he was even old enough to know them, but also the young boy who had lost his parents after having had them long enough to feel the loss. Neither situation was one she'd wish on any child. "I'm so sorry."

"I barely knew them," he said gruffly. "They didn't spend a great deal of time with my sisters and me. We were all far closer to Nanny Meadows, who had taken over the care of Adrian by then."

"About Adrian," she said, into the silence that hung between them.

She saw him open his mouth to cut her off, but for Violet's sake, she pressed on. "Were you able to contact him about the Amazon railway scheme as you suggested to Sir Geoffrey Stannings last evening? It's just that if he leaves London before you make the request then we will have to wait until the house party is at an end and..."

She let her statement trail off, and there was a beat of silence between them as if he was waiting for her to finish. When it was clear she was not going to say anything more, he spoke up.

"You are relentless, are you not?" he asked, with a shake of his head. "If you must know, I sent a messenger to London with a letter for Adrian first thing this morning."

"But if he is to arrive here this afternoon—" she began, but he cut her off.

"He will have time enough to ask a few questions of his colleagues this morning and can take the afternoon train. Have no fear he will give short shrift to the task. If there is one thing my brother loves it's digging for information."

Poppy worried that the man wouldn't have time to make the necessary inquiries, but she was grateful all the same. "Thank you, Langham. Truly."

She placed her hand on his arm to emphasize her gratitude and was immediately distracted by the warmth she felt emanating from beneath his coat. Not to mention the hard muscle there. So distracted that she hadn't realized he'd brought the curricle to a halt until he'd turned to face her. Meeting his gaze with her own, she saw something akin to disappointment flicker across his face. Had he changed his mind about taking her to the tower?

Langham cleared his throat, and she had the distinct impression he was hesitating over whatever it was he wanted to say. "I made a commitment to assist your sister," Langham said, then stopped to clear his throat again. Her stomach dropped. Whatever it was he was struggling to tell her couldn't be good. "Whatever you may think of me, Poppy, I keep my promises. Even when they entail enlisting the aid of my brother."

His expression was fierce, and the relief she felt was matched only by the nagging thought that she'd underestimated him once again. Before she could ponder that thought further, Langham pointed to the signs at the junction of the two diverging roads.

"This way will take us to the caves and St. Lucy's," he said, pointing to the lane on the left. "This other one, toward the village of Little Kidding and on the way,

Rothwell Grange. Are you quite sure you wish to climb up to St. Lucy's?"

Recognizing that their discussion of his brother was at an end, she nodded. "If you are willing, yes. I would like to see the site of the murder."

With a nod, he prodded the horses into a brisk walk.

Recalling what he'd just said, she asked, "What did you mean when you mentioned 'the caves'?"

At that, he laughed darkly. "Have you not heard of St. Lucy's storied history?"

"No," she said, puzzled. "I am not overly familiar with this area of the country."

"My dear lady." He spoke as if he were confiding some dark secret, and despite her prosaically commonsensical bent, she felt a slight thrill of fear creep down her spine. "St. Lucy's is short for St. Lucifer's, and it and all the chalk caves that lie beneath it were used by my great-grandfather's club to perform their hedonistic rituals. They were called the Lucifer Society."

Chapter Twelve

⸻❧❦❧⸻

Lucifer?" Poppy echoed, her voice unnaturally high. "As in…"

"Old Scratch, Satan, the Devil," Langham finished for her. He'd wondered what, aside from her family troubles, would shock the unflappable Miss Delamere. It would appear that his great-grandfather's exploits had done the trick. "If it gives you any comfort, I suspect there was little actual glorification of the dark lord going on. From what I've learned it was more an excuse for licentious behavior in a novel locale."

When he glanced over, he noted the pink tinge in her cheeks and wished anything but his great-grandfather's exploits had put it there.

"Wasn't there outcry from the villagers, or the Church for that matter?" Poppy asked, her sharp mind at once discerning who would be most likely to object to such activity in a rural village. "I can't imagine they were happy to welcome such goings-on in their vicinity."

"As has always been the case, my great-grandfather's title did much to keep them from publicly objecting. And since many members of the church hierarchy were members of other such clubs they could hardly do anything about this one. In fact, most of the members were otherwise upstanding members of the community." Pulling the curricle to a stop, he leapt down and reached up to help Poppy down.

"So the very people who would typically be raising a hue and cry over the shocking behavior were involved?" she asked as she stepped to the edge. "Why doesn't that surprise me?"

It was only the work of a moment to fit his hands about her waist and lift her down, but by the time he set her feet on the ground they were both a little breathless.

After securing the horses, Langham led Poppy to the path that wound its way up to St. Lucy's. It was slightly hidden by the overgrowth, but despite the decades between his last ramble in these woods and now, he recalled the area as if no time had passed at all.

"It must have been difficult," Poppy said as they began to push through the tangle of briars, "growing up with the evidence of your great-grandfather's misdeeds peppering the landscape."

"I didn't even know about the society until I went away to school," Langham replied, recalling just how astonished he'd been to learn that the austere man in the abbey's portrait gallery, whose powder and lace he'd always found amusing, had been one of the most notorious men of his day. "Boys have a tendency to exaggerate, so even then I didn't really think it was as bad as all that. Then when I was sixteen I found a cache of papers and journals hidden in a secret compartment in the library, which were Thaddeus's records of the Lucifer Society. That was his given name—Thaddeus."

"Were you shocked?" Poppy asked, pausing to catch her breath after navigating a steep curve on the hill.

Langham gave a bark of laughter. "Not so much shocked as delighted. I'd spent my whole life being told by my uncles, who were my trustees until I came of age, that my every move was a reflection on the Fielding name, only to find out there was very little I could do that would make as black a mark as Thaddeus had left. It was quite...liberating."

Poppy, he noted, was watching him carefully. "What prompted him to assemble such a group in the first place? Surely it didn't improve his standing among the *ton*."

"You'd be surprised," Langham said dryly. "Sir Francis Dashwood's Hellfire Club boasted members from the highest echelons of society, government, the arts. It was as coveted a membership as any of the most prestigious gentlemen's clubs. But Thaddeus, for some reason, was denied entry. So, he founded his own, had tunnels built into the existing caves, and had St. Lucifer's constructed—though you'll see when we get there that it's a folly and not an actual chapel."

"He went to the expense of having tunnels dug and a chapel built simply out of pique at being excluded from Dashwood's club?" Poppy asked, aghast.

"He did," Langham confirmed ruefully.

Thaddeus had depleted the family coffers to such an extent that it had taken Langham's grandfather and father decades to replenish them through judicious investments and farming improvements.

"Even more galling," he continued, "was the fact that the Lucifer Society was far less popular than the Hellfire

Club, and thus the membership not as robust. After his death, my grandfather—Thaddeus's eldest son—locked up St. Lucy's and allowed it to fall into disrepair."

"So, the chapel folly was a folly in more ways than one?" Poppy laughed. "I'm sorry to find joy in your great-grandfather's failure, but honestly."

"Don't apologize on my account," Langham assured her, matching her smile with his own. "I came to the conclusion long ago that he was the last person who deserved my admiration."

"Didn't..." She paused, as if she was choosing her words carefully. "Didn't the people in the village object to a chapel—whether they knew it to be an actual place of worship or not—called St. Lucifer's?"

Langham held back a branch that blocked her way. "There was an early Christian saint called Lucifer, but most importantly, St. Lucy's is on the ducal estate. Whatever the townspeople thought or didn't think hardly mattered."

There was no arrogance in his words—he was simply stating fact—yet he caught the wince on Poppy's face before she turned herself away from him.

"What did the dowager say about Thaddeus's papers?" she asked pleasantly, and if he hadn't seen her expression moments earlier, he wouldn't have believed she'd been affected at all by his words.

She has spent the past two years playing a part.

He would do well to remember that.

"I never told her," he admitted finally. "At the time, I didn't wish to call attention to the fact that my grandfather, her husband, had been the son of a villain. But I later learned she'd been told all about the Lucifer Society by my grandfather. He hadn't wanted for them to begin their marriage with secrets between them, or so she said.

Apparently, he was smitten with her and had made it his mission to rehabilitate the family name when they wed."

"And clearly succeeded, if one goes by the quality of guests gathered at the abbey this week," Poppy said, stooping again to slide beneath a particular thorny branch he held out of her way.

But just as she did so, she stepped on a root and lost her balance, falling against him with a gasp. "Oh!"

Poppy's eyes met his and the moment stretched out between them.

"Careful," Langham said, grasping her arms as he felt her hands press against his chest. In their current position, with her standing just above him on the hill path, they were at eye level, and his gaze went unerringly to her plump red lips. She smelled of roses and something else— something citrusy and clean. When he glanced up, he saw her lashes lower, and without even thinking, he tilted his head as they moved closer together, in the timeless preamble to a kiss.

"Your Grace!" came an unwelcome voice from the path below, just as their lips touched. "Your Grace, are you there? Is everything well?"

As if he were made of flames, Poppy stepped back from him in alarm, and he was forced to steady her as she lost her balance and nearly went tumbling back down the way they'd come.

"Careful," he said again, only this time it was more of a growl. He didn't know who the devil was coming up after them, but he would be more than happy to shake them senseless.

Poppy's nostrils flared as she inhaled, attempting, it seemed, to get hold of her senses. Was she just as affected as he was by the attraction between them? He hoped so.

Turning, he saw that a man of middle years wearing the uniform of a village constable was fast approaching.

"Mr. Rhodes, I presume," Langham said, glaring down at the man as he huffed his way closer.

"Indeed, Your Grace," the other man said, glancing from Langham to Poppy and back again. "We haven't had the pleasure, but I'd heard you were up at the abbey for the dowager duchess's birthday celebration, and with a betrothed, no less."

The man glanced pointedly at Poppy, as if waiting for an introduction, and Langham bit back a sigh. "Rhodes, may I introduce you to my fiancée, Miss Poppy Delamere. Poppy, Constable Rhodes."

Despite the interruption, or perhaps because of it, for all Langham knew, Poppy smiled warmly at the man. Which was, he thought, an odd way to greet the man who intended to lock up your sister for murder.

"A pleasure, miss," said Rhodes, his moustache trembling as he bent over her hand in a courtly gesture. "I'd been told you were a beauty, but your looks are even more stunning than I expected, Miss Delamere."

Poppy's smile lit up her whole face, and to Langham's surprise he felt an unfamiliar pang of jealousy. Which was ridiculous considering he and Poppy were barely acquainted and Rhodes was old enough to be her father.

"You're too kind, Mr. Rhodes," she said with a breathiness that was entirely unlike her usual no-nonsense manner. And again he was reminded just how adept she was at slipping from one role into another.

But the constable's next words erased the smile from Poppy's face.

"You are, I understand, the sister of Mrs. Violet Lovell, are you not?" Rhodes sounded apologetic as he asked the question, but he clearly wasn't so remorseful that he didn't ask the question at all. "May I ask if you are heading up to St. Lucy's?"

Poppy took Langham's arm with a grasp that he suspected owed only a small debt to the unevenness of the path. "We are," she answered calmly, but Langham was certain he could hear the tremble beneath the words as she fought to retain her composure. "I wish you to know that I don't believe my sister is responsible for her husband's death, Mr. Rhodes. And I intend to prove it."

Rhodes scowled and made to respond, but Langham cut him off. "We're going up to see the scene of the crime, Rhodes. It will be a great help if you'll come along with us."

The way Poppy pinched his arm let Langham know that she wasn't best pleased with this plan, but he intended to question the man and gain insight into why it seemed everyone was convinced Violet had committed the crime. It would also give Poppy the opportunity to make a case for her sister's innocence.

Rhodes beamed in response to the duke's invitation. "I would be honored, Your Grace. Miss Delamere."

Then, almost as if he'd just remembered why they were there, he said, "Though I regret to inform you, Miss Delamere, that the evidence against your sister is quite bad."

"And what evidence is that?" Langham asked mildly as he pushed aside a branch so that Poppy could go forward. "I heard something about a knife wound?" He asked the question with an air of idle curiosity, hoping to disarm the man.

"That was supposed to be kept quiet," said the constable, irritation evident in his tone. "There are some details that we don't like getting out for public consumption."

"Because you don't wish for the public to be frightened?" Poppy asked, turning to look at him.

And because she'd stopped, Langham did so as well. The constable's face was glistening with perspiration, and his cheeks were ruddy. Clearly, he wasn't accustomed to this much exertion.

"That," Rhodes agreed, "but also because only the true killer will know of the knife wound's existence. And until I have a chance to speak to Mrs. Lovell, I had hoped to keep the fact of it a secret."

This made Langham turn to the other man in disbelief. "You haven't spoken to her yet either? How is that possible?"

Rhodes looked sheepish. "Lord and Lady Short have refused thus far to let me interview her." He turned to Poppy with a rueful smile. "Would you be able to help me with that, Miss Delamere?"

Poppy looked at the constable as if he had been eating opium. "Why would I help you prove that my sister murdered her husband?" she asked in a tone of disbelief. "I just informed you that I intend to prove that she did not."

The news that Rhodes was also denied access to Violet was troubling beyond measure. Why were Lord and Lady Short so intent on keeping her from being interviewed? If they were willing to defy the law, and a duke, was there something that Violet could reveal that they meant to keep private?

"Despite the evidence I've already gathered," Rhodes said as they resumed their climb, "I do like to keep an open mind. What I have thus far is only based on the word of people who have told me your sister and her husband had an unhappy marriage. And that he was not the most faithful of men."

"Even so," Poppy argued, "that doesn't mean I'll help you. There have been far too many times when the authorities have pursued the wrong person for a crime, and I intend to see to it that in this case, at least, the right person is apprehended."

"Then help me speak to your sister," Rhodes persisted, though his breathlessness indicated that the climb was becoming too much for him. Fortunately for the man, they were almost to the top.

As they neared the top of the hill, it became clear that Ned's description of the path's impassability was only accurate to a point. There were, indeed, many parts of the route that were difficult to maneuver, where he was forced to use brute force to break off branches or hold them back so that Poppy could go on.

But he'd expected there to be even more brambles and overgrowth to get through. It was obvious someone had ensured the way leading to St. Lucy's was easily traversable despite its having been abandoned for decades.

"Oh, how lovely," Poppy said as she looked up at the stone structure that had the appearance of being a thousand years old but had been constructed in Thaddeus Fielding's time. There was even a faux graveyard to add verisimilitude to what was, in fact, merely the outer shell of a chapel. "But I stand by my assertion that there is no way my sister would voluntarily climb to the top of that tower."

They all three stared up at the cupola containing the bell. "It's not quite as lovely when you know why it was built— if you don't mind my saying so, Your Grace. Apologies, Miss Delamere." Rhodes glanced at Langham guiltily, as if he'd just realized who he was speaking to.

"Oh, I know all about the Lucifer Society, Mr. Rhodes,"

Poppy said before Langham could respond. "There are no secrets between us, are there, darling?"

She took his arm and looked at him adoringly, and Langham bit back a laugh. "There certainly aren't, my little cabbage."

He pressed a kiss onto her wrist and didn't miss the way her pulse leapt at his touch. A glance at her face showed her eyes had darkened, and she touched a finger to her lips. Was she thinking about their almost kiss just before Rhodes had interrupted them? He certainly was.

If Rhodes found their byplay suspect, he didn't say so. Instead he stepped forward so that he could face Poppy. "It makes it easier that you know about the Lucifer Society, Miss Delamere. Because I have reason to believe this murder may be connected to it. At least in part."

"Since the Lucifer Society died with my great-grandfather, Constable, I'd say it's very unlikely that its members are committing murders in the present day." Langham scoffed, wondering suddenly if the climb had affected the constable more than he'd realized.

"That's what I meant by connected, Your Grace," Rhodes explained. "It's not club members who killed Mr. Lovell. Of course it wasn't. But that doesn't mean the club isn't involved in his death."

"You'd better explain yourself, man," Langham said sharply.

Rhodes looked conflicted for a moment, then let out a heavy sigh. "I suppose since you know about the knife wound you may as well know that we found the knife a few feet away from the body."

The duke frowned. "I suppose that makes sense. It would have been forced from the body with the strength of the body's impact. You were able to connect the knife with the club somehow? I find that hard to believe since it's been defunct since the turn of the century."

"That's just it, Your Grace. I suspect that someone has resurrected the club." Rhodes paused, and Langham got the distinct sense the constable was enjoying his dramatic revelation. "Not only was Lovell wearing a necklace with a pendant inscribed with the crest of the Lucifer Society, but the knife found near the body is inscribed with it as well."

Chapter Thirteen

At Rhodes's revelation, Langham swore eloquently. "Surely you don't believe my family has anything to do with Lovell's murder."

"Of course not, Your Grace," said Rhodes with alacrity. "But it does harken back to a dark time for the area, doesn't it? Especially what with Lovell being killed at the old chapel. It makes one wonder if someone has revived the Lucifer Society."

"It seems more likely to me," Poppy said, with a sympathetic glance at Langham, "that someone either had the knife in their possession and purposely used it in Lovell's murder in order to tie the crime to Langham, or they came upon it by chance and used it, having no notion of the crest's significance. Any suggestion that the Lucifer Society has been re-formed seems premature at best."

At her chiding, the constable's ears reddened a little. But Poppy had had quite enough talk of mysterious societies for one morning. Her sister stood accused of murder, and Rhodes seemed more interested in tying the crime to a defunct club for debauched noblemen than finding the real culprit.

Leaving Langham to soothe the constable's ruffled feathers, she set out at a brisk pace through the wooded area that bordered the stone façade of St. Lucy's and approached the chapel itself. Alongside, she noted the cemetery Langham had spoken of. She tried to imagine him as a boy, climbing over the stones and chasing Stannings and other friends through the headstones.

"It's much the worse for wear since I was here last." Langham's voice just behind her gave Poppy a start.

"Easy," he said taking her arm in his. "You're meant to be the more level-headed of us."

She gave him a speaking look. It was all well and good for him to tease, but it would take some time for her heartbeat to slow. "The graves may not be real, but the atmosphere is no less eerie for it."

"Thaddeus was nothing if not attentive to detail," Langham said pointing toward a small grave that was clearly meant to be that of an infant.

Poppy suppressed a shudder and turned away from the tiny grave. "Yes, it's very realistic. Though I've never felt this unsettled by a real cemetery."

"I suspect some of that is due to the isolated location," Langham said, surveying the area. "The trees and undergrowth have grown up around it so that it seems like its own little world."

Rhodes, who had trailed them at a bit of a distance, now followed Poppy and Langham past the cemetery and toward the cobblestone expanse that jutted out from the entrance of the chapel. "Over there, on the stones, is where we found your brother-in-law's body, Miss Delamere," he said in a somber tone, as if recalling the gruesome sight. "Mr. Jarvis had come searching for one of the sheep from the estate—the fool creature got itself tangled up in a bramble over by the mausoleum—and found more than he bargained for. Jarvis turned the dead man over, of course, to determine who he was, and that's when he found the knife wound."

Poppy stared at the irregularly shaped dark spot on the rocks where it was clear that blood, or some other fluid she didn't wish to contemplate, had stained the surface.

She had been no admirer of Alistair Lovell, but it was unspeakable to think that the man had lost his life in such a ghastly manner mere steps from where she now stood.

Trying to turn her mind away from the horror of the man's death and toward unraveling who might have caused it, she asked, "Were you able to determine if he was stabbed before or after he fell? I should imagine the depth of the wound would be an indicator. The amount of force a person—even a very strong one—can wield is no match for the power of gravity from that height."

Langham gave a soft laugh. "Why does it not surprise me you are familiar with Newton's second law as it pertains to falling objects?"

"I am a lady, Langham," Poppy said with a roll of her eyes, "not an ignoramus."

"No, Miss Delamere," Rhodes said, ignoring their little exchange altogether. "It makes no sense for the killer to stab him after. The fall would have killed him, so there'd be no need to use the knife. No, it's clear that Lovell was attacked up there"—he pointed toward the bell tower looming above them—"and fell from the tower after he was stabbed."

"But wouldn't that mean he'd have fallen on his back?" Poppy asked, not bothering to keep her frustration from her voice. "It makes no sense for him to be stabbed in the chest, then spun around by the killer so that he'd fall to land on his front."

"Now, Miss Delamere," the constable said in a condescending tone, "I know you're a clever lady, but there are some matters that are best left to those of us who investigate such things for a living."

Poppy was about to explain to the man that the rules of logic were the same no matter the profession, but Langham's hand on her arm silenced her.

"Let's make our way up to the tower," he said, his eyes indicating that the argument with Rhodes wouldn't be worth the trouble. To Rhodes he said in a hearty voice, "Perhaps you can remain down here, Constable, and stand where Lovell's body was discovered. That way we can determine the most likely spot from which he fell."

The relief in Rhodes's face was not feigned, Poppy noted. Whether it was because he was weary of her questioning his methods or thankful to avoid the steep climb, she didn't know. But whichever the case, she was grateful for the chance to be away from him for a time.

"Of course, Your Grace," the constable said with a nod. "A sensible plan."

Leaving Rhodes at the base of the path, Poppy and Langham approached the gate separating the yard from the few steps going up to the door. To her surprise, when Langham pushed the gate open, it made no sound at all. "Someone has been maintaining the chapel, if not the cemetery," she said, glancing up at him with a raised brow.

"Indeed. Likely the same person who cleared the way to the yard. I've made a note to ask Ned about it when we're back at the abbey," the duke said as he let the gate clang shut behind them. He had a difficult time imagining a reason for his cousin to order that sort of upkeep for an area of the estate that he'd ordered be left alone.

"Is it possible Mr. Jarvis planned to reopen St. Lucy's?" Poppy asked, peering into the interior of the chapel once Langham had pulled open the heavy door by its iron ring.

"I doubt it," Langham said, following her inside and fumbling at the base of a torchiere along the wall. "Ned would have asked me before entertaining such an idea. He knows as well as anyone how poorly this place reflects on the family. For all that we found it thrilling as boys, I made myself clear about how it was to be left to nature after I had the caves and the connected tunnels blocked off."

Poppy heard the strike of a match, and with the illumination of a large lamp that Langham had lit, she was soon able to see that, rather than being an actual chapel, with pews, altar and the like, the interior of St. Lucy's was simply a vast empty room with several small alcoves.

"It truly is nothing more than a chapel folly," she said in wonder as she scanned the area, from the stone floors to the stained-glass windows through which sunlight streamed, giving the space an otherworldly glow.

"In his diaries, Thaddeus called it an anti-church," Langham said as he stepped farther inside. "But the stained-glass windows rather ruin that idea. Grotesque as their subjects might be, the effect is far more Church of England or Roman Catholic than I suspect he wished."

Poppy studied the windows one by one and realized that Langham was right. Though the depiction of St. Sebastian, who according to legend had been shot through with countless arrows, was far more gruesome than Poppy had seen before, the blood pouring from his eyes, mouth, and various other places in his body did follow the story. As did another one showing, by Poppy's guess, St. Stephen, who had been stoned to death.

She was unable to place the subject of the third window, however. It showed a man writhing on the ground while what looked eerily like small demons pierced him with knives.

When Langham noticed her puzzled expression, he told her, "St. Cassian. He was a teacher hacked to death by his students."

"Heavens," Poppy said with a shake of her head. "Thaddeus must have had a particularly disturbing aesthetic sensibility."

"Or a particularly disturbing sense of humor," Langham replied. "It's said St. Cassian bears a striking resemblance to one of my great-grandfather's most hated tutors at Eton."

Poppy shuddered, even though the sunlight that had been trapped inside the building for hours had kept it somewhat warm.

"The last," Langham said as they stepped toward the fourth window, "is the chapel's namesake, St. Lucifer."

It was not, Poppy noted, the iconic image of St. Michael expelling Lucifer from heaven that had been painted time and again by the Old Masters. No, this depiction of Satan was before his fall. He stood proudly, surrounded by long, narrow white strips of glass, which were, she knew, meant to denote sunbeams.

"Lucifer. Light bringer," she said and felt an unexpected poignance at knowing the brightest of God's angels had met his downfall.

"I'm really rather surprised no one has ever come to tear the place down stone by stone," Langham said wryly. "Though I suppose, technically, it is merely celebrating an angel and a saint. But in another time, this is the sort of thing that would get one burned at the stake."

"Even dukes?" Poppy asked, with a sideways glance.

"Perhaps not dukes," he conceded with a laugh, then his expression turned pensive. "I'll need to revisit the notion of having this place torn down when I've got a family of my own. As much as I enjoyed my rambles around here as a boy, I don't like the idea of perpetuating this history on another generation."

Poppy was assailed by an unexpected pang of jealousy for that nameless, faceless lady who would one day be his wife. Determined to distract herself, she glanced around the large room. "How do we get to the bell tower from here?" There didn't seem to be any stairs or doorways through which they could access a flight leading up to the cupola.

"The stairs are over here," Langham said, taking her by the hand to lead her to the other side of the room.

He might only have intended to hurry her along, but the warmth of his hand on hers sent a frisson of awareness through her. Between their near kiss earlier and the demonstration for Rhodes's benefit, Poppy was as taut as a bowstring.

As he reached the far-right corner of the room, he pressed a stone that from all appearances was the same as all the others. But when a whole section of wall swung outward to reveal an interior room, Poppy knew the stone in question had hidden a mechanism of some sort.

"One amusing aspect of Thaddeus's machinations," Langham said as he set the lantern on a hook inside the recess, "is that he had secret doors and passageways installed all over the estate. As a boy I found them particularly useful when I wished to annoy my sisters or avoid punishments."

"I can imagine," she said, though she noticed that despite his attempt at humor, there were lines of tension around his mouth.

"Are you sure you wish to go into the tower with me?" she asked. "I can climb up and look around, try to determine where Lovell was when he fell. There's really no need for both of us to go."

Langham bit back a curse. "I most heartily wish you would forget I said anything about my problem with enclosed spaces."

"You told me less than an hour ago," she said dryly. "I'm hardly likely to forget it."

Without meeting her gaze, he simply went ahead of her into the shadowed stairwell.

"Very well," she said, following him into the inky darkness. "But I would like to state for posterity's sake that you are an exceedingly stubborn man."

Langham hadn't set foot on these winding stairs since he'd been trapped here over two decades ago. And yet the passage of time had done little to expand the breathing space in the blasted stairwell that seemed narrower still now that he was a grown man.

"Is it much farther?" she asked, as they came to a recess in the wall that held a skull gleaming in the lamplight. "I don't much care for the style of the décor here."

"We're almost there," he said to Poppy, glancing back

to see that she was pink cheeked and a little winded. "We should see sunlight around one of the next turns."

And indeed, in moments they saw a ray of light that made them both cry out in pain as their eyes adjusted to the change.

"I never realized how grateful I could be for the sight of the sky," Poppy said as they emerged in a square cupola, in the center of which hung a bell with a rope running through a chimney-like opening that went all the way down to the lower level of the chapel.

"Nor I," said Langham, and as if by instinctive agreement, they grasped hands and moved to stand against the stone wall that ran along the edges of the cupola. The wind was strong up here, and though he knew they were likely in no danger of being carried off by it, he felt a need to hold on to her nonetheless.

He didn't wish to examine the reasons for that feeling too closely.

They peered down at the ground below and saw Rhodes waving up at them. "Ho, Your Grace," Rhodes shouted. "This is where Lovell's body was found. Can you tell where he might have been standing when he fell?"

Langham moved to stand directly above where Rhodes had indicated Lovell had landed and glanced around at the floor surrounding the area. There was an accumulation of leaves and other natural debris that had likely been blown onto the platform by the wind. "What do you think?" he asked Poppy. "Was he standing somewhere near this spot?"

She moved to stare down at the ground below, and to Langham's alarm, she began to sway on her feet.

"Oh!" she gasped and he pulled her against him, his own heart thundering in his chest as his mind leapt ahead to the thought of what might have happened if she fell. He held her against him for a moment, and the warm scent of her reminded him once again of that unfulfilled kiss. "I have you. I won't let you fall."

"I hadn't realized just how disturbing it would be to look down," she said, pulling away from him, and reluctantly he let her go. "There's no possible way Violet would be able to maintain her composure up here, much less stab her husband and push him over the edge."

"And that's what we'll remind Rhodes of when we return to the ground," Langham said as he turned to lead her back down the stairs. He had no desire to tarry up here longer than necessary.

"Let's wait a moment before we go back down," Poppy said, a determined expression on her face. "I want to look around a bit more to see if there is any trace of who might have been up here with Lovell."

"As you wish," Langham said, admonishing himself silently for not thinking of that himself. His desire to be away from this place was clearly overriding his thinking.

They explored the tower in silence for several moments, and Langham was almost ready to declare the task a failure when he noticed a light-colored bit of cloth peeking from a crevice between the stones that made up the floor.

Frowning, he grasped the fabric and pulled on it gently so as not to tear it. Ever so slowly, he realized it was a lady's handkerchief. A knot formed in his gut as he unraveled it to reveal initials neatly embroidered in the corner. VSL. *Violet Short Lovell.*

Damn it.

He was about to show Poppy what he'd found when she gave a cry. "I've found something," she said with excitement. "It's a pipe."

Langham tucked the handkerchief in his coat and turned to examine the pipe she held out to him. He would allow her this moment of triumph before telling her of the handkerchief.

"Do you recognize it?" she asked, holding the silver filigreed men's tobacco pipe in the palm of her hand so that he could examine it. "I know it didn't belong to Lovell. He was rather adamantly against the use of tobacco of any kind. Claimed it was a filthy habit."

Langham removed his quizzing glass from an inner pocket and used it to look more closely at the decorations on the pipe. It was finely made, the sort of item that could be purchased at a high-end haberdasher.

"I've never seen it before," he said thoughtfully before handing it back to her. "It could very well have belonged to whoever killed Lovell."

Would it matter, he wondered, if Rhodes saw the handkerchief? He had to tell Poppy about it before they reached the other man.

But Poppy was already halfway down the stairs before he caught up to her. "We have to show this to Rhodes," she called to him over her shoulder. "It proves there was someone else here. A man!"

"Poppy wait." Langham followed at her heels, trying not to send them both tumbling downward in his haste.

"I thought you'd be more enthusiastic," she said, pausing halfway down and turning to scowl at him. "If we can trace this back to the shop it came from, it can lead to the real killer. It could clear Violet's name."

Crushing her hope was the last thing he wanted to do, but she needed to know the truth, before they reached Rhodes.

"I need to show you something," he said in a low voice.

"Why are you whispering?" she asked in an answering hiss, her brows lowered.

Wordlessly, he pulled the handkerchief from his pocket and handed it to her.

She stared down at the delicately embroidered square of cotton in confusion for a moment, then her eyes widened. *"No,"* she said, looking up at him with such misery that he wanted more than anything to tell her it was a jest.

But it was all too real.

"She didn't do this, Langham."

"It may not mean she did it," he said gently, "but it very likely means she was here."

"Rhodes won't make that distinction," she spat out. "He'll use this to prove her guilt whether it's warranted or not."

"I'll use every ounce of my power to make sure every avenue of inquiry is explored," he said. "We'll send for Eversham. He can see to it that the real story comes out, not whatever tale Rhodes concocts. We'll make it right."

"It can't be made right," she said in a voice that made him want to gather her in his arms and protect her from this darkness. "Detective Inspector Eversham's opinions might wield influence in London, but he holds no such regard in Little Kidding, where the villagers have already painted Violet as a murderess. They are the ones who will serve on the jury after all. Even you, with all your horses and all your men, cannot repair this da—"

"Your Grace," Rhodes's voice was suddenly there at the foot of the stairs, and from the sound of it, he was on his way up.

"He cannot see this," Poppy hissed, squeezing up against him in the small space as she reached out to pluck the handkerchief from his hand.

Just then Rhodes's ruddy face appeared in the stairwell, and his eyes darted back and forth between Poppy and Langham, suspicion clouding his face.

Poppy, resourceful as ever, threw her arms about his neck.

"Kiss me," she breathed, and lifting her face she pressed her mouth to his.

Chapter Fourteen

A week ago, Poppy would never have imagined she'd be so brazen as to kiss the Duke of Langham as if her very life depended on it. But, as Hippocrates said, desperate times called for desperate measures.

Rhodes's voice had sent alarm coursing through her, but once her lips touched Langham's, she was so caught up in the maelstrom of sensation his nearness brought that all thoughts of the constable were swept from her mind.

She'd been kissed before, by a dance partner at a local assembly before she left for London, but the experience had been more embarrassing than pleasurable. And she'd never felt the need to repeat it.

Langham, though. His kiss she felt from the top of her head to the tips of her toes. It had never occurred to her that a kiss could be playful, but his teasing strokes, which invited her to answer with her own, gave her a strange lightness in her chest.

He'd just moved to kiss down over her jaw and along

the curve of her neck, one hand caressing up from her waist and over her breast when the sound of Rhodes's surprised "ahem" cut through the fog of her desire.

Langham's head snapped up, and he took a step back from her, looking all the while like a man awakening from a trance. "We'll follow you down, Rhodes. If you will, please wait for us outside the entrance. Miss Delamere is feeling a little unwell from the height."

Poppy, despite feeling a little breathless from the abrupt shift in Langham, was none too pleased at Langham's subterfuge. "I am not unwell," she hissed. Far from it, if she were being honest with herself. But she was hardly going to give him the satisfaction of telling him that.

"It gives him a plausible reason to discount what he just saw with his own eyes," Langham hissed back, with an equally annoyed look. "I'm attempting to preserve your reputation. Once our betrothal is at its end you will need to go about your life without the whisper of scandal."

The reminder that whatever this was between them was temporary brought Poppy up short. He was right, of course. Their ease with one another had become so familiar that she'd forgotten for the space of a few minutes that they would soon go back to their former lives.

Turning away from him, she set about smoothing her gown and straightening her hat, which felt a little askew.

"Here," Langham said with ill-concealed impatience, though whether it was for her or himself Poppy could not tell. With a surprisingly impersonal touch, given how familiar he'd been a moment ago with her person, he tucked a stray lock of hair behind her ear and straightened the ribbons of her bonnet beneath her chin. "We can't do anything about your reddened complexion, but at the very least you no longer look as if you've just been thoroughly kissed."

If only it were as easy to remove the evidence of what had just happened from her mind, she thought wryly.

Aloud she said, "That's something, I suppose."

Wordlessly, she began the descent toward the ground floor of the chapel.

"I'm sorry you became unwell, Miss Delamere," Rhodes said as she stepped out of the doorway. "I suppose you have that in common with your sister. Ladies can be sensitive that way. It is nothing to be ashamed of. Especially given your reasons for climbing the bell tower in the first place."

"Thank you," she said to the constable through her teeth. "But I'm afraid we'll need to make haste back down the hill. The duke and I wish to pay a call at Rothwell Grange."

"I do wonder if it might be better for us to return to the abbey so that you might rest, my angel," Langham said, coming up beside her and taking her arm with what Poppy considered to be an overly solicitous manner. "I'm sure your sister will understand."

"In matters such as these, Miss Delamere," said Rhodes, with an approving look at the duke, "it is best to let yourself be led by those who have your best interest at heart."

"I should still like to meet with my sister, Mr. Rhodes." To Langham she turned a look of blind adoration. "There is no need to worry, my pumpkin. I assure you that I am feeling ever so much better now, and as alarming as this situation with my family is, I know I will have you at my side."

She wasn't sure if Langham winced at the endearment or her expression, but she was relieved when he finally spoke. "Of course, my dear. If traveling to the grange is what you wish, then we shall make it so."

When they arrived back to where the horses and curricle awaited them, the constable bowed over Poppy's hand and gave a bow to Langham. "I am sorry for the circumstances under which we had to meet, Miss Delamere," he said with a troubled look, "but I wish you both happy. And I do believe that once you accept the fact that your sister is very likely guilty of her husband's death, you will find some peace."

And bidding them farewell, he set off down the lane in the direction of Little Kidding.

"What an insufferable man," Poppy said once she and Langham were seated far too close to one another in the curricle. "As if he could have any notion of what feelings I might have about my sister's situation. How dare he?"

"He has rather let his role go to his head," Langham agreed as he steered the horses in the direction of Rothwell Grange. "But given the handkerchief we found, you must admit he may not be as far off the mark as we first believed."

"I will admit no such thing," Poppy retorted. "Someone might have placed that handkerchief there to implicate her." There had to be another explanation for its appearance in the bell tower—an explanation she intended to get from Violet herself.

"But surely if that were the intention, it would have been put somewhere more easily detected," Langham argued.

"And the pipe?" Poppy demanded. "Surely you are not suggesting she has taken up that foul habit while I've been in London? It's far more likely it was left there by a man. The man who was responsible for Lovell's murder."

"That's possible," Langham said in an irritatingly reasonable manner. "But it's also possible the pipe did belong to Lovell, and you aren't as familiar with the man's habits as you once were."

He was right and Poppy knew it, but she was unwilling to give in just yet. In the bell tower, she'd feared for the fraction of second that her sister might be guilty, but back here on the ground she was able to see more clearly that the pipe did more to make her sister look innocent than the handkerchief did to make her seem guilty.

"I want to hear Violet's side of the story," she insisted, grateful to see the chimneys of Rothwell Grange rising in the distance. "The only accounts of her whereabouts that night have come from other people. I want to hear the tale from her. I know my sister. If she is responsible for her husband's death, I will know as soon as I speak to her."

"You've been away from her for two years," Langham said gently. "It's possible that you don't know her as well as you used to. Or that she's learned how to lie while you were away."

"She was my only playmate and my dearest confidante when we were girls. I think sometimes I understood her better than myself." Poppy knew she sounded foolish, but she could not believe that Violet would lie to her. "She will tell me the truth."

"I hope you are right," he said grimly. "For your sake, I hope you are right."

As the curricle drew closer to the entrance of the grange, Poppy felt a frisson of nerves run through her. The last time she'd come here, she'd been convinced of Violet's innocence. This time she wasn't so certain.

Langham handed the reins to a waiting groom, and when he reached to lift Poppy down he could feel the tension radiating from her.

"I'll be with you," he said, hoping to reassure her. "I won't let Short bully you again. And if your sister is in this house, we *will* see her."

Langham had no doubt Poppy could have managed on her own, but he was glad to be at her side as they climbed the steps of the grange and made their way to the door.

"Thank you," she said, slipping her arm through his. "Truly."

"Do not become maudlin on me, Poppy," he said bracingly. "We are friends, are we not? Friends help one another."

By kissing each other senseless in bell towers?

"I suppose so," she said as Langham rapped none too gently on the door, though she didn't sound any more convinced than he was.

He was saved from further discussion by the butler opening the door. Langham handed the man his card and said in his most commanding tone, "We are here to see Mrs. Violet Lovell. Take us to her at once."

Whether it was Langham's hauteur or the mention of Violet, the butler's eyes widened with alarm.

"Begging your pardon, Your Grace, Miss Delamere, I'm afraid I've been instructed that Mrs. Lovell is to have no visitors. I will let Lord Short know that you are here, Your Grace—"

"Violet is my sister, and I insist on seeing her at once," Poppy interrupted the butler, who seemed ready to collapse at having to deny them. "I do not require permission from Lord Short."

Langham had already followed Poppy into the entryway when he saw Lady Short approaching. She looked haggard. Clearly the hours since their visit yesterday had not been restful ones.

"Please do not make a scene, Poppy," Lady Short hissed, as if she didn't wish to be overheard. "It will not make your father any more inclined to let you see Violet, and he will likely take out his anger on us once you are gone."

Beside him, he heard Poppy give a sharp intake of breath.

"Lady Short," Langham said, as Poppy rushed forward to take her mother's hand, "if you are in fear for either your or your daughter's safety, then you both must come with us to Langham Abbey. I can ensure that you both will be safe there."

At his words, Poppy shot him a look of gratitude.

"Let us fetch Violet, and we will remove you both from this house before he returns," she implored her mother.

But they'd barely got past the entry hall before Lord Short himself appeared at the top of the stairs, his eyes cold with fury. "I would not have thought you would be so foolish as to attempt to come between a man and his wife, Langham. There are laws about such things after all. My wife will be back with me before you reach the end of the drive. I've got friends who will see to it."

"We'll see about that," Langham said levelly, making a note to look into these so-called friends who Lord Short was so certain would support him.

"As for your sister," Short said to Poppy as he reached the base of the stairs, "she is not here." There was something about the smug way he uttered the words that sent a chill through Langham.

"What do you mean, she's not here?" Poppy demanded, and Langham saw that though she hadn't relaxed her spine, her stepfather's words had alarmed her as well. "I don't believe for a moment that you allowed her to leave this house on her own."

"Believe what you want," Short said with a shrug. "I

assure you Violet is not here. Tell them, my dear." He put his arm around his wife's waist then, and his message was clear: Poppy would find no allies here.

Lady Short flinched at her husband's touch, then said in a quavering voice, "He speaks the truth, Poppy. Violet has gone."

Chapter Fifteen

I don't believe you," Poppy said firmly, looking back and forth between her mother and stepfather. "I want to see her bedchamber. I want proof that she's not locked away somewhere in this house."

Langham laid a hand on her shoulder, silently signaling his support.

"Are you calling your mother a liar?" But instead of sounding outraged, Short sounded bored.

When Poppy didn't answer, only held her stepfather's gaze, the man sighed.

"The rooms she shared with Mr. Lovell are on the second floor, third on the right," Short said with a wave of his hand toward the upper floors. "You are welcome to search the rest of the house, but I can assure you she is not here."

It occurred to Langham then, though he would never put the idea in Poppy's head before she got there on her own, that it was entirely possible that Violet had been killed by the same person who had killed her husband. If so, then their search for her in this house was doomed to be fruitless. But at the very least they might be able to find some clue as to whether she'd left on her own or against her will.

Beside him, Poppy said in an undertone, "Let's go look. Even if she isn't here, we may be able to find something that points to Lovell's killer."

With a nod, he followed her as she swept past her mother and stepfather and up the stairs toward the upper floors of the house.

"If he has any proof of his illegal activities in the house," Langham said in a low voice once they were out of earshot, "then they aren't kept up here."

Poppy shot him a surprised look, and he gave her a wry smile. "I suspect you are accustomed to being the cleverest person in whatever room you happen to be in. Never fear, you still are. Indeed, it's one of the things I like best about you."

Then, realizing he'd said more than he intended, he pressed forward to the door Short had said was Violet's and turned the handle.

It was, as Short had indicated, empty.

"I don't know why I'm disappointed," Poppy said with a tremor in her voice. "He told us she wasn't here."

"We'll find her," Langham said, squeezing her hand. "I promise you."

Langham stepped into the attached dressing room while Poppy explored Violet's bedchamber. Opening drawer after drawer, then cabinet after cabinet, he noted that however Poppy might dislike Lovell, it didn't seem that he'd stinted his wife on her clothing allowance. There were rows and rows of gowns in the wardrobes, and the drawers held any number of stockings and underthings. The last wardrobe, however, was nearly empty of gowns.

"There's no valise or trunk here," he said to Poppy as he crossed back into the bedchamber. "And you'll have to check for yourself, but it looks to me as if there are some gowns missing. I would say that in this instance your step-father was telling the truth. Your sister has left. Whether of her own volition or not, we can't know yet."

"But why would she leave?" Poppy asked, frustration heavy in her voice. "If she has run, then it will only serve to make her look more guilty in the eyes of the law."

"She may have thought it was her only option," Langham said with a shrug. "It's not as if she can count on her father for help. He's the one who gave her name to the authorities in the first place."

"But she has me," Poppy protested, and it was impossible to miss the sheen of tears in her eyes. "Though how she could possibly have guessed I would come, I don't know. I'm just as responsible for this mess as anyone. If I hadn't run away and left her here to take my place—"

"—you would have been trapped in marriage to that cretin Lovell," Langham said, stepping forward to brush a tear from her cheek. "You cannot blame yourself for thinking your sister would be safer under her own father's roof than you were."

"I should have stayed," Poppy repeated, pulling away from him. "I should have protected her. I was the eldest. She was my responsibility."

Langham watched helplessly as Poppy stalked into the dressing room. He followed as she opened the door on the far side, which led into another dressing chamber, this one presumably Lovell's.

Going through to the bedroom beyond, Poppy opened the draperies there just as she had those in Violet's room. Whereas the other bedchamber had been light and airy, this one, decorated in claret-colored fabrics and with darkly patterned paper on the walls, felt heavy and oppressive.

"The décor rather makes one want to check under the bed for monsters doesn't it?" Langham asked.

As if in silent agreement, they each took a bedside table to search. Pulling open the drawer of the one nearest the window, Langham began pulling out various bits and bobs. A comb, a volume of Catullus with a leaf serving as a bookmark, a tin of lemon drops. In the back of the drawer—whether it was hidden there by chance or purpose he could not say—he found a book of pornographic drawings.

Flipping through the well-thumbed pages—he would not think about *that* just now—Langham noted with clinical detachment that it was neither the most lurid collection of erotic images he'd ever seen nor the tamest. He considered putting the book back in the drawer and forgetting about it. But he knew Poppy would not thank him for shielding her from it.

"Why would Lovell have a bagful of earbobs?" the lady mused aloud as Langham walked round the bed to stand beside her.

"Let me see," he said, leaning forward to look at the velvet bag she held in one hand and the several odd earrings in the palm of the other. Realization struck him, and much as he disliked it, this was apparently the day for revealing to Poppy just how much worse men were than she'd even guessed. "I suspect they are trophies of a sort."

"Trophies?" Poppy's nose wrinkled adorably.

"Some men keep lists of the women they bed," Langham said, feeling shame for the entirety of his sex, "but it isn't unheard of that one would ask for a piece of jewelry or an item of clothing."

Poppy dropped the jewels back into the bag as if they were made of hot coals. She turned to him with wide eyes, an unasked question in them.

"No," he said, feeling his ears redden. "I've never seen the need. And despite what you may think of me, the number of my conquests isn't so great that I'm in danger of forgetting their names."

"I never said a thing," she said primly before turning back to the drawer where she'd found the bag. "What's that book in your hand?"

"Oh, just a volume of artistic prints," he said truthfully as he slipped the book into his pocket. After the earbobs discussion, now was not the time to launch into another example of men's debauchery.

She didn't press him and was soon distracted by something in the drawer she searched. "I've found something," she said, excitement in her voice. "There's a page wedged into the back of the cabinet."

Then, with a cry of triumph, she pulled out a folded piece of paper.

Breathlessly, she pressed it open, and together they scanned the words that had been written in a neat copperplate hand.

"It's a list in some sort of code," Poppy said finally. "And there are numbers that look like monetary amounts to the right of each, as well as dates."

"What the hell was Lovell playing at?" Langham said, turning the note over but finding nothing of consequence on the back. "And why the secrecy?"

Poppy scanned the column of nonsense words for any

hint of what they might mean. "You did mention that some men keep lists of their lovers."

"Unless the identities of his paramours are a state secret," Langham said with a raised brow, "then I fail to see why he would feel the need to encrypt their names."

"Good point," she said, frowning down at the unintelligible words. "And though I have no experience with such matters, some of these costs seem rather exorbitant for ladies of the night."

She heard Langham choke on a surprised laugh and frowned at him. "I'm hardly a green girl. I know about such things."

"My apologies," he said mildly. "I'll try not to make assumptions in the future."

"See that you do," Poppy said with a sniff. It was bad enough having to paw through the detritus of Alistair Lovell's life without having the man who'd just kissed her breathless presume she was as innocent as a newborn babe. She *had* lived on her own in London for two full years, after all. She'd learned some things.

"You don't recognize the hand, do you?" Langham asked, wisely changing the subject. "I certainly do not."

Poppy shook her head. "It isn't my sister's or my mother's. And I saw Lovell's and Lord Short's writing so infrequently I couldn't say with any certainty whether it's either of theirs."

Then, reaching toward a stack of books piled on the bedside table, she picked up a volume of poetry and flipped open the front cover. As she'd hoped, Lovell had inscribed his name and the date of acquisition on the flyleaf.

"Look," she said, showing the inscription to Langham, whose eyes widened at seeing the title. "It matches," she said before he could remark upon the book's contents.

"So, Lovell wrote the list," Langham said glancing at the page again. "I was rather good at ciphers as a youth. Perhaps I'll be able to unravel it once we're back at the abbey."

"I too am quite good at codes," Poppy said, remembering the hours she'd spent with Lady Kate and Caro, decrypting the letters sent to *The London Gazette* by the XYZ Killer after they'd covered the case in their column.

"Ah. Of course," he said, his eyes meeting hers with a glint of challenge. "Then the prize goes to whoever can untangle it first."

Poppy swallowed, feeling the color rise in her cheeks. "What is this prize?"

Langham took a step closer to her. "I shall have to think on it," he said softly. "Perhaps a kiss?"

The sound of voices in Violet's bedchamber, however, had them breaking apart.

Langham took the note and folded it back into its original shape and tucked it into the inside pocket of his coat, while Poppy quickly replaced the bag of earrings inside the drawer.

When Lord and Lady Short burst into the room, Poppy and Langham were standing innocently before the window, the duke pointing to something in the distance. "Stannings's estate is just over that hillock. You can see the roof of his stables just there."

"We said you could search Violet's bedchamber," said Short in a tight voice. "Not Lovell's. But of course you would have no respect for the dead, would you, Poppy? You never liked the man from the moment he came to work for me."

Glaring at her stepfather, Poppy refused to be cowed by him. "No, I never did. But then I've never been fond of men who use their strength to prey upon those who are weaker than they are. But you would know all about that, wouldn't you, stepfather?"

Lord Short, whose forehead was shiny with perspiration, shook his head. "My dear daughter, I was only trying to see that you were cared for. You were hardly going to attract a suitable husband on your own, what with your managing ways."

Poppy felt Langham slip an arm about her waist. "She is well cared for now, Lord Short," the duke said as he escorted her toward the door. "And I must assume that your other daughter was also managing if you found it necessary to wed her to Lovell after Poppy left."

"I had promised him Poppy's hand," Short said tightly as the butler ushered them over the threshold. "You understand what it is to give your word, Langham. I had to make good on that promise after Poppy ran off."

Langham stopped in the doorway and turned back to look sharply at Lord Short. "You make it sound as if you owed the man, Short."

The look that her stepfather directed toward Langham was simmering with hatred, and suddenly Poppy was convinced the duke had hit on the truth. The thought that her sister had been traded to Lovell by her own father made Poppy feel ill.

"Come my dear," Langham said from beside her, "let us get you away from here."

They were nearing the entry hall when they heard the butler speaking to someone. As they turned the corner, Poppy saw it was Sir Geoffrey Stannings and her heart sank. There was no way he would interpret Violet's disappearance as anything but an attempt to flee justice.

Violet, where are you?

"Langham, Miss Delamere," the magistrate said with a sober nod. "I take it you have come to see Mrs. Lovell? I hope she is ready to speak with me at last. I have delayed the coroner's inquest for as long as I can but justice cannot wait forever."

Perhaps having felt Poppy stiffen beside him, Langham spoke up before she could do so. "Stannings, Miss Delamere, as you can imagine, is overset. We'll leave you to your work."

And without another word, he ushered her from the house and into the waiting curricle.

Once they were under way, Poppy said, "Thank you. I do not think I could have borne speaking to him about Violet's disappearance."

Moving to hold the reins in one hand, he gripped her left in his right. "Stannings might be one of my oldest friends, but I am hardly going to put you in the position of informing him your sister may have fled. He can do his own damned investigating."

"And if he determines she *has* run away?" Poppy asked, concentrating on the warmth of his hand clasping hers, trying not to let her alarm overwhelm her.

"One calamity at a time, Poppy," he said gently. "One calamity at a time."

Chapter Sixteen

Once they'd returned to Langham Abbey, Poppy wanted nothing other than to retire to her bedchamber. She needed to think. About the handkerchief and the pipe they'd found. About the encoded list from Lovell's bedchamber. About the fact that Violet was now missing. And, once she was alone, she could let herself ponder the kiss she and Langham had shared in the bell tower.

But having agreed to play the part of Langham's betrothed, she could hardly tell him to find someone else to fill the role for the rest of the afternoon. And so it was that as soon as she'd washed off the dirt from the climb, changed into fresh clothes, and repaired her hair, she headed back downstairs for luncheon.

To her surprise, one of the footmen was waiting for her at the second-floor landing. Langham, it seemed, had requested her presence in his study.

Poppy arrived just as Langham was ordering tea brought up from the kitchens.

"Tea here? Won't your grandmama be cross with us?"

she asked, frowning. "I thought she was expecting us to join her in the dining room?"

"I think she'll forgive us this once," Langham said, taking her hand and leading her into the room. She was startled to see a man was already in the study, leaning casually against the mantel.

"Poppy, this is my brother, Lord Adrian Fielding."

To his brother, he said, "Adrian, this is my betrothed, Miss Poppy Delamere."

"I am delighted to meet you, Miss Delamere," Lord Adrian said as he bowed over her hand. "I find it hard to believe that a lady as lovely as yourself would agree to marry my irascible brother, but I can only assume he's been hiding his true nature."

Poppy couldn't suppress a laugh. "I'm afraid that could not be further from the truth, Lord Adrian. Indeed, I had not known your brother more than a few minutes before I had decided him to be thoroughly disagreeable."

Adrian's eyes, so like his brother's, widened. "Did you, indeed?" he asked with a smirk. "And here I thought you were said to be a charmer with the ladies, Langham. No wonder it has taken so long for you to find a wife."

"I wasn't looking for a wife," Langham said testily. Then taking a seat beside Poppy on a nearby sofa, he added, "Besides, we have come to an understanding about my churlish behavior that day. Miss Delamere has forgiven me."

Poppy didn't quite recall it that way, but she was willing to allow him the deception just this once for the sake of the present goodwill between the brothers.

Just then the tea tray arrived, and soon they were too busy partaking of sandwiches, biscuits, tarts, thinly sliced ham, and all manner of other delectable offerings for there to be more than anything but the most superficial conversation.

Once they'd all had their fill, Langham turned to Poppy, who was pouring more tea, and said, "I'd asked Adrian to hold off sharing any information he might have gleaned about the railroad scheme until you joined us."

Accepting a cup from Poppy, Adrian nodded his thanks. "Now, as my brother wrote to me, you overheard a conversation between your stepfather and another man about a scheme they'd devised to raise funds for a railroad they were claiming to build in the Amazon, is that right?"

"Yes." Poppy nodded. "And they were alarmed because Lord Twombley, one of the investors, had asked a friend at the Foreign Office about the plan's viability."

Adrian nodded. "Yes. And because I wasn't sure which of my colleagues he consulted, I simply asked at the Traveler's Club—that's the gentlemen's club for those of us in the diplomatic corps, Miss Delamere—if anyone knew about the scheme."

"And?" Langham asked, with a slight roll of his eyes at his brother's dramatic pause. "What did you find?"

But Lord Adrian was not in the least bit bothered by Langham's impatience. "I discovered that it was my colleague Henry Riggle who had been inquiring after the project. And as it turned out, just as you suspected, Miss Delamere, there are no plans for a railroad to be erected in that location. It's far too treacherous."

Poppy sighed. "I hope you will give your friend Mr. Riggle my thanks, Lord Adrian."

"Unfortunately, I cannot," the younger man said, a line appearing between his brows. "Riggle was killed on the way home from White's two years ago. Footpads, it was believed to be, but I don't think the Metropolitan Police were ever able to find the actual culprit."

"Oh my heavens." Poppy shook her head. "Lord Twombley, Mr. Riggle, and now Mr. Lovell. It cannot be a coincidence that three of the men who were mentioned in or participated in that conversation are now dead."

She turned to look at Langham, searching his face for some sign that she was overreacting. Unfortunately, his expression, far from placating, was grim.

"It is possible," he said, squeezing her hand, "but unlikely, I'd say."

"I agree," Adrian replied.

Langham bit out a curse and went to the bellpull. "This investigation is far too complicated to leave in Rhodes's bumbling hands. It is time to call in Eversham."

Once he'd rung the bell, he strode over to his desk, sat, then took up a quill and ink and began writing.

"It's customary for Scotland Yard to wait until the local authorities have requested their assistance before becoming involved in an investigation. Do you think Rhodes will put up a fight?" Poppy asked as she reached for another biscuit.

"If he does, I'll damned well tell him that he needs the assistance," Langham ground out. "If a duke of the realm cannot request Scotland Yard's help, then what is the point of holding the title at all?"

"I daresay the practice is in place to keep dukes and the like from directing criminal investigations in their favor," Adrian said dryly.

At the glare directed at him by his brother, Lord Adrian winced. "I didn't say I thought you were wrong to call for this Eversham fellow," he said, raising his hands in a gesture of innocence. "Just attempting to clarify why the rule is in place."

The younger man was saved from further explanation by the arrival of a footman.

Langham proffered the note he'd just sanded and sealed to the servant. "Thomas, have one of the grooms take this to Detective Inspector Eversham at Scotland Yard in London."

Adrian stood and intervened before the footman could take the message. "I can take it, Langham. There's no need to send a groom."

"Not so fast," the duke said to his brother. Reaching around Adrian, he put the missive in the footman's hand. "Take this, Thomas."

Once the footman was gone, Adrian scowled at his brother. "Why will you not let me take it. I can at least be of help."

"I know you would be happy enough to escape from the melee of young ladies who are here for the week," Langham said tartly, "but it would break Grandmama's heart if you were to go back to London after such a brief visit. Especially since you haven't even had time to share a meal with her yet."

Poppy was amused to see the heat in Adrian's cheeks.

"You cannot blame a chap for trying," Langham's brother said, looking sheepish. "Especially since I suspect many of the guests are eager for *my* acquaintance now that you've been taken off the market."

"Regardless," the duke said, "it would be badly done for you to leave when you've promised the dowager that you would be here for her party."

"You're right, I suppose." Adrian didn't sound particularly happy about the fact, however.

Deciding that it would be best for her to leave the brothers alone so that they could continue their conversation, Poppy rose. "I believe I will go rest for a short while after the day's excitement. Thank you for bringing the news about Mr. Riggle, Lord Adrian. I am grateful for your assistance."

"Of course," said Lord Adrian, bowing over her hand. "It was my pleasure to meet the lady who has ensnared the heart of my brother, though I must admit to a certain concern on your behalf. Especially given how short-tempered he can be."

She glanced at Langham, who merely rolled his eyes at his brother's impertinence. "I have no worries on that front. I, too, am short-tempered."

"I beg leave to differ, my dear," Langham said with a smile. Rising, he began to move toward her. "Shall I escort you to your bedchamber?"

She had a good idea of what he might be considering if she read the hooded expression in his eyes aright. But as much as contemplating a repetition of the kiss they'd shared in the bell tower made her heart race, it was more important, she told herself, for him to have a private conversation with his brother. Especially if their relationship was as fractious as his sisters had told her it was.

"No," she said aloud. "You stay here and have a chat with Lord Adrian. I have little doubt there is much for the two of you to catch up on."

And before he could argue, she slipped from the room and hurried toward the privacy of her bedchamber.

"It was good of you to look into the Amazon railroad matter," Langham said to Adrian once Poppy had closed the door behind her.

Truth be told, he hadn't been sure his brother would do

it. When they'd quarreled over Adrian's decision to join the Foreign Office, Langham had feared the rift between them would become a permanent one.

Deciding that the occasion called for something stronger than tea, Langham crossed to the cabinet behind his desk and poured them both tumblers of whisky. Handing a tumbler to Adrian, he said, "Thank you. You may not credit it, but I do appreciate your assistance. And I know Poppy does as well."

Taking the glass from Langham, the younger man shook his head in exasperation. "You must truly think me a churl if you believe I would refuse to help. For pity's sake, you're my brother."

"And the last time we spoke," Langham said, equally piqued, "you told me to go to the devil."

"That is because you were being an arse."

"For insisting you accept the allowance you're entitled to as my heir."

Adrian took a generous drink of whisky before replying. "I receive a salary from the government," he explained, his voice clipped. "I made some lucky investments and no longer have need of the family's money. But for some bloody reason, you refuse to take no for an answer."

"Because I want to do right by you." Langham hadn't intended to raise his voice, but Adrian could aggravate him as no other could. "And don't think I don't know that you're so dead set against taking the money because you think it comes with strings."

Adrian tilted his head. "And you're saying it doesn't?"

"It may have in the past," Langham admitted without shame. There had been a time when he thought the best way to get his brother to do as he wished was by controlling the purse strings. It was how his guardians had managed him before he reached his majority. "But it's been some years since I thought of it that way. It might have been wise for me to explain that to you, I realize now."

"I suppose I didn't really give you an opportunity to do so," Adrian admitted with a wry twist of his lips.

"Clearly," Langham said, raising his glass, "intractability is a family trait."

"I hope your Miss Delamere knows what she is in for." Adrian relaxed into his chair now that they'd cleared the air. "Though from what I saw of her she seems able to hold her own."

Langham thought about the ways in which Poppy had refused to bow to him. Indeed, it was one of the first things he'd noticed about her. And now that he'd had the chance to know her more intimately, he could see that this quality of hers was just one of the myriad that made her exceptional. That made her a woman he could see spending the rest of his life with.

"From the lovesick expression on your face," Adrian said with a snort, "it is a love match. I'm happy for you."

Coming back to himself with a start, Langham felt warmth creep into his face. "Hardly," he said dryly. "Though we did allow Grandmama and her guests to think so. Especially given how far their noses were put out of joint by our arrival. No," he continued, gesturing with his tumbler, "Miss Delamere and I are compatible enough, but neither of us is looking for a love match." That neither of them were in the market for a match at all, he didn't bother explaining to his brother.

"If you say so," Adrian said skeptically. "Though having seen the way you look at one another, I believe that if you haven't reached that point yet, the day isn't far off."

"If you're such an expert on love these days," Langham

said, "then perhaps I should tell Grandmama you're ready to settle down. I feel sure she'll be happy to inform her friends in the *ton*."

"That's just cruel," Adrian said, aghast.

At his brother's horrified expression, Langham laughed despite himself. It was good to have him home.

They sat in companionable silence for a few moments before Adrian spoke.

"It was Ned who found Lovell's body, I heard?" He gave a shudder. "Poor chap. Not exactly what he was expecting I daresay."

"Not at all," Langham agreed. "I'd say he shook it off well enough, but I'm not sure that's the case."

Adrian's brows lowered. "What makes you say that? I saw him on my way in and he seemed fine to me."

Langham thought back to his interview with his cousin that morning. "To be frank, I'm not sure if it was finding the body, or it's something else that has him off balance. But when I spoke with him about it he seemed unsettled somehow."

"You don't think it's something else, do you?" Adrian asked, swirling the whisky in his glass. "Perhaps he's thinking of leaving. I know I'd be nervous about telling you something like that."

"I'm not that bad," Langham protested. "Am I?"

"At the risk of endangering our newfound rapport," his brother said wryly, "I will refrain from answering that."

The duke sighed. "Point taken. But as for Ned, I honestly don't know what it is that has him so ill at ease. I suppose if he does want to leave he'll tell me when he's ready. With Poppy's sister gone missing and the threat of the gallows hanging over her head there is enough trouble to deal with at the moment."

"I didn't like to bring it up while Miss Delamere was here, but we cannot discount the possibility that Mrs. Lovell was killed by the same person who murdered her husband."

"The notion had occurred to me," Langham said, scowling. "But until we have some proof besides her absence from Rothwell Grange, I will not entertain the idea seriously."

"Perhaps your friend Eversham will be able to unravel this tangle," Adrian said. "At the very least he can look into the deaths of Riggle and Twombley. Though I recognize that those are not the most pressing of issues for you and Miss Delamere at the moment."

"Anything that can more firmly tie the knot of justice around Short's neck," Langham said firmly, "is a pressing matter in my estimation. And the sooner we get him behind bars, the sooner Poppy, her sister, and her mother are safe from the man's influence."

Setting his glass down on the desk, Adrian rose from his chair. "If there is anything more I can do to be of assistance, please let me know."

Langham rose as well. "I will," he said, and with a move born of impulse, he clapped his brother on the shoulder.

When Adrian turned the gesture into a hug, he found himself touched more than he could say.

"It's about time we both stopped behaving like nodcocks," Langham said with a rueful grin once they'd separated.

"Agreed," Adrian said with a nod. "Now, I suppose I'd better go play the dutiful grandson before Grandmama has me dancing attendance on every last young lady who came to the abbey intent upon leaving betrothed. Because as happy as I am for your decision to marry, I have no intention of following you into the state."

"May the odds be in your favor," Langham said with a laugh. "Though if I were to bet on it, my money would be on the dowager."

Adrian made a rude hand gesture over his shoulder, then shut the door behind him with a snap.

Chapter Seventeen

Mary was just putting the finishing touches on Poppy's hair when a brisk knock sounded on the door. Frowning, Poppy rose from the dressing table and was surprised when the maid opened the door to reveal Langham looking almost criminally handsome in evening wear.

His blond hair glinted gold in the candlelight, and when he saw her, his blue eyes darkened for just the fraction of a second—so quickly she almost thought she'd imagined it.

Stepping into the room, he surveyed her from head to toe. Her gown tonight was another of his sisters', a pink creation that should have looked insipid, but the way it hugged her bosom and revealed her shoulders saved it from any hint of girlishness. She felt a flush building within her from her center to her cheeks, and the look in Langham's gaze reminded her of their kiss in the tower earlier that day.

When Langham took her hand in his and brought it to

his lips, Poppy felt her breath quicken. And from the way his eyes met hers, he was well aware of the effect he was having on her.

"I know it's a cliché to say you look beautiful," he said, his voice stroking down her spine like a caress, "but words fail me at the moment, darling."

The endearment pricked the bubble of her enthrallment as no amount of self-lecturing would have done. It was a reminder that he was practiced in the ways of seduction and that whatever this was between them, it was very likely little more than a moment's diversion to him. And she could not afford to let herself fall under his spell. She might have enjoyed that kiss, but whatever this was between them, it wasn't real.

"Thank you, truly," she said, pulling her hand back. "But you must know how improper it is for you to be here."

A glance told her that Mary, whose loyalty was to the master of the house, of course, had discreetly disappeared into the dressing room. So much for chaperonage.

"Since when have you been concerned with the proprieties, Poppy?" he asked with a crooked smile that was more winning than she was comfortable with. "Not that I plan on taking advantage of the situation, no matter how tempting it may be to stand alone with you in this bedchamber with you looking like Venus incarnate."

She shook her head at his words. "It is one thing to be alone with you when I am trying to help my sister. It is quite another to be closed up with you in a bedchamber."

"Surely it is unexceptional for a fiancé to visit his betrothed in order to give her a gift," he said, not looking repentant in the least.

And for the first time she noticed the velvet box he held in his hand. "Why are you giving me a gift?" she demanded, unable to keep the butterflies in her stomach at bay despite her harsh tone. Her physical reaction to this man was going to get her into trouble. She knew it, but somehow she was powerless to control it.

Langham gave a long-suffering sort of sigh. "Because, my suspicious little Poppy, as I have reminded you before, I am the Duke of Langham, and there are standards to be maintained."

Opening the box, he held it out to show her the ring inside.

Given that he was a duke, Poppy had been expecting something showy, even a little vulgar, if she were honest with herself. But the sapphire nestled between two smaller diamonds, in an understated gold setting, was nothing like that. It was, she thought with a pang of wistfulness, just what she'd have chosen for herself if given the chance.

He must have misread her silence as she stared at the ring, because he said in an almost sheepish tone, "I thought it would suit you, but there are dozens more in the family collection if you'd like to choose your own. I will take you to pick something out tomorrow."

Then, as if reminding them both, he added, "It's only temporary. And we must make a good showing for the family, if nothing else. I can't have my sisters or the dowager suspecting this betrothal is false before the house party ends. It would defeat the whole purpose of our ruse."

She gave herself a mental shake and said, "Of course. It was clever on your part to consider it. Thank you." Taking the box from him, she removed the ring from its cushion and slipped it over the third finger of her left hand. It fit perfectly.

They both looked down at her hand for the space of a breath—as if sensing something momentous about the occasion but neither one wanting to remark on it.

Finally, Langham took the box from her and slipped it back in his pocket. But when he withdrew his hand, he extracted a folded slip of paper, which he offered to her.

Frowning, Poppy took it from him. "What's this?"

"The list we found in Lovell's chambers," Langham explained, locking his hands behind his back. "Perhaps you'll find some time later this evening to unravel it."

"I thought we were going to decipher it together," she said, confused, since he'd seemed so keen to work out the garbled words earlier in the day. "What's changed your mind?"

He gave her a half smile that revealed his dimple. "I realized that of the pair of us, you are by far the cleverer. If you run into problems, I will attempt to help, of course, but otherwise I leave it in your capable hands."

Though he'd only moments ago given her a family heirloom, albeit temporarily, Poppy felt somehow that the page in her hand was of greater value.

"Thank you." She stepped away to slip the list in her reticule, which was lying on a bureau near the door.

When she turned back to the duke, he was looking at her with a puzzled expression. "For what? Acknowledging that you are a person of intelligence?"

"You say that as if any man would do so," she said dryly, "but I can assure you that is not the case."

"My dear Miss Delamere," Langham said. "I should hope that I am not just any man. Because I have known from the moment we met that you are not just any woman."

And never taking his eyes from hers, he lifted her hand to his lips. Poppy felt the gaze as surely as if he'd run a finger down her spine.

Heavens.

"Now," he said, tucking her hand into his arm. "Let's go down to dinner."

Dinner was a lively affair, and when the ladies left the gentlemen to their port, Poppy was swept along to the drawing room by Charlotte on one side and Genia on the other.

"I see my brother has finally done his duty and given you the Chatham sapphire," said Charlotte with an approving nod toward Poppy's hand. "I thought I would have to do the thing myself."

"Well, really, Char," chided Genia, as the three entered the chamber where the dowager had already taken a seat near the fire with her two dearest friends flanking her. "It's only been a little over a day since they arrived. You must give Josh time to get his bearings. He's never been in love before, after all."

"Oh, no, I think you must—" Poppy said, trying to pull away from the sisters, but they clung to her like limpets. "That is to say, we have never—"

"No need to dissemble with us, Poppy," said Charlotte, patting her on the arm as they pulled her toward the settee. "We have worked it all out for ourselves."

"I can understand why you wouldn't wish for word to get about," Genia added from her other side. "The way the gossip papers breathlessly recount his every affair is indeed daunting. But, in truth, he's no more rakish than any other peer. And less than many, I'd wager."

Since she, herself, had been an avid consumer of those gossip columns detailing Langham's romantic exploits, Poppy winced in shame. She was just as guilty as anyone in the *ton* of reducing him to an object for amusement.

"Just be sure to ignore whatever attempts they make to drive a wedge between you," Charlotte said firmly. "They simply wish to sell papers. And, unfortunately, the demise of a love match is the sort of story that interests far too many who buy Fleet Street's rags."

"That's enough of that, Charlotte," said Genia, putting an arm around Poppy's shoulders. "You'll have the poor girl terrified of seeing Langham's name in print."

"Oh, I think our Poppy is made of sterner stuff than that," said Charlotte with a twinkle in her eyes. "She'd need to be to get mixed up with this family."

Poppy might have offered her own opinion on the matter, but it was clear that the sisters didn't need her input, so she opted to simply be amused by their rapid-fire conversation.

"We aren't as bad as all that," Genia protested. "Though I must admit that I am terribly glad to have her among our number. Or soon to be among our number, that is."

"As am I," Charlotte agreed.

Then, turning to Poppy, she said, "You cannot imagine how many times we have speculated over what sort of wife Langham would choose. Having the head of the family marry someone who doesn't fit in can truly dampen the spirits of everyone. But I am convinced you will fit right in. Even Grandmama seems to like you, which, I don't mind telling you, is unthinkable."

Now that she'd been included in the conversation, Poppy found herself wishing she had not. The kind words of Langham's sisters—especially in the face of her dishonesty—was too much to endure.

She had to get out of the drawing room before she burst into tears—or worse, since it would mean breaking her word to Langham, who had stood by her without fail, confessing all.

Standing abruptly, she said to Charlotte and Genia, "I'm feeling a little overwarm. I'm going to step out onto the terrace for a moment." Before the sisters could argue, Poppy brushed past them and through the throng of ladies who were crowding toward the tea table.

Someone—the servants, no doubt—had opened the French doors and lit torches that illuminated the gardens beyond. Lifting her skirts, Poppy hurried down the steps of the terrace toward the winding path that led to the lake.

It had been too long since she'd been outdoors in the country at night. Her time in London had involved its share of late nights working at the newspaper, but because of the pervasive smoke and fog from coal fires, it had been impossible to tell night from day at times. Certainly there had never been a chance to see the stars as she could now.

She breathed in the fresh, crisp air, lightly scented with the fragrance of the roses climbing the wall at the far edge of the garden. The darkness beyond gradually became less opaque as her eyes adjusted to the lack of light, and she was soon able to make out the shapes of trees, and even caught the glint of the moon on the lake when it emerged from behind a cloud.

It is so beautiful here, she thought, clutching her arms about herself. She looked up at the stars and wondered if Violet was out here somewhere, looking at those same stars.

"Here you are." The relieved voice came from behind her, and Poppy nearly jumped out of her skin.

"I didn't mean to startle you," Langham said, softly. "I did call out, but you seemed miles away."

She turned to look at him and saw that he was standing with his hands behind his back. She almost wished he would put his arms around her. She could use a bit of human warmth at the moment. And he was the only other person in the world who would understand the reasons why she was feeling so downcast.

"Just thinking," she said, and despite her misgivings, she reached out for his hand. It was a risk, maybe, but she was tired of hiding so much of her true self. For this one moment, she needed to feel something real.

He looked at her extended hand for a moment, and she feared he'd reject her. But then, without speaking or even glancing up at her, he took it.

Unwilling to imbue the moment with any more significance than it deserved, Poppy simply enjoyed the strength and warmth of his grip, and they both looked out toward the lake and, on the other side, the temple folly, which was visible now that the moon had fully escaped the curtain of the clouds.

"About what are you thinking?" he asked after a bit of companionable silence. "If I may be so rude as to ask, that is. I know you'll tell me to go to the devil if you don't wish to tell me."

"When have I ever told you to go to the devil?" she asked with a suppressed laugh.

"Poppy," he said chidingly. "You may not have said it in so many words, but from the moment we met you've been telling me. I'm amazed I haven't simply vanished in a cloud of brimstone smoke from one of your withering looks at this point."

"Perhaps I haven't always been as deferential as your title deserves," she admitted in a dry voice. "But neither of us has been all sweetness and light."

"No, we haven't," he agreed with a laugh. "But I think it's been a long time since we've been at loggerheads in the same way we were when we first met. I'd even venture to say we're friends of a sort now."

He turned to her and looked down at their joined hands. The sapphire and diamonds on her ring finger glinted in the moonlight.

"Wouldn't you agree?" he asked, pulling her into his arms and staring into her eyes—his own blue ones nearly black in the dim light.

Though she'd only just been wishing he'd take her in his arms, the reality of it—in the full moonlight, with the scent of roses surrounding them—was headier than she'd imagined it would be.

"Do friends do this?" she asked lightly, lifting her hand to his shoulder. From this angle, she could see a patch of whiskers his valet must have missed when shaving him before dinner, and the sight endeared him to her as no polished façade could have done. He was, despite his elevated title and great wealth, simply a man. The warmth of his body so near hers told her as much.

"Our kind of friends do," he said in a low voice that made her heart quicken. "We even do other things when we choose to."

"Like what?" she whispered, hearing the tremble in her voice, but not caring.

"We kiss when we want to," he said softly. "So, the real question, Poppy, is do we want to?"

"*I* do," she said, going up on her toes.

She had nearly touched her lips to his when he must have seen something behind her because he lifted his chin and stared off into the distance.

"What is it?" she asked, turning in his arms to follow his gaze.

There, on the other side of the lake, she saw a gleam of

light bobbing in the darkness near the temple folly. Almost as if someone was carrying a torch.

Her breath caught. What if it was Violet? She'd need some kind of shelter if she were still in the area, and the folly would offer that.

Before she could think better of it, Poppy hiked up her skirts and rushed down the path toward the lake.

Chapter Eighteen

One minute Langham had been about to kiss Poppy, and the next he was chasing after her.

"Where are you going?" he hissed, not wanting to draw attention to them from the house. "Slow down, for pity's sake."

She was surprisingly swift given that she was hampered by her skirts.

"It could be Violet," she called out without even bothering to glance back at him.

Knowing how desperate she was to find her sister, he forbore from pointing out that it was far more likely that the light had come from a poacher or some other ne'er-do-well roaming the grounds. So when he caught up to her, he simply grasped her hand to ensure they remained together.

As if by mutual agreement, they were silent as they hurried along the path around the lake. At least it was a well-trod one, Langham thought, as Poppy stumbled over a stone.

"Careful," he warned, though she didn't seem to notice as she continued her trek.

When they finally reached the other side of the lake, there was no sign of illumination anywhere near the temple folly, but it was possible whoever was out there had heard them—they hadn't been precisely quiet as they made their way here—and was now hiding.

Wishing his groundskeepers weren't quite so diligent about removing stray branches from these paths, Langham resigned himself to his lack of weaponry and forged ahead.

Poppy grasped him by the arm. "Do you smell that?" she hissed. "It's smoke. There was a torch here."

Langham didn't like this one bit. But if Violet was inside the temple, then they needed to find her—if not for her own sake, then for Poppy's. He greatly feared her own sense of guilt over leaving her sister behind would follow her until she made it right somehow.

He would have liked for Poppy to remain behind while he investigated the interior, but he knew her well enough now to realize that was a vain hope. Instead, he took her by the arms. "Remember to let me lead. If something happens, run as fast as you can back to the house and get help."

It was possible he was being overcautious, but given that there was a murderer in the vicinity and Poppy's sister was missing, Langham was willing to risk it.

She nodded, her blue eyes wide in the moonlight. He kissed her swiftly and, taking her by the hand, led her up the stairs onto the pillared portico and through the darkened doorway into the folly interior.

"What is that sound?" she whispered. "It sounds like humming."

"I don't know," Langham said in a low tone. But the sound was unnerving.

The smell of smoke was strong, but as they stood

silently just inside the door, he got the sense that they
were alone. Feeling along the wall, he found what he was
looking for—a lantern hanging from a hook. Using one of
the matches he'd stuck in his interior coat pocket for his
after-dinner cigar, he lit the wick.

The flame hissed as it caught and illuminated the room.

"There's no one here," Poppy breathed as she scanned
the chamber, the disappointment in her voice almost palpable. "I was so certain she'd be here."

But despite the emptiness of the room, Langham wasn't
so sure their errand had been in vain.

"There's an entrance to the caves over here," he
whispered, pulling her with him toward the far corner of
the room.

"But I thought you had them all sealed up years ago?"
Poppy hissed, sounding accusatory.

"It's not as if I added an iron door over them all. A lock
was sufficient for most of them. And of all the entrances,
this is the one I thought would need the least fortification.
Like in St. Lucy's, there's a hidden door here. Only a
handful of people know of it, and I'd trust them all with my
life. Besides," he added, "we don't know for sure someone
has gone through this one yet. We won't know until we go
in ourselves."

Handing the lantern to Poppy, he began pressing on the
wall, searching for the mechanism that would unlatch the
hidden door. As he looked, the hum, which he could tell
now was coming from below them, grew louder.

"It almost sounds like..." Poppy seemed to search for
the right word. "Bees," she settled on, with what sounded
like a shudder.

He hid his amusement that a woman who'd just run
willy-nilly through the dark of night was frightened of

stinging insects. "I don't believe it's bees you're hearing," he said, pressing stone after stone. "I think that might be the sound of voices."

Poppy stared at him. "But who?"

"I don't know, but I aim to find out," he said, just as he finally hit on the stone hiding the opening mechanism. What had at first glance seemed to be a solid stone wall began to silently slide inward, revealing an interior recess above a flight of steps leading down into darkness.

As the door opened, the sound of the humming grew louder, and Langham recognized the noise for what it was: chanting.

"Not bees," Poppy said staring down into the darkness.

"Indeed," Langham agreed, feeling his chest constrict as his old discomfort in the face of closed-off spaces made itself known. "We needn't go down there just now. Tomorrow, in the light of day will be soon enough to investigate the mat—"

But before he could finish, Poppy had already descended several feet farther into the depths of the cave.

As much as he'd have liked to turn tail and flee in the opposite direction, there was no way in hell he would let Poppy face whoever had gathered at the bottom of that darkened staircase.

Pushing past his alarm, he followed her down, holding the lantern up to light the way.

As he moved, he tried to remember the diagram he'd found among his great-grandfather's papers. It had shown a series of corridors leading from the various outbuildings of the estate into a central open space, which was where the large gatherings of the Lucifer Society had taken place. There were, however, several rooms off the main one where small groups or those who wished for privacy might retreat. The reverberation of the chanting that emanated from the caves below suggested that they were approaching one of the larger chambers.

How many people can possibly be down here, he wondered in puzzlement. It wasn't as if a large influx of people into a village the size of Little Kidding could go unnoticed. And as far as he could tell, his own house was where most of the visitors to the area were currently gathered.

Not wishing for their light to alert the people in the cave to their arrival, he hung the lamp from a hook on the stone wall of the stairwell and moved to stop Poppy. "Your gown will give you away," he whispered into her ear, unable to steel himself against the sweet perfume of roses and citrus that clung to her. "It's too light to blend into the dimness."

She nodded silently and allowed him to step in front of her. Once again, he took her hand and was reassured by the warmth of it as they continued their descent.

As they approached the bottom of the stairs, the sound of voices grew louder until he was finally able to make out what they were saying.

"Prosperity through strength. Prosperity through discipline. Prosperity through love."

What the devil did it even mean?

Finally, as they rounded a curve in the stairs, the flicker of lights within the large chamber below began to illuminate the way. When they reached the bottom of the steps, he saw there was a small squared-off anteroom of sorts that opened into the main area, where the chanters were gathered. If he and Poppy hid to either side of the open doorway, they should be able to watch the proceedings without being seen.

Before he could whisper this to her, she crept forward

and took up a place to the left of the door and peered around the corner. He quickly followed and, thanks to their height difference, was able to see over her and out at the spectacle before them.

It was like something out of a lurid gothic novel, Poppy thought, not quite able to believe the scene laid out before them in the dimly lit interior of the cave.

She didn't stop to count, but there must have been close to fifty robed figures surrounding the raised dais. As they chanted, the masked and naked man in the center raised something red and bloody above his head.

It was impossible to tell the man's identity, but he was too young and fit to be her stepfather—for which she was all too grateful, considering the man's nudity. Around his neck hung a long chain. It was difficult to be sure from this distance but the golden pendant attached to the necklace seemed to be a jeweled depiction of the Lucifer Society crest.

"Silence," the naked man barked in a voice that reverberated through the chamber. "We come to honor our fallen brother, Alistair, who gave his life in service to St. Lucifer. All praise to him that gives us power."

"All praise," repeated the gathering.

"It is only fitting that we honor him by eating of his heart," said the leader, and Poppy suddenly realized what it was he held aloft was...she couldn't even finish the thought. She gripped Langham's hand tighter, and he squeezed back. It wasn't much but she was grateful to have another witness to this madness, because she was quite sure no one would believe her if she told the tale.

And as they watched, the man, who wore a golden demi-mask that hid the upper half of his face, brought the bloody mass to his mouth and bit into it. Poppy felt bile rise in her throat as she watched him lift the meat again and saw the red of blood coating his teeth.

"Who will be next?" he cried out.

There were multiple cries of "I will," until finally the man in the center handed down the bloody mass to one of the others—from the height Poppy would guess a man, but from this angle the face was impossible to make out. And as they passed it around the chanting began again, "All hail St. Lucifer."

The man in the middle turned as the heart made its way around the circle, and as he turned Poppy was able to see that on his right shoulder there looked to be a brand of the sun.

She wondered about the symbol for only a moment before recalling that Lucifer meant "light bringer."

Before them, as each member of the group partook of the gruesome feast, he or she would push back the hood on their robe and throw off the garment, revealing a black demi-mask and their nakedness beneath.

"Now, children," the man in the golden mask said as the members formed a circle around him, "you will each come forward to be marked as one of our number."

Poppy watched in stunned fascination as one by one the members of the circle came forward. The golden-masked man placed what looked to be a long chain bearing a circular pendant over each of their bowed heads. She would have given much to see what the pendant looked like, but it was impossible from where she and Langham watched the odd ceremony.

As the individual members of the circle received their

necklaces, they began to break off into small groups around the chamber, speaking quietly—surreally, it looked like nothing so much as the sort of fellowship church members enjoyed after Sunday service.

One pair, however, seemed to be approaching the corridor where she and Langham hid.

Behind her, Langham whispered a curse and tried to pull her back toward the stairs. But Poppy saw that the approaching couple had stopped their progress and had begun kissing. Farther into the large chamber, the members of the group looked to be engaging in amorous activity. She was fascinated despite the prurience of the scene before her.

"Come away before we are discovered." The whispered heat of his words against her ear sent a shiver down Poppy's spine, and she allowed him to nudge her away from their hiding place and toward the stairs.

Neither of them spoke as they climbed the circular stairway, pausing when they reached the lamp—its bright light making Poppy squint after the dimness of the cave—and then continuing on.

They were soon back inside the interior of the temple folly. Langham felt around on the wall for a moment until he found the mechanism that slid the secret door back into its place.

Poppy noted that whereas before there had been moonlight coming into the interior from the outdoors, now it was completely dark. She was grateful for the light of the lantern in Langham's hand.

Watching as he hung the light on the hook, she burst out with the question that had been on the tip of her tongue as soon as they'd turned away from the gathering in the cave.

"What in heaven's name did we just see?" She wasn't sure what she'd imagined a meeting of the Lucifer Society or even the Hellfire Club would look like, but it hadn't been nearly as lurid as what they'd just witnessed.

Turning to her with a shake of his head, Langham said dryly, "I suppose that is what happens when men have more money than good sense. The mask the leader was wearing looked to be molded from actual gold. And if the requirements for membership are anything like those of the Lucifer Society, then they paid a small fortune for the privilege of joining."

"They weren't all men," Poppy said, remembering the woman and her lover who had come near the spot where she and Langham had hidden. "I must admit I was shocked to see there were ladies partaking of that bloodied flesh. Though I suppose neither men nor women are all possessed of good sense when it comes down to it."

"Men or women," Langham said with a scowl, turning toward the door, "none of them had permission to hold their macabre meeting on my land. We need to get back to the abbey so that I can come back with Ned and see if we can catch some of these trespassers in the act."

It wasn't until he stopped dead and muttered a curse that Poppy realized something was wrong. Moving to stand beside him, she saw that what she'd previously thought was an entryway without a door was now blocked.

"This explains why it was so much darker in this room than when we were here earlier," Poppy said, a pang of alarm running through her. "I didn't even realize there was a door here to close."

"It's a pocket door," Langham said through clenched teeth, feeling along the now closed entrance. "We keep it open in case one of the gardeners or a member of the family needs to seek shelter during unexpected storms. It hasn't been shut in decades."

"What are you looking for?" She watched as he felt from the top of the door, which she could now make out in the light of the lantern, to the bottom.

"There's a brass handle that can be used to pull the door open." His voice sounded tight, and Poppy recalled how unnerved he'd been in the bell tower. The prospect of being locked inside the folly must be unsettling for him.

Finally, he said "aha," and Poppy watched as he lifted the large brass handle from where it lay against the surface of the door and wrenched it.

Nothing happened.

"It must be stuck," he said, and there was no mistaking the annoyance in his tone.

"I'm going to have someone come out and take this entire bloody door off tomorrow," Langham ground out as he pulled again and again on the handle to no avail.

"Langham, stop," she said, placing a hand on his arm, "Clearly the mechanism is broken."

He tried once more to pull the door open, as if doubting the previous attempts had been enough to do the trick. But the result was the same.

"I know you dislike enclosed spaces, but we must remain calm," she soothed, tugging him by the hand away from the door. If he remained there, he'd just keep trying, which would only frustrate him further. "We *will* find a way out."

"I dislike kippers," he said pettishly. "I dislike rain. I am terrified by enclosed spaces."

The admission hung in the dimness between them like a London fog. Poppy realized then—as she should have guessed if she weren't so distracted by Violet's predicament—he'd downplayed the degree of anxiety his fear truly caused him. And yet, for the second time in less than a day, he'd accompanied her to just the sort of place that grieved him. The foolish, gallant man.

"You're disgusted, no doubt," he said pulling away from her to lean against the wall. His breathing was shallow, and she could sense his growing agitation.

"Not at all," she said, stepping closer to him and reaching down to take his hand in hers. He squeezed it and held on as if she were the only thing stopping him from disappearing into some unseen abyss.

She looked up to see that his jaw was tight, and his eyes were bright with pain. "You should be," he muttered. "I am supposed to be the one calming you."

"I thought we had dispensed with those antiquated notions of how men and women are supposed to behave," Poppy said, though she didn't put any real heat into her words. "Let us just agree that there are times when every person needs a bit of comfort."

His mouth was tight with frustration, but he allowed her to pull him away from the door and into one of the alcoves beside it.

"Come," Poppy said in an even tone, "let's sit down and make ourselves comfortable while we wait for help."

But when she went to sit down, the cage crinoline beneath her gown made that action impossible.

Diverted from his anxiety over the enclosed room, Langham said, "You're going to have to take it off." There was no mistaking the glint of amusement in his eyes.

Poppy drew upon her innermost schoolmarm. "Sit down and cover your eyes, then," she ordered.

"Yes, ma'am," the duke said, lowering himself to the floor and leaning back against the wall behind him. At a glare from her, he covered his eyes with both hands.

"I have to admit," he said conversationally as she reached

beneath her skirts to untie the fastening of the crinoline and stepped out of it, "this is not the way I'd imagined the moment when you'd remove your underclothes in my presence."

Despite her embarrassment at the situation, Poppy couldn't stop the laugh his words surprised out of her. "You are incorrigible."

"But at least I'm no longer in danger of fainting," he said reaching for her hand. When she sat on the floor beside him, he didn't let go, and when he turned to face her, his eyes were grave. "Thank you for that."

"Of course," she said, suddenly unable to meet his gaze.

Leaning his head back against the wall, Langham said, "Once the... activity in the cave has died down and the gathering has dispersed, we should be able to find our way out through the connected tunnels."

"Or," Poppy said, hoping it was true, "someone from the house will have noticed our absence, and they've already formed a search party."

"I wish you were right," Langham said, "but it's entirely possible that they've assumed that we, as a betrothed couple, have simply gone off to be alone, and they are all pretending not to have noticed."

"Surely, your grandmother and sister would not simply stand aside and allow us to do such a thing," she argued. What she did not mention was that their disappearance would mean that once they ended their betrothal, she would be well and truly compromised. Ineligible. Ruined.

Poppy knew Kate didn't give a fig for whether her private secretary's reputation was intact. However, there were those who subscribed to *The London Gazette* who did. And if they got wind of Poppy's exploits in Little Kidding, they might decide to patronize a newspaper whose employees were more well behaved. She couldn't bring that sort of trouble to Kate's doorstep. She wouldn't.

"As much as they like to think they are the ones who manage things, I am still the head of this family," he said with a slight frown. "It is not for them to allow or forbid me from doing anything."

Despite her dark thoughts a moment before, Poppy couldn't help but laugh at his arrogant words. "I'm sure you believe that," she said patting him on the arm.

"Are you condescending to me?" he asked, looking at her in wonder, his head tilted to the side.

"Of course not, Your Grace," she said lightly. "I have the utmost respect for your elevated title."

"Now I am *quite* sure you're insulting me," he said with a shake of his head. "Wretch." But the epithet was said lightly, and they sat for a moment in companionable silence.

After a few moments, however, he asked. "Do you think she was there in the cave? Your sister, I mean."

"I don't know," she said thinking back to the gathering they'd witnessed. With the masks it had been impossible to tell the identity of any one individual there. "I hope not. Who the others were, I cannot say. Though given the age of the man in the golden mask, I know for a fact that he wasn't my stepfather."

She wasn't sure she'd have been able to endure the sight of Lord Short like that. She suppressed a shudder at the thought.

"It was very likely an animal heart obtained from the butcher's shop in the village," he said after a moment. "In case you were thinking they were actually biting into Lovell's heart. Aside from that, he's been dead for several days, so I cannot think it would be as . . . fresh as that one was."

Poppy shuddered. "What could possibly motivate people

to engage in such a barbaric act?" Whether it had been an animal heart or not, the ritual had been gruesome.

"If my great-grandfather Thaddeus's journals are anything to go by," he said, "it can be a number of different things. Boredom with everyday vice. A need to prove oneself to be as bold as one's fellows. Or in the case of the man who was leading the travesty, I'd guess a craving for power. Did you see how gleeful he was as he watched them taking and eating the heart after him? He enjoyed having encouraged them, even persuaded them, to do it. He was aroused by it."

Poppy remembered how the man's...member...had seemed to grow as they passed the bloody mass from person to person.

She shuddered. "Is that how it is for men?" she asked, not daring to look at him as she spoke. "Do you all derive enjoyment from such things?"

"Good God no!" Langham burst out. "That was an abomination. I know of no man who would find pleasure in such a thing."

"What about the couple coming toward us?" she asked. "It looked as if they were planning to engage in coitus while there were other people doing the same around them. Is that common?"

At her mention of coitus, Langham coughed a little. She thought he might have done it to cover a laugh, but it was too late to take her question back.

Before he could answer her question, she went on. "Have you ever done that? Made love to a woman in a room where there were others doing the same, I mean?" Her voice trembled a little as she spoke. It was a bold question, and she wouldn't be surprised if he told her to mind her own business.

He'd been holding her hand in his, stroking his thumb over the back, but he'd let it go at the first mention of the couples in the cave. She felt oddly bereft.

Running a hand through his hair, Langham stared out into the darkness beyond their half circle of lamplight. "I have not been a saint, Poppy. Nor have I ever claimed to be."

"I did not say you had," she said firmly. "But you seem to be familiar with things of a carnal nature. And in the gossip papers, at least, you have a reputation as something of a rake."

"Will I never live down those blasted scurrilous tales?" he asked heatedly. Turning to her with a fierce look, he said firmly, "I haven't done half the things those tattlers have attributed to me. You must know that."

"You seemed to indicate their account of your affair with Nell Burgoyne was true enough," she said, picking at the skirt of her gown.

"That doesn't mean they are right about everything, for pity's sake," he said, brushing a hand over his face.

Turning to look at her, his blue eyes sincere despite his obvious exasperation, he said, "I have done a great many things—a number of them in my misspent youth—which would no doubt make your ears turn crimson if you were to learn of them."

Poppy nodded, certain her ears were at least a little pink at simply the thought.

"But I have never," the duke said, taking her chin between his thumb and forefinger, "in all my years of debauchery, witnessed anything as depraved as what we've seen tonight. I wish, in fact, I'd been able to shield you from it."

This made her still. "I'm not a child, Langham." Clearly, she'd revealed too much of her naivete to him.

But his rueful laugh gave her pause. "I am all too aware of the fact."

"Then why would you shield me from the realities of the adult world?" she asked, puzzled. "If you see me as an adult, then you should treat me as an equal."

"Poppy, sex can be joyful, glorious. And while I feel sure those people were enjoying themselves, something about it—especially the way the fellow in charge seemed to be controlling them—was disquieting. I would have spared you that if I could. And that doesn't make me disrespectful of you."

She looked at him and felt a flutter of nerves in her tummy at the idea that was forming in her head.

It was an outrageous idea. But hadn't she just resigned herself to the fact that she was ruined now? She and Langham—Joshua—had been gone from the abbey for over an hour. They'd been alone together before, but an open-air carriage on a public thoroughfare was not the same thing as an enclosed temple folly in the dark of night.

Illogical as she knew the societal conventions surrounding a lady's reputation to be, they would nonetheless be applied to her. Even if she and Langham were found right now, she'd still find her reputation in tatters once she left Little Kidding—especially given those guests at the house party who would love nothing more than to see her brought down a peg.

If she was to live out the rest of her days as a spinster, then this might be her only chance to taste the sort of passion he spoke of—the joyful, glorious sort.

"Perhaps," she said, her voice strangely calm, "you should show me what you mean."

Chapter Nineteen

He wasn't sure he'd heard her correctly.

"Show you?" he repeated, as if suddenly incapable of comprehending English.

Her blue eyes, luminous in the lamplight, darted away. "Forgive me. I know better than to think a duke would find a woman like me of interest when he could have any woman he desired."

Her voice trembled a little and he hated it.

He gathered her hands in his, and even that simple touch between them was charged enough that he had to steel himself against his response to her.

"Poppy, my dear." He dipped his head so that he could look into her eyes. "Our kiss today should be proof enough that I've no lack of desire for you. If you must know, I would like nothing more than to show you all the ways we could pleasure each other."

He'd been up half the night thinking about them.

"But...?" To her credit, she didn't look away now, but lifted her chin and stared him boldly in the eye.

"But," he said, trying to be as gentle as possible,

"though I do not account myself to be a particularly good man, I do have lines I am unwilling to cross. One of those is ruining virgins."

She shook her head, her pretty mouth tight with some negative emotion he couldn't read. She pulled her hands away, and he fought the urge to grab them back. Finally, she said, "Aside from the fact that the very notion of ruination is a ridiculous concept created by men in order to subjugate women, there's also the fact that—whether you believe it or not—I am ruined already. Just the fact of my being here with you now means that I will be a pariah in polite society once we end our betrothal."

He felt her words like a punch in the gut. "I will not let that happen," he ground out.

"You won't have a choice," Poppy snapped. "You seem to think you are able to control the world around you with the snap of your fingers, but that is not the case."

He glared at her, wanting to argue, but also knowing full well that she was right. He had the power of his title, but that didn't mean he could ensure that polite society accepted Poppy among their numbers once it was revealed how she'd been compromised tonight.

"It's not as if I have any real care for what society thinks of me," Poppy continued. "And it is very likely that I will remain a spinster once we go our separate ways. I only mean to indicate that since I'm already ruined, your objection is a moot point."

"You don't know that to be absolute," he argued, unable to think of someone as vibrant and lovely as Poppy spending the rest of her life alone. "There may come a day when you meet a man who is able to convince you to marry him. And that man may very well object to what you propose here tonight."

Her brows narrowed. "Any man I decide to marry would not care whether I'd had lovers in the past or not. And frankly, if you believe I'd give a fig about what some hypothetical man in the future would think about what I did with my own person, then you clearly don't know me at all."

Langham cursed and ran a hand through his hair in agitation. "I did not intend to insult you. But you must know that this proposition is not without risk. And all that risk would be on your side. What if I get you with child? We would have no choice but to marry, something you have said you do not want."

If he'd thought that would bring her up short, however, he was to be sorely disappointed.

"There are ways of preventing conception," she said with a frown. "I should have thought a man of the world like yourself would know about them."

He closed his eyes and asked the heavens for patience. "Yes, of course I know of them," he said with a frown as his traitorous mind whispered that if she was so hell-bent on giving herself to him, then it was foolish of him to deny her.

"Then I fail to see what the proble—"

He cut her off with an exasperated growl. "I don't want to hurt you."

Poppy pulled back from him with a start. "Hurt me how?"

Langham pinched the bridge of his nose in agitation.

"I could hurt you physically," he said finally, unable to stop himself from taking her hand, needing to touch her even as he tried to dissuade her from this action neither of them could take back. "The first time is often painful, and you deserve better than to be introduced to lovemaking by being taken on the floor in a damned folly, for pity's sake."

Her expression softened, and she reached up to place

her palm over his cheek. "You foolish man," she said in a tender voice. "I don't care about that. I care that it will be with you. Someone I care about. My friend. None of the other worries will matter."

The way she called him friend made his heart lurch in his chest. When she made as if to pull her hand away from his face, he placed his over it.

His objections died away in the light of the mix of bravado and fondness he saw in her eyes. "Whatever am I to do with you?"

In answer, she gave a smile that spoke of triumph but also incalculable sweetness.

With a sigh of relief, he covered her mouth with his own, savoring the soft feel of her lips against his, and the little moan of pleasure when he took the kiss deeper. Once they were both breathless, he rested his forehead against hers. "If it was your intention to distract me from my apprehension over being trapped in this godforsaken folly, then you've succeeded admirably."

She just managed to stifle her laugh.

Poppy should have been nervous, considering what they were about to do, but instead she was filled with a giddy sort of elation at finally giving full rein to the desire—and yes, affection—that had been building in her for days. A week ago she'd have thought anyone who suggested she'd feel comfortable seated on the lap of the Duke of Langham was a prime candidate for the nearest asylum. But the joy she felt in this moment was so far removed from her initial feelings for him that she might as well be a different person.

With an eagerness that made her tremble a little, she slid her hands into his surprisingly soft hair while he worshipped her mouth with his. Slowly, decadently, he stroked his tongue over hers. At the same time, his hand caressed her collarbone and downward over the exposed skin of her upper chest. His every touch ignited a path of flame along her skin. She'd heard passion described as burning before, but she'd never quite understood why until now. It was as if her whole body was on fire for him.

When he lowered her bodice to reveal her breasts, she gasped at the sensation of the cool air on her exposed flesh. But her surprise soon turned to pleasure when he stroked his palm over her. With an unexpectedly gentle touch, he slid a thumb over the hardened peak. Poppy felt the contact all the way down to her core, and when he replaced his hand with his hot mouth, she inhaled sharply.

Suddenly, desperately, she felt the emptiness at her center, and almost as if he could read her mind, Langham rucked up her skirts and shifted her so that she straddled him.

The position placed her aching core against his hardness, and when he took her mouth again, she flexed her hips and almost cried out at the friction.

"Gently, sweet," he hissed, as if in pain, gripping her hips to curtail her movements. "Much more of that and we'll be finished before we begin."

Poppy wasn't quite sure what that meant, but since he was the expert and she the novice, she was willing to accept his tuition. Once she'd stopped shifting on his lap, he reached up and brushed a lock of hair from her brow. "I knew you'd be gorgeous all mussed and flushed like this. From the moment we met, I knew."

That took her aback. "You were thinking of this when

we first met?" she asked, aghast. At their first meeting she'd been torn between running him through or putting a bullet in him. She was definitely not thinking of the way his mouth would feel on her—oh dear Lord, was that his mouth on her bosom again?

He gave a decadent pull on her nipple with his mouth, and Poppy couldn't stop herself from moaning. "Of course I was," he said, as he kissed his way back up her chest and over her throat and settled his mouth over hers again, biting down a little on her lower lip. He said, "I wanted you from that moment. But you were determined to hate me, so I put you from my mind."

She frowned, wanting to reply, but the way he scraped his teeth over the place where her neck met her shoulder sent a shiver of sensation through her, and any coherent thought she might have held was lost in the maelstrom. When Langham's wandering hand gathered her skirts and slipped beneath them to stroke up her stockinged leg, she dropped her forehead to rest against his shoulder.

So slowly that she almost cried out with frustration he caressed up her inner thigh, lightly gliding a finger over the moisture gathered there, in that place where only she had ever touched herself before.

The touch was almost unbearably pleasurable, and when he dipped inside her, she moaned at the sensation.

"That's it," he whispered, adding another finger to his ministrations as she moved mindlessly against him, striving toward something she couldn't name.

When he sped up the movement of his hand, she too increased her pace, and soon she was rocking against him, holding on to his shoulders for leverage.

When Langham somehow managed to flick the sensitive bud above where his fingers thrust into her, she felt herself come apart. She didn't know what was happening, just that she was mindless with pleasure. For a brief moment she was outside of herself somehow and at the same time more herself than she had ever been before.

"Perfection," Langham whispered in her ear.

But something didn't feel finished somehow. "That wasn't it, was it?" she asked with a frown. She slipped a hand between them and felt where his erection tented the front of his trousers.

Langham made a strangled noise. "That wasn't all of it, no," he said, gently removing her hand from where she'd continued to stroke him through the fabric. "But it's easier for an untried lady if she has reached completion before being breached for the first time." At her stare, he said hastily, "Or so I have heard. As I said before, I don't make it a habit of falling upon virgins."

His expression softened, and he took her cheek in his hand. "I want this to be pleasurable for you, Poppy. The last thing I wish is to cause you pain."

He kissed her sweetly, as if making a promise, and Poppy felt her heart constrict with affection for this man who was, she knew now, one of the kindest, most honorable she'd ever met. She no longer questioned whether she was making the right decision to share this intimacy with him—she questioned whether she'd ever want to share this with anyone but him ever again.

"I'm not worried," she said against his mouth as she began pushing his evening coat from his shoulders.

Following her lead, he made swift work of removing coats, neckcloth, and shirt.

When his chest was finally bare, she drew in a breath at the sight of him. The muscles of his sculpted chest, lightly covered in golden hair, shone to advantage in the lamplight. Unable to curb the impulse, Poppy leaned forward and nipped his shoulder.

"Ow," he cried with a laugh. "What was that for?"

"I couldn't resist," she said softly, and leaned back to sit on her heels. Running her hands over the hardness of his chest, she marveled at just how well made a man he was. "You really should not hide all this beneath clothing all the time."

"I think the populace at large would have some objection to my going about in only the suit I was born with," he snorted, then, pulling her against him, he kissed her hard. "But I think you're far lovelier."

The feeling of his heated skin against her own was intoxicating, and as he caressed her breasts with first his hands and then his mouth, Poppy began to feel that aching in her center again. But this time when the instinct to move threatened to overtake her, she felt Langham adjust his trousers between them and realized he'd freed himself. Curious, she reached and caressed a hand over the evidence of his desire for her.

He inhaled harshly but didn't complain as she closed her fingers around the silken heat of him. When he placed his hand over hers and slid them up and down his length, Poppy gasped at the intimacy of the act.

After another stroke, however, he pulled her hand away and kissed the palm before placing it on his shoulder. Reaching beneath her skirts, he lifted her by the hips and pulled her up onto her knees. With one hand holding her upright, he used the other to place himself at the apex of her thighs.

"Just lower yourself slowly onto me," he said in a strained voice. "You can control the pace."

She looked up then and saw that his eyes were dark

with some emotion she couldn't name, but she couldn't have looked away if she'd wanted to. Settling herself over him, inch by slow inch she welcomed his body into hers. She watched as Langham's jaw tightened with every infinitesimal motion, until finally she felt fully impaled, and he closed his eyes as if in pain.

"All right?" he asked, hoarsely.

"Ye-es." Her own voice was a little breathless as she shimmied a little to get her bearings. "It feels odd. But good."

He laughed, but it sounded more strained than joyful.

"Is it all right if I move now?" she asked, not wanting to cause him discomfort.

"God yes," he muttered, before lifting her a little himself. The sensation was similar to the one she'd felt before when he'd used his fingers on her, but this time it was different. *More.*

Bracing herself on his shoulders, she lifted almost all the way off of him, then let herself back down and felt her body close around him as she moved. Soon they found a rhythm that pleased them both, and she felt the now familiar euphoria building within her. When Langham reached out to kiss her, she was reminded of the line from the marriage ceremony "with my body I thee worship," and for the barest moment she faltered. But then he reached between them to touch the bud just above where they were joined and the sensation was enough to send her spiraling over the edge into oblivion.

She cried out as bliss overtook her and a moment later heard Langham say her name in a guttural tone as he lifted her off him. She felt a warm moisture against her stomach.

Unable to hold herself up, Poppy collapsed against him as they both struggled for breath.

Joshua's—she didn't think she could ever think of him only by his title ever again—shoulder was slick with sweat where she rested her cheek, and she took comfort in the contact even as she felt tears threaten. In the aftermath of their passion, she realized just how much of a miscalculation it had been on her part to think she could simply share her body with this man then go back to her solitary life as if nothing had changed.

As if *she* hadn't changed.

Chapter Twenty

Langham stroked his hand down Poppy's bare back and forced himself to remain calm. Making love with Poppy was perhaps the most reckless thing he'd ever done. And yet, if given the chance to go back in time and change things, he wouldn't do it.

He'd known from the first that she'd be passionate—it was impossible to be in Poppy's company for more than a moment before one realized she felt things very deeply. But the reality of making love to her had been both more arousing and more soul stirring than he could have imagined.

Perhaps because of their heightened awareness from what they'd seen in the cave—though he suspected it had more to do with the woman now cuddled against him—he'd reveled in the reality of tasting, touching, claiming her, and some distant part of his mind had marveled at how right Poppy felt in his arms.

Unfortunately, as much as she'd enjoyed herself—and

he made damned sure she had—Poppy was the one woman in England who would most definitely not leap at the chance to become the next Duchess of Langham.

More than once she'd spoken of how she valued the independence she'd achieved while working in London with Kate and Caro on their crime column. It was clear she enjoyed the research she performed at *The London Gazette* as Kate's assistant there, and before she'd been forced to leave London to come to Little Kidding, he'd seen first-hand how her investigative work had helped her friends search for a missing friend.

He'd be a fool to think that even the kind of earth-shattering lovemaking they'd just shared would be enough to make Poppy give up that hard-won autonomy. Nor, as much as he now knew there was no woman he'd rather have as his duchess, would he wish that complicated and constricting role on her.

What a coil.

The sense of well-being that satiety had brought him evaporated in the onslaught of his dour thoughts, and Langham groaned.

"What is it?" Poppy asked, raising her head to look at him. With her hair falling down from its pins and her cheeks flushed, she looked exactly like what she was—a lady who had just been thoroughly tumbled.

He looked into her wide blue eyes and tried to read her thoughts. But apparently sexual congress did not imbue you with omniscience.

"Just a stone digging into my back," he lied.

"Oh, I'm sorry," she said, moving to climb off of him. He wanted to protest, but there was no use in clinging to these final moments of closeness when he knew all too well that their false betrothal would be ending soon. They could hardly remain holed up in the folly forever, no matter how much he might wish it.

Before she could stand, however, he retrieved his handkerchief from the pocket of his discarded coat and would have used it to tidy her, but blushing, she rose hastily and turned her back on him to do the job herself.

Hiding the smile that had formed as he watched his ever-independent Poppy set herself to rights, he took the opportunity to tuck himself back into his trousers and redon his shirt and coats. His neckcloth he stuffed into an inner pocket.

"May I assist you in any way?" he asked as he watched Poppy coil her shining golden hair into a knot and begin pinning it up.

"No," she said with a laugh as she turned to look at him. "One benefit of having gone without a maid is that I'm able to dress my own hair. Of course, it won't be in the same style it was in when we left the house, but at least it is neat and won't invite too much conjecture, I hope."

She was right. If he hadn't known what they'd just been up to, he'd never have known it by looking at her. With the exception of some smudges of dirt on the skirt of her pink gown, and her differently dressed hair, she looked tidy if not perfectly turned out.

"It should be safe to go back into the main room of the caves now," he said locking his hands behind his back to keep from reaching for her. The buzzing sound of the voices of the revelers had ceased long ago, and a glance at his pocket watch a moment earlier had shown nearly an hour had passed since they'd first left the drawing room. "I'll go down and make sure they're gone first."

He didn't wait for her response but turned toward the hidden door and was about to press the opening mechanism when a loud scraping sound came from the door of the folly.

On the other side, he could hear someone—Jarvis?— shouting their names.

"Hello?" Poppy yelled back. "Hello? We're in here! Help us!"

It took a few minutes, but soon the pocket door was sliding open and they were met by the sight of Ned Jarvis, several footmen, a few grooms, and even Charlotte and her husband, Felton, peering in at them.

"Thank heavens," Charlotte cried and rushed forward to engulf Poppy in her arms as soon as she stepped out onto the portico. "We thought you must have been taken by whoever it was that killed Alistair Lovell. We even sent for Constable Rhodes."

"Someone locked you in there," said Felton in a not uncommon for him statement of the obvious.

"There's a latch up here," said Ned, pointing out the simple sliding bolt that had been installed at the top of the door and the jamb. "I don't know who fastened it. It's so rarely used that I'm surprised anyone knew it was even there. I can't recall the last time the door was shut, much less latched closed."

"Nor I," said Langham with a scowl as he stared up at the bolt. Someone must have seen Poppy and him go into the folly and locked it once they went through the hidden door. Whether they were affiliated with the group they'd seen in the caves, he didn't know. But surely it couldn't be a coincidence that their imprisonment had occurred while they were spying on the revelers.

To his cousin, he said, "I'd like you to see to it tomorrow that all the grounds are searched for signs of similar misdeeds. Poppy and I went through the hidden door into the caves below this evening and saw a group meeting there who certainly did not have leave from me to do so."

Quickly he explained that they'd seen a light at the folly when they were in the gardens and had come out to investigate. If any of their rescue party thought the explanation was suspect, none of them said anything. Though he did note the speculative gleam in his sister's eyes as she looked from Poppy's rearranged hair to his missing neckcloth.

Charlotte was many things, but a fool she was not.

"What sort of group?" demanded Felton, his chest puffed out at the notion of someone trespassing on abbey grounds. "This is private property."

Langham caught Poppy's eye and shook his head slightly. For now, he thought, it would be best to keep the truth of what they'd seen in the cave to themselves. Once the depravity of what they'd seen—especially the eating of what the leader had claimed was human flesh—was revealed, the village would be rife with gossip and innuendo that would overshadow their goal of finding Violet and proving her innocence.

Before he could even offer an expurgated story of what they'd witnessed, however, a shout rose from the edge of the lake, where he could see Constable Rhodes running toward them from the path.

"Miss Delamere," he cried as he ran toward them. "You must come at once."

"What's going on, Rhodes?" demanded Langham, moving to stand next to Poppy and slipping his arm about her waist. "What's happened?"

"It's Miss Delamere's sister, Your Grace," the constable said as he reached them, leaning over to place his hands on his knees in an obvious attempt to catch his breath.

"Well, spit it out, man," said Charlotte, her voice cross. "You cannot leave poor Miss Delamere in suspense."

Rhodes stood upright and moved to take Poppy's hand, but she crossed her arms protectively across her chest.

"What is it, Mr. Rhodes?" she asked, and Langham could feel a tremor run through her as she spoke.

"Your sister has turned up at the abbey." Rhodes looked from Langham to Poppy and back again, his eyes lingering on Langham for a beat longer than was necessary. "She claims she's been locked away somewhere but won't say anything more, just insists on speaking to you. She's in bad shape, but she's alive. His Grace's sister, Lady Bellwood, has seen to it that she's been placed in a bedchamber to rest. And she's also sent for the physician."

The constable looked as if he wished to say something more, but before he could speak, Poppy ran down the steps of the folly and hurried off in the direction of the path around the lake.

"I'll go after her," Charlotte said to Langham with a squeeze of his arm.

He gave his sister a nod of thanks, then turned to Rhodes. "What is it you aren't telling us?"

"She's burned up with fever," said Rhodes. "It's clear wherever she was hiding was cold and damp. A cellar perhaps, foolish chit. She might have saved the crown the expense of a hanging."

Langham scowled at the man, grateful Poppy had left before being exposed to the constable's cruel words. "You don't know how she came to be locked away, Rhodes, and I'll thank you to keep your comments to yourself in Miss Delamere's presence."

"I'm just stating the facts, Your Grace," said Rhodes, looking mulish. "But I'll do as you wish. Your lady is going to get her heart broken when her sister is charged with her husband's murder at the coroner's inquest the day after next. You'd do well to prepare her."

The duke clenched his jaw. "When was that decided? We've heard nothing of it." So much for the power and influence he'd boasted of to Poppy when they'd made their bargain. Admittedly, he wasn't particularly well versed in the workings of these proceedings, but he'd thought there would be more time before the inquest was held. At the very least he thought that asking Stannings for his assistance would have delayed things.

"I received word just this evening, Your Grace," the constable said, not quite able to hide his smugness at having heard the news before the duke. "Mr. Trowbridge, the coroner for this county, likes to hold the proceedings as soon after the body is found as possible. And because he reckons this death is like to draw a crowd on account of the dead man being a gentleman, he decided to hold it sooner rather than later."

Langham had never heard of Trowbridge. He pondered the idea of sending the man a note and asking him to postpone the proceedings. But he knew enough of how tightly local officials clung to their power to know that the missive might have the opposite effect. He'd ask Stannings about the man before he risked putting Violet in any more jeopardy than she already faced.

For the moment, however, he needed to get back to the abbey and ensure that Poppy and her sister received every assistance they might need at the moment.

Leaving Rhodes to his petty triumph, Langham set off at a run for the house.

As Poppy ran toward the abbey, she turned over the constable's words about Violet's condition over and over again in her mind. "Bad shape" could mean anything from terribly ill to at death's door. The days could get quite warm, but the nights were still quite cold—and if she'd been kept in some place damp or without a fire, she could have caught a chill. Or had she been beaten or injured in some way by the person who had taken her? It was impossible to stop her thoughts from racing.

By the time she arrived at the entrance to the abbey, Poppy was quite sure she'd dissolve into a fit of tears if anyone attempted to stop her before she reached Violet's side.

Which is precisely what happened when Genia met her in the entry hall and took her in a fierce hug. "There, there my dear," Langham's sister said in a soothing voice. "She's here and she's safe. Let it all out."

Once Poppy had regained her composure and gratefully accepted the handkerchief Genia placed in her hand, she wiped her eyes, blew her nose, and allowed the other lady to lead her upstairs.

"She's been placed in a bedchamber down the hall from yours," Eugenia said in a low voice as they made their way upstairs. "We could not put her closer because of the other guests, but this one was empty and is a pleasant room overlooking the gardens. I have always liked it, and I'm sure she'll be quite comfortable."

So long as Violet was safe and in the confines of the abbey, Poppy had little care for the view or luxury of her bedchamber. But she knew that Genia meant well and made no comment on her assurances. Instead, she asked the questions foremost in her mind. "How is she? Is she conscious? Did she say where she's been?"

Not blinking an eye at the string of questions, Genia

slipped Poppy's arm through hers. "She is awake, but feverish. I've sent my own maid in to look after her until the physician arrives. And she's asked for you. So of course, I assured her that you were on your way to her."

It was, Poppy thought, the best she could have hoped for under the circumstances. "Thank you, Genia. You cannot know how much this means to me."

"Of course I do, dear girl," the other lady assured her. "If it were any of my siblings, I'd feel the same. And though you have only been here for a short time, you've become dear to all of us—not just to Joshua. You're part of the family."

Her words sent a stab of guilt through Poppy. But she had no room for it just now, so she simply squeezed Genia's hand and said nothing.

By the time they reached Violet's bedchamber, she felt composed enough to see her sister without succumbing to her emotions. Once Genia left her with an assurance that she would bring the physician as soon as he arrived, Poppy took a deep breath and stepped inside.

The bedchamber was, as Genia had said, a pretty one, with blue and silver bed hangings and a vase of peonies on a table near the window. But it was the figure in the bed who drew Poppy's eye.

Violet's eyes were closed, and her cheeks were flushed with fever, but there was no visible sign that she'd been struck or beaten in any way. Her light brown hair was down and far longer than Poppy remembered it being when she'd left for London. And, most strikingly, in the intervening two years, her sister had grown from a child into a woman.

"Violet?" she said softly, perching in the chair that had been drawn up to the bedside. "Violet, I'm here. It's me, Poppy."

At the sound of her voice, Violet's blue eyes, so like her own, flew open. "Poppy? You're here? It's not a dream?"

Gripping her sister's hand in hers, Poppy leaned forward to kiss her softly on the cheek. "I'm really here, dearest. I'm sorry it's taken so long for me to find you."

When Poppy leaned down to hug her, Violet's grasp was surprisingly strong. "I never dreamed your father would force you into marriage with Mr. Lovell," she said pulling away to sit, but taking hold of Violet's hand. "If I had had any notion that—"

Violet interrupted her with a shake of her head. "You could not have known. I thought as you did that he would not insist upon the marriage. Especially not after the way Mr. Lovell intruded into your bedchamber. But Papa would not be moved, no matter how much Mama or I pleaded with him. I was glad you were able to leave when you did."

It was far more than she deserved, Poppy thought, though she was grateful for her sister's forgiving nature. But she could not shake the guilt that dogged her as she took in the shadows beneath her sister's eyes and the flush of fever in her cheeks.

Still, it would do Violet no good if Poppy succumbed to her own feelings now. They needed to know who had killed Lovell, and sooner rather than later.

"Violet, where have you been? Do you know that the authorities are saying you followed Mr. Lovell to St. Lucy's and pushed him from the tower? Your father told the magistrate that he saw you, and though the duke and I both spoke with Sir Geoffrey Stannings on your behalf, I don't know whether he believed us or not. And the constable, Mr. Rhodes, certainly believes you're guilty. I will do what I can to find the best barrister possible for your defense, but I am afraid that—"

To Poppy's shame, Violet was forced to interrupt her once again—she had not meant to run at her with so many questions and explanations at once—and she stopped in midsentence.

"Please, slow down, Poppy," Violet said, squeezing her hand gently. "I know how dire my situation is, but we will not resolve anything if you are dead of an apoplexy. For now, let me assure you that I did not kill my husband, no matter what my father might have to say about it."

Poppy frowned. "How did you know that Lord Short had accused you of killing Lovell?"

"I overheard him speaking to the constable before he forced me into hiding." Violet's mouth tightened at the memory. "I planned to flee as soon as I heard him, but I was too late. He locked me away that very afternoon."

"At Rothwell?" Poppy asked. "But we searched the house. And found no sign of you."

"No, you wouldn't have done. I was locked in the cellar of the dower house," Violet said. "I only knew you'd come because the footman that had been bringing me my meals—such as they were—told me."

Violet's expression changed to one of joy. "He also told me that you were betrothed to the Duke of Langham. I am pleased for you, sister. I always knew you would do well for yourself, what with your clever way with words and interest in learning. I suppose it was he who helped orchestrate my removal from the dower house?"

Poppy frowned. She would need to inform her sister of the real reason behind the betrothal, but that could wait. Now, she was concerned that Violet might be suffering from the effects of the fever.

"Violet," she said, gripping her sister's hand. "Neither I nor the duke had anything to do with saving you from the dower house. We went to the grange to search for you, but there was no sign of you. And Lord Short assured us you'd run away. I would have dearly loved to get you away from him, but I had nothing to do with your escape."

"You didn't?" Violet's brow furrowed. "I was sure you must have been the one to make sure the door to the dower house was left unlocked this evening. I'd checked every few hours, since my father didn't insist on me being bound—I suppose he thought I wasn't clever enough to find a way to escape on my own—and finally tonight I tried the door and it swung open. When I ensured there was no one lurking about outside, I fled."

"On foot?" Poppy demanded, thinking of how far the drive she and Langham had taken from the abbey to the grange had been. By carriage it wasn't so very daunting, but in Violet's weakened state, it must have felt interminable. "That must have been a walk of several miles. Did you have shoes at least?"

Violet shook her head. "Papa made sure to take them as soon as he had me locked away." She tilted her head. "You're sure it wasn't you that had someone unlock the door?"

"If it had been me, I would have seen to it you had some sort of conveyance to carry you here." That her sister thought she'd have left her to find her own way away from the grange was perhaps a sign of how the fever had confused her mind. At least Poppy hoped that was the reason.

"It wasn't so far," Violet said squeezing her hand. "I was afraid the whole time that I would be found. And you know I've never liked the dark, but I followed the path and the moon lighted my way. I don't remember very much after I started up the drive to the abbey, though. I was weak and must have collapsed at some point. When I woke up, I was here in this bedchamber. Lady Bellwood has been very kind. And I don't believe I've ever seen a lovelier room, have you?"

"No," Poppy said smiling at her sister's enthusiasm. "I'm pleased you like it."

They were silent for a moment, and Violet's eyes began to drift closed with fatigue.

Hoping to ask one more question before her sister fell into slumber, Poppy murmured in a soft voice, "Why did your father lock you away, Violet?"

But it was clear that Violet was either unable or unwilling to answer.

Contenting herself to sit by Violet's side, holding her sister's hand between both of her own, Poppy watched over Violet for several moments until she was startled by a brisk knock.

"My dear," Langham said quietly as he entered the room, followed by a man of middle years she didn't recognize. "Here is Dr. Howard come to see to your sister."

With a nod, Poppy stood in order to make room for the physician, but Violet, who had awakened at the entrance of the two men, clung to her sister's hand. "You will come back, won't you?"

Poppy's chest constricted with emotion. "Of course," she assured Violet, kissing her on the forehead. "I'll return once the doctor has finished with you. I promise."

With a slow nod, Violet let go of her hand, and Poppy stepped over to stand beside Langham.

"We'll be in my study, Howard," Langham told the doctor. "Just have the maid send for us once you're ready."

Then he tucked Poppy's arm into his and led her from the room.

Once the door was closed behind them, Poppy felt exhaustion descend upon her like a heavy cloak. Some part of her knew she should pull away from Langham—especially after their intimacy in the folly—but she was honest enough to admit that she needed his support. Their betrothal would end soon enough, but she would be a fool to push him away at the moment she needed him most.

They were halfway to his study when she realized how selfish her thoughts had been. What right had she to be tired when Violet had walked miles to reach the abbey tonight? And had possibly made herself ill as a result? Shaking off her mood, she stood straighter, and as soon as they were inside Langham's inner sanctum, she pulled away from him.

Unaware of her inner struggle, the duke went to a sideboard and poured two generous glasses of whisky. He brought one of the drinks to Poppy and pressed it into her hand. When she tried to resist, he curled his hands over hers around the glass. "Drink it," he ordered. "It will calm your nerves, if nothing else."

She wanted to argue that her nerves didn't need calming but knew he wouldn't believe her.

"Fine." Taking the cut crystal goblet from him, she took a large gulp. A mistake, she soon realized, as she coughed and sputtered. "My throat is on fire."

"You're supposed to sip it," Langham chided, taking the glass from her before patting her on the back until she caught her breath. "I might have known you'd drink spirits in the same way you do everything else."

"And how is that?" she asked, her voice still hoarse from the alcohol.

"Full on," he said with an affectionate grin.

She laughed in spite of herself, but then the reality of all that had happened tonight settled over her, and she found herself swaying on her feet.

Langham caught her by the arm. "Easy. I would never forgive myself if you were to collapse on my watch."

Ushering her over to the settee, he assisted her onto the cushioned seat. Then, for a reason known only to him, he took a seat behind the desk. Poppy knew the distance was for the best, but she wished desperately that he'd have put his arms around her instead.

"How is your sister?" he asked, stroking a hand over his mussed hair.

The gesture reminded Poppy of how that same hand had caressed her bare back earlier, and she looked down at her lap even as she felt her cheeks heat.

"She's exhausted but in good spirits. Beyond that, I look to Dr. Howard's expertise." Poppy's voice sounded wobbly even to her own ears.

"Did Violet say what happened?" If Langham noticed her agitation, he was kind enough not to acknowledge it and in any case most likely attributed it to her concern for her sister's well-being, "Where she was being held?"

Having regained her composure, Poppy told him what Violet had said about her father locking her in the cellar of the dower house.

"It didn't occur to me to check there," he said with a curse. "I should have realized he was lying about not knowing where she was."

"You're not omniscient, Langham," Poppy told him. It was just like the man to blame himself for an inability to see through solid stone walls.

But instead of laughing, he clenched his jaw. "I know that all too well," he said tightly. "Especially after what Rhodes told me once you left us at the folly."

Something in his tone sent a spiral of fear through her. Whatever the constable had revealed, she knew it would be very bad.

"The coroner's inquest has been set for two days from now in Aylesbury," he said, with a gentleness that only emphasized the gravity of the news. "I'm unfamiliar with the coroner, a man named Trowbridge, but I will speak to Stannings first thing tomorrow to learn more. And perhaps I'll send another note to Eversham to let him know the latest developments."

Poppy had known that there would be an inquest, of course. She had followed enough murder cases with Kate and Caro that she was quite familiar with the ways in which violent deaths were investigated. But when the inquest was held was up to the discretion of the coroner, and since neither Rhodes nor Stannings had mentioned the proceeding, she'd assumed they'd have sufficient time to prove Violet's innocence before it was scheduled.

She realized now just how naive that assumption had been.

"I am sorry, my dear," Langham said, grasping her hand. "I should have known better."

"You can hardly have known the exact date when the coroner would schedule the inquest, Langham."

He gave a hollow laugh. "That's not what I'm apologizing for. I was so damned arrogant that it never occurred to me that I wouldn't be able to stop the suspicions against your sister in their tracks with a few words. Clearly, I was wrong."

There was genuine regret in his eyes, and though a few days earlier she'd not have believed him capable of it, now she knew him well enough to know he was not only frustrated at himself, but also hurting on her behalf. There was so much more depth of emotion lurking beneath the façade of hauteur he presented to the world. And she was one of the few people outside of his family he'd ever allowed to see it.

Blinking back tears, she realized that once their sham betrothal was at an end, she would likely never see him again. The realization hurt her more than she'd ever have believed. Her own emotions were in a turmoil, but one thing she knew now was that she would never forget this dear, dear man who had somehow managed to make her fall in love with him.

Misinterpreting the moistness in her eyes, Langham crossed to sit beside her on the settee. "Do not fear. I have been unsuccessful thus far, but I have faith that Eversham will be able to bring the weight of all the authority of his position with the Yard to bear on Violet's case. He'll figure out who really killed Lovell, whether it was your stepfather attempting to keep him from revealing the extent of their swindle or one of the revelers in the cave."

Poppy took his hand in hers and squeezed it. They'd long ago abandoned gloves, and the answering warmth of his strong fingers around hers gave her a jolt of much needed confidence. She might be afraid for Violet's life now, but like Langham, she trusted Eversham. And despite his own disappointment in himself, she trusted the man beside her as well. Her sister might be in danger, but she was not without powerful friends.

Which reminded her of something her sister had told her. "Violet said the door of the dower house was unaccountably unlocked tonight. She'd been told of our betrothal by one of the servants sent to bring her food and water, and so when she escaped, she made for the abbey to look for me. That is how she arrived here tonight."

"Unlocked?" Langham repeated, pulling away to look her fully in the face. "Were they really so careless as to leave the door open so that she could escape? I find that hard to believe, given your stepfather's no doubt strict way with his servants."

"As do I," said Poppy with a grim nod. "Your assessment of his way with the household staff is accurate. He does not suffer mistakes easily, and I cannot imagine that whichever of them he put in charge of seeing to Violet's needs would have made such a foolish error. Perhaps Violet has another ally in Rothwell Grange?"

She had a guess, but it seemed too childishly hopeful to be true.

"Your mother?" Langham asked, speaking her own conjecture aloud. "It did seem when we visited that she disagreed with your stepfather's treatment of both you and your sister."

Poppy felt her chest constrict at the notion Mama had finally found the strength to stand up to Lord Short. She only hoped that her stepfather didn't punish her for it. "Perhaps," she agreed aloud.

They were silent then, as she contemplated what would happen when her stepfather learned that Violet had escaped.

"Poppy," the duke said into the stillness. "We should talk about what happened in the folly. I believe the nature of our agreement has—"

But whatever it was he'd been about to say was cut short by a knock at the study door. "Enter."

Poppy clasped her hands in her lap and watched as Dr. Howard entered the room. Her heart in her throat, she waited for the physician's assessment of Violet's condition.

Chapter Twenty-One

Howard," Langham said, gesturing for the other man to come in and take a seat. "Can I offer you a whisky?"

But the physician shook his head and, perhaps noting Poppy's agitation as she looked up at him, said, "I'll get straight to the point, Miss Delamere. Your sister is in fine health. She should suffer no consequences from her time locked away."

"Oh, thank heavens," Poppy exhaled in relief. "And her fever?"

"A result of being kept in the cold and damp for too long," he said with a reassuring smile. "But she is a healthy young woman and should recover from the effects with a few days' rest."

Langham felt his shoulders relax at hearing the prognosis. He'd feared that Lord Short might have had Poppy's sister beaten in order to ensure her compliance, but thankfully it sounded as if he'd been content with simply keeping her away from Poppy.

"She had several cuts and scrapes on her feet and lower

legs," Howard continued, "and I'm afraid she is suffering from weakness due to a lack of water and sustenance while she was locked in the dower house. It would seem that she was given only a few bread crusts a day and her water pitcher was not refilled once it was empty."

"She didn't tell me that," Poppy said lifting a hand to her chest.

"I daresay she didn't want to worry you." Langham squeezed her shoulder.

"Quite so," Howard agreed. "I suspect it is just as His Grace said. She was trying to save you from worrying. We often have a difficult time telling those closest to us about the worst things we've endured. As a physician, I am often the recipient of such confidences."

"Thank you, Dr. Howard," Poppy said with a smile. "That does give me some comfort."

Langham was grateful that at least someone had been able to give Poppy good news tonight.

"I dressed the superficial injuries," Howard continued, "and gave her a sleeping powder to allow her to rest. I expect you'll see much improvement in her by the morning."

Waiting for the physician to take his leave, Langham was surprised when the man cleared his throat and addressed Poppy again.

"In the interest of offering you a bit more uplifting news, Miss Delamere," Dr. Howard said, "I can reassure you that while I can have no notion of who pushed your sister's husband from the tower, he was very likely stabbed before he fell and whoever landed the fatal blow had far more strength than your sister does."

Poppy gasped.

"How can you know this?" Langham demanded. "I thought Rhodes called in someone from the neighboring village to examine the fellow's wounds because he claimed you were too close to Lovell."

"He did, but Stannings insisted I be there as well." Howard turned to Poppy to explain. "I was no more familiar with Lovell than anyone else in the village. I simply took the place of old Dr. Matthews, who was very close to Constable Rhodes's family, and he's never forgiven me for it."

"What more can you tell us about Lovell's injuries?" the duke asked. If it was true that Violet didn't possess the strength to have stabbed her husband, then perhaps they could have Howard testify on her behalf.

"In addition to the strength needed to stab through the man's sternum," Howard said, "the angle of the wound indicated that the blow was dealt by someone as tall or taller than him. There's also the impossibility of a woman of your sister's build having the strength to toss a man of Lovell's size over the tower wall. It is simply not possible."

"Oh, you cannot know how happy I am to hear you say all of this, Dr. Howard." Poppy smiled through her tears, and Langham felt his heart lurch at the sight of her relief. If he'd known the physician had the power to put that smile on her face, he'd have sent for the man as soon as they'd arrived in Little Kidding.

There were, he realized suddenly, few things he *wouldn't* do in order to make Poppy happy. Oh, he wasn't fool enough to think she couldn't take care of herself. She'd proved again and again that despite her desperation when they'd reconnected in the train station, she was more than capable of making her own way in the world. But they'd been good together in the folly. And aside from his ability to bring her physical pleasure, there was also the fact that for all of its drawbacks, life as his duchess would give her a comfortable life. Comfort that he would be happy to extend to her sister and mother.

He watched her expression as she spoke quietly with Dr. Howard, and he was struck by the thought that he'd come to know this woman as well as he knew himself. And ensuring her happiness was becoming essential to his own. She was strong and proud and beautiful, and he wanted more than anything in the world to call her his wife.

The idea that she would agree to make their betrothal a true one was preposterous, he reminded himself. They'd both seemed to pull away after the intensity of their time in the folly. But he'd done so because he knew that all too soon, he'd have to give her up. Perhaps she had done so for similar reasons? If there was even the slightest chance that she'd agree to a real proposal, then he had to try.

Damn it.

As if in a dream Langham said his goodbyes to the doctor and watched as Poppy shut the door behind him.

"Now that my mind has been put at ease," she said, turning to face him, "I believe I shall go to bed. Thank you again for all of your help. I don't know what I'd have done tonight if you and your family hadn't been here to assist Violet in her time of need."

"It was my pleasure," he said, and as much as he wished to give them both time to digest the events of the evening, he somehow found himself unable to stop his next words. "Before you go, there is something we should discuss."

Her blue eyes, luminous in the lamplight, grew round. "Is something wrong?" she asked. For the barest moment he thought about making up something inconsequential to talk with her about instead of forging ahead with his proposal.

But the idea of going to his lonely bed to wonder what

her reaction would be to a true accounting of his feelings for her was too much to bear.

"No, not at all." Langham stepped closer to her and took her left hand, lifting it so that he could examine his family sapphire on her fourth finger. "I wanted to talk about this."

Her brows knitted. "You wish me to give it back? I had thought to keep it until the end of the week, but—"

"No," he said hastily, pulling her toward him. "Quite the opposite. I want you to keep it. Until death do us part."

But she braced her hands against his chest. There was no mistaking the surprise in her blue eyes. "What? I think the events of this evening have affected you more than I realized."

It wasn't the ecstatic acceptance he'd hoped for, to say the least. And something told him that revealing that he'd come to have tender feelings for her wasn't the best way to convince her that his offer was genuine. She was a rational, level-headed woman. So, he would simply have to give her the logical case for why they would be better married than apart.

"That was before we'd spent so much time together," he said lifting one of the hands she'd pressed against him to kiss its palm. When she didn't pull her hand away, he counted it a small victory. "I realize we weren't the best of friends when we embarked on this journey, but as we've run into obstacle after obstacle—whether it was a drawing room full of angry candidates for my hand or the nasty insinuations of Constable Rhodes about your sister—I've come to value your wit and strength. Your loyalty to Violet is something I can't help but admire, because it is so similar to my own loyalty to my family."

He lowered his voice and added, "God knows our time

in the folly proved that we have passion between us. With that and friendship we can make a better marriage than most *ton* unions."

Poppy's mouth tightened and her expression turned blank, as if she'd dropped a curtain over her thoughts. She pulled away from him, and he had no choice but to let her go.

He wasn't sure what he'd said that had annoyed her. Should he have kept silent about the folly? He hadn't thought she was the sort to be embarrassed about such things. Especially given how frank and open she'd been when they were together.

Before he could try to smooth things over, however, she spoke first.

"You're saying that we should marry because we're such good friends?" she asked carefully. Her smile was perfectly pleasant if one didn't see that the light in her eyes had been snuffed out like a candle at bedtime.

"Friends who enjoy kissing," he said, trying for a levity that he knew would fall flat even as the words came out of his mouth. This was not going as well as he'd hoped.

"You keep bringing up the time in the folly," she said aloud. Her arms crossed over her chest in a protective manner. "I realize that you're likely sincere about friendship and passion being a reason for us to wed, but I wonder if there isn't another reason why you're pressing me to accept you tonight of all nights."

Langham tilted his head. "I don't know what you mean."

Poppy dropped her arms to the side and sighed. "You're a gentleman. You think that because you compromised me, you are honor bound to offer me marriage. You've tried to wrap it up in ribbons of friendship and passion, but that's really what is behind your proposal."

It was at that moment that Langham knew he'd well and truly bungled this.

"That's not it at all. If you'd just let me explai—"

But Poppy would have none of it. "You're a good man, Langham. And I value the friendship we've formed in the past few days. But I don't mean for either one of us to be trapped in a marriage simply because we succumbed to desire in a moment of weakness."

Going up on her toes, she kissed his cheek. Then without a backward glance, she opened the study door, stepped into the hall, and shut the door behind her.

Langham stared after her in disbelief.

If this was love, then no wonder poets were always so bloody miserable.

Despite having lain awake long into the night, Poppy awoke the next morning at her usual time, thoughts of Langham's proposal still weighing heavily on her mind.

Once she'd had time to think about it, she realized that she should have expected his proposal. For all that he had let down his guard with her since they'd arrived from London, he was, nevertheless, a gentleman. He might have decided to hoodwink his grandmother and her guests about their betrothal, but he was hardly going to let something like taking her virginity pass without a proposal of marriage.

Never mind that no one but them knew what had happened between them. He'd compromised her, and his sense of honor dictated that he ask her to marry him. It was as simple as that.

But oh, for a heart stopping few seconds she'd thought

he might be about to tell her that he'd come to love her just as much as she did him. Her chest had swelled with hope, and it had taken every iota of self-control she had not to blurt out how much she'd come to trust and admire and, yes, love him.

Thank heavens she'd stopped herself. Because his very next words had been about friendship and passion.

Yes, there was no denying that there was passion there. She had read accounts of such encounters before, and though the descriptions had made her breathless and warm, she'd wondered all the same whether the diarists had exaggerated. Happily, Langham had proved that rather than an exaggeration, the writings she'd pored over had, if anything, underrated the experience.

She closed her eyes and was once more in the folly, with his hard muscles under her hands and his mouth on hers as he thrust into her.

No, she thought, feeling a little flushed, not an exaggeration at all.

But even knowing that they could be so spectacular together in the bedchamber—or anywhere, it would seem—that wasn't enough to make a marriage between them work.

When she'd first gone to London, she'd thought she'd never want to marry. She'd seen just how awful her mother's marriage to Lord Short had turned out. And she never wanted to give a man that much power over her.

But then she'd seen first Kate and then Caro marry men whom they truly seemed to be head over ears for. And more importantly, their husbands felt the same about them. And far from controlling Kate or trying to constrain her writing or the way she ran the newspaper, Detective Inspector Eversham seemed proud of his wife's accomplishments.

And Poppy had seen how Lord Wrackham looked at Caro, and it was that kind of adoration that Poppy had come to desire.

If she was going to marry and trust a man to have legal control over her, then she would only do so if he was just as in love with her as Eversham and Lord Wrackham were with her friends.

Or, a tiny voice whispered, as much in love with her as she was with him.

That wasn't to say she hadn't been tempted by Langham's proposal. While she wasn't particularly enthralled by the idea of becoming a duchess, she would very much like to be *his* duchess. But only if he could offer her love.

Because despite the fact that as a duke he was one of the most powerful men in England—or perhaps because of it—if they ever did marry, there would be opposition from all sides. Lady Carlyle and Miss Beaconfield's revelation of Poppy's work in London at the dinner table was only a small preview of the kind of public attempts to embarrass both Poppy and Langham that would occur once they were wed. There were those who would accept their marriage as a fait accompli, but many more who would see it as an invitation for them to make an example of Poppy. To serve as a warning to any other woman of lesser birth who considered marrying above her.

If she and Langham were to face that kind of opposition for the rest of their lives, then Poppy would settle for nothing less than a love match.

She sighed.

A glance at the clock reminded her that she needed to get dressed and check on Violet. After she'd bathed, she donned a jonquil silk morning gown with Mary's help and dressed her hair in a simple chignon. Then she set off down the hall for her sister's bedchamber.

Her knock was answered by a maid, who informed her that Mrs. Lovell was bathing, but from the adjoining dressing room, Poppy heard her sister call out for her to come in.

In the adjoining dressing room, she found Violet swathed in a robe and brushing through her wet hair.

"I did not realize how grateful I would be for something as simple as a hot bath," Violet said once Poppy had come into the chamber and taken a seat on a tufted stool near the wardrobe.

This wing, where the family rooms were located, had been outfitted with modern running water and plumbing. Poppy suspected it must have cost Langham a small fortune to do so, but he didn't seem concerned about the estate's coffers. If it had been an issue, she had no doubt he'd have taken up one of the heiresses the dowager had been parading before him long before now.

He still might take up with one of them, now that you've turned him down.

Poppy chose to ignore the chiding voice in her head that sounded remarkably like one of the more sour-tempered governesses whom Lord Short had employed for her and Poppy when they were girls. She had enough trouble without having an imaginary Miss Renfrow in her head.

Turning her attention back to Violet, she noted that the shadows that had lingered beneath her sister's eyes last night were gone. And her color seemed healthier now. "You're looking much better this morning, I'm relieved to see. I don't mind telling you that you gave me quite a scare last night."

Violet met her eyes in the mirror and gave a rueful

smile. "I'm sorry I worried you. In truth I was a bit worried for myself. But the sleeping powder the doctor left for me worked splendidly. And before I took it, the cook sent up a tonic for the fever. So by the time I awakened this morning, I felt as if I'd never been ill at all."

Poppy made a mental note to go down later this morning and thank the cook for her assistance. Still, there was no medicine that could help the murder accusation that was still hanging over Violet's head.

Dr. Howard had said he would inform Sir Geoffrey Stannings and Mr. Rhodes that he didn't believe Violet could have stabbed her husband, but since he wasn't the physician Mr. Rhodes had asked to view the body, his words might not matter to the constable. And she knew from her work with Kate and Caro that eyewitness testimony like that of Lord Short against Violet counted more with juries than the sometimes dry words of physicians.

Restless, Poppy rose to her feet and idly examined the various trinkets and bits of jewelry that had been laid out atop the chest as Violet bathed. She recognized a simple silver chain with a topaz pendant that her sister had received as a gift for her sixteenth birthday. And beside it, there was a simple gold wedding band that made Poppy's stomach turn, as it reminded her that Violet's union with Alistair Lovell had been all too real.

But to the side of these items was something that turned Poppy's blood cold.

Lifting the long gold chain with an all too familiar pendant hanging from it, she crossed to Violet and showed it to her. "Where did you get this?"

The round pendant was decorated with a jeweled re-creation of the Lucifer figure from the stained glass window at St. Lucy's.

Violet had finished brushing her hair and had begun rubbing cream into her hands. But when Poppy showed her the pendant, she closed her eyes briefly. When she opened them, she shook her head. "It's nothing. Please forget you ever saw it."

Rising from the padded chair where she'd been seated, Violet crossed to the door leading back into the bed-chamber.

But Poppy wasn't about to let the matter drop. "I can't forget it, Violet," she said, following her sister into the bedroom. "This is the symbol of the Lucifer Society. Langham's great-grandfather founded it here nearly a century ago, and it's meant to be disbanded. What do you know of it?"

"I don't know anything about this Lucifer Society you're talking of. And really, this is just a necklace Papa gave me. I don't know why you're so upset by it," Violet said, going to a pair of chairs arranged near the fire and taking a seat.

"Your husband was wearing just such a necklace when he died," Poppy said. "A necklace remarkably like those worn by a group of hooded figures Langham and I saw in the supposedly abandoned caves where the Lucifer Society used to meet. Not to mention the fact that a knife with the same symbol engraved on it was found near Lovell's body and is believed to have caused the wound in his chest."

Violet gasped. Perhaps not surprisingly it was the news about the stab wound that she remarked upon. "What? I thought my husband died from falling from the top of the tower. Edw— that is, no one told me anything about Alistair being stabbed."

It was impossible for Poppy to miss the slip Violet had just made. She'd been about to say the name Edward. And as far as she knew the only man with that name in the area was Langham's cousin Edward Jarvis, who just so happened to be the man who had discovered Lovell's body.

For the moment she would not mention that she'd noticed Violet's slip of the tongue. It was clear to her, however, that there must be more to her sister's relationship with the man than mere friendship. Her sister would not call an unmarried man by his given name unless there was more between them.

Quickly, Poppy gave a brief history of the Lucifer Society and how it had been connected to the chapel on the hill as well as the temple folly. "And last night, Langham and I were walking in the garden after supper and saw lights in the temple folly across the lake. I thought perhaps someone was keeping you there, but when we went to investigate, we instead found a large gathering of people in the caves beneath the folly. They were participating in a ceremony where they were each given a necklace just like this one."

She didn't tell her sister about the other part of the ritual, where the group members took bloody bites of what had been purported to be Lovell's heart. There were some details that were simply too gruesome to share—no matter how much her sister might have disliked the man.

What she had told Violet had been startling enough, if her sister's reaction was anything to go by. "What? I know nothing about such an odd assembly. Certainly not involving necklaces like mine." She placed her hand to her chest. Then, her eyes troubled, she asked, "Did you see my father there?"

"No," Poppy said, "though everyone was wearing a mask. So, I have no way of knowing whether Lord Short was among those gathered. Though the fact that he gave you that necklace seems to indicate he is involved in some way with the group."

Violet pursed her lips, thinking.

"Did he say anything when he gave you the necklace?" Poppy asked. Perhaps if she understood the context of the gift, she could better understand her stepfather's reason for giving Violet a pendant connected with the Lucifer Society, and what reason he might have to be involved with such a group. There would be some sort of rationale for him to do so. Of that she was certain. Lord Short did nothing out of happenstance.

"You know how Papa and Alistair were always meeting with various men from the neighborhood over business dealings and investments?" Violet said. "Even before you left, they did that in whichever city or town we lived in."

Poppy nodded. As soon as they settled into a new locale, Lord Short would begin seeking out the prominent members of the area so that he and Alistair could lure new prey into whichever scheme they were conducting at the time. She hadn't realized what it had meant until just before she fled for London. But it was not a surprise to learn her stepfather and his cohort had continued the practice once they moved to Little Kidding.

"One night about a year ago," Violet explained, "I thought Papa and Mr. Lovell were gone for the evening, and I went into the study to find a book. I walked in, and to my surprise they were seated at one of the library tables with a number of necklaces just like mine spread out over the table. As soon as I walked in and realized they were there, I turned to leave at once."

Poppy saw the way her sister's lips tightened at the memory. "What happened?"

"I'd interrupted them when they were working on their

business matters before and had been scolded roundly," Violet explained. "And I had no intention of having it happen again. Only I must have gasped when I saw them because Alistair saw me and grabbed me by the arm and dragged me inside."

It made Poppy's blood boil to think of her sister at the mercy of such an awful man. But she held her tongue, knowing that it would do Violet no good to speak of it just now.

"Normally, Papa would have joined in with Alistair's chastisement," Violet continued, "but this time, he laughed. 'Let her come in and see what a celebration we're planning for our neighbors,' he said. And plucking one of the necklaces from the table, he stood and came to slip it over my neck. It was clear from Alistair's expression that he was livid, but he made no protest, only said 'We've already spent far too much on these baubles. We can't afford to simply give them away.'"

Thinking of the argument she'd overheard between Lovell and her stepfather the night she ran away, when Lovell had warned that Lord Twombley was suspicious of their fraudulent investment scheme in the Amazon, Poppy wondered if the two men had become more hostile to one another in the intervening year.

Violet continued, "But Papa told him to stop being such a pinchpenny. If he couldn't give his daughter a gift every now and then, why were they working so hard?"

Poppy felt a pang of sympathy as she realized Violet had teared up.

"He'd never really given me a gift before," she said shaking her head ruefully. "Even knowing it was tied up with one of their illegal schemes, I was touched."

"Did they say anything else about their plans for the

necklaces?" Poppy asked, curious if they'd made mention of the caves or the revival of the Lucifer Society.

"No," Violet said. "Alistair told me to leave, and for the most part, Papa left it to my husband to be the one to manage me."

Poppy thought with a sickness in her belly about the ways in which that management might have been meted out by Lovell's hands. "I'm so sorry for what you must have had to endure from him, Violet," she said reaching out to squeeze her sister's hand. "I will never forgive myself for leaving you to that man's mercy."

But Violet merely looked at her knowingly. "To my great relief, Alistair didn't seem to be interested in *that* side of marriage."

Poppy was shocked. "But he seemed so intent on— well, there was the time he intruded upon me in the bath. I thought he must want the marriage for carnal reasons."

Violet shrugged. "I don't know why he wasn't interested, but I was grateful. Though I suspect he had his heart set on you. I overheard him complaining to Papa once that he should never have agreed to take me in your stead, that he should have gone through with his plan to expose Papa to the world as soon as it was revealed you'd left."

"He was blackmailing Lord Short?" Poppy wondered suddenly if Lovell had threatened to expose Lord Short's crimes. If so, it made sense that her stepfather would agree to dance to the other man's tune.

Violet nodded. "And though he never insisted on exerting his marital rights, he was very determined that we cut a dash in the neighborhood. He bought me all sorts of gowns and jewels. And made sure we accepted every invitation that came our way. I suspect his true reason for wanting to marry into our family was a desire for the status it would bring him."

It made some sense. Poppy could recall how much Lovell had loathed being treated like a servant. As Lord Short's private secretary, he'd occupied an in-between status where he wasn't the equal of Lord Short and his family, but he wasn't as low in station as the rest of the staff below stairs, either. As a member of the family, however, he could claim the connection to the baronet—even one whose title Poppy now knew to be fraudulent.

"I suspect one reason for not asserting his rights with me," Violet said, "was that he had a lover in the neighborhood. Though I don't know who."

Poppy's eyes narrowed. Perhaps Lovell's murder had nothing to do with his crimes with her stepfather and was instead connected with his mistress, whomever she might be.

Which reminded her of one more unpleasant topic she needed to broach. "Violet, your father said he saw you follow Alistair from the grange on the evening he was killed. He said you were walking in the direction of St. Lucifer's."

Violet's mouth twisted with disgust. "My father would betray anyone in an effort to save his own hide. Even his own daughter."

She lifted a hand to her forehead. "No, to answer your question, I didn't follow my husband to the tower and murder him. You know how I feel about heights. I would never have gone up there in the daylight, much less in the evening."

Poppy related how she and Langham had found her handkerchief atop the chapel's tower, and Violet looked perplexed. "I don't know how it got there, but it wasn't left there by me."

"Do you think your father could have taken it up there?" Poppy asked, thinking about what her sister had just said about Lord Short's determination to save himself.

"I think it's a distinct possibility, just as I think it's possible he killed Alistair himself." Violet scowled. "Even before I'd had time to make sense of the news—Papa took me into his study and tried to make me sign over my rights to my inheritance from Alistair. It is quite a sizable sum, though of course, given how it was acquired, I have little wish for it."

"He was wealthy?" Poppy asked. Though now that she considered it, Lovell must have made a great deal of money as a result of his schemes with her stepfather.

"I don't know the true extent of his holdings," Violet said, "but he was clearly managing well enough. And if he successfully blackmailed Papa to marry one of us, then perhaps he was blackmailing others for money."

If the note she and Langham had found in Lovell's bedchamber was any indication, then it was likely he *had* been blackmailing others besides Lord Short, Poppy thought.

"How did you react to your father's demand to sign over your inheritance?" Poppy asked.

"I refused, of course." Violet's jaw was tight, and Poppy was proud of her sister's determination. "But he was angrier at my refusal than I've ever seen him."

"What did he do?" Poppy asked, terrified to hear her sister's answer.

"When I wouldn't sign the papers," Violet continued, "Papa locked me in the cellar of the dower house and said that if I didn't change my mind in a few days he'd have me declared mad and send me to an asylum, and he'd get the money that way."

Lord Short had long ago proved to Poppy that he was

ruthless when he wanted something, but she could never have imagined that he would do such a cruel thing as to send his only daughter to the hell of an asylum.

"How could he?" she asked, her hands clenched with rage. "You must never go back to his household, Violet. I will ask Langham to do what he can to have Mama brought here. But it will be difficult to manage it until we find a way to have Lord Short arrested for his financial misdeeds. Langham has sent for a detective we know from Scotland Yard, but it might take time to find evidence to charge him. And until then, it is illegal to come between a man and his wife. No matter how cruel he is to her."

"She tried so many times to help me," Violet said sadly. "But Mama has been under his thumb for so long now that I fear she may never truly be able to escape him. She does love us, though. When you left, she was inconsolable. And so very angry at Papa. I've never seen her stand up to him the way she did when she learned you'd gone."

Poppy had been so caught up in the reality of her flight to London and then trying to get settled there that she hadn't given much thought to how her mother had reacted to her running away. Hearing that her flight had hurt her made Poppy's eyes burn. "I will do what I can to get her away from him," she told her sister now.

"Good," said Violet. "Because the more I think of it, the more I think that it was Papa who planted my handkerchief in the tower. I remember the last time I had it was in the library at the grange the day before Alistair was killed. I left it behind when I was called away to answer a question from the housekeeper, and when I came back to retrieve it, Papa was there. He denied having seen it."

"So, he could have taken it," Poppy said, her mouth tightening.

"I feel certain he must have."

At the sound of dejection in her sister's voice, Poppy took her in her arms. "We're going to see him punished, Violet. I promise."

But even as she said the words, she wondered whether, even with the evidence mounting against him, Lord Short would find yet another way to escape justice.

Chapter Twenty-Two

Though he was still smarting from the way Poppy had turned down his proposal the night before, Langham nevertheless chose a seat beside her the next morning in the breakfast room. It might be an uncomfortable situation for both of them, but with Violet's arrival he was more mindful than ever of the need to keep up the pretense of their false betrothal.

Any worries he might have had about disturbing Poppy with his presence flew away when she greeted him. "Finally," she said in an undertone as he picked up his fork. "I thought you'd sleep the day away."

The pink tinge in her cheeks gave him pause as he contemplated what it might be like not to have Poppy by his side. He'd been a fool to offer her friendship when what he felt was so much more, to think that she wouldn't want to hear how much she meant to him, how much he cared for her. He was determined to right his mistake. But first, they needed to clear Violet's name.

"I am here now," he said mildly, tucking into his eggs.

"What has you so agitated this morning? You look as if you are ready to levitate like the table at a séance."

"You might well say that," Poppy said, and this time when he looked at her he could see it was excitement—not anger—making her eyes shine and her cheeks flush. "I knew from the first that we needed to speak with Violet in order to make better sense of things, and I was right."

Quickly, she related to him the key points of her conversation with Violet.

When she was finished, Langham shook his head in wonder. "Now I understand why you were so eager to share this news. None of it looks particularly good for Lord Short."

The duke ticked off the reasons one by one. "He is connected to the Lucifer Society by the pendant he gave your sister. He has reason to want Lovell dead given that the man threatened to expose him to the world as a swindler. And there is strong reason to suspect he stole Violet's handkerchief and planted it at the tower to implicate her in Lovell's murder."

Poppy nodded, but Langham could see the shadow of doubt in her eyes. "What troubles you?"

"I came away from my meeting with Violet thinking that he must be the one who killed Lovell. But after turning it over in my mind later, I realized that I cannot believe he would be so foolish as to leave a knife that linked back to the Lucifer Society so near Lovell's body. He has been a successful swindler for decades. He hasn't managed to escape capture for all these years by calling attention to his crimes. I believe he would have made Lovell's death look like an accident."

"Like that of Lord Twombley," Langham said, referring to the victim of Short's Amazon railway scheme who made the mistake of threatening Short and Lovell with exposure.

"We don't know that my stepfather and Lovell were responsible for Lord Twombley's death," Poppy reminded him. "But it is quite the coincidence that his death, as well as that of Mr. Riggle at the Foreign Office, who confirmed for Twombley that the railway project was impossible, both came so soon after Lord Twombley's threat."

"So, we are agreed those other deaths are suspicious," Langham said thoughtfully. "What else about your step-father as a suspect in Lovell's death doesn't ring true for you? Because when one discounts that particular inconsistency, he certainly seemed to have plenty of reason to want the man dead. His fortune alone is a logical enough reason for me to think it's more likely than not he's the killer."

Poppy rubbed the spot between her brows, as if warding off a headache. "But even that motive is not as straight-forward as it appears at first. Why, for instance, if he'd already decided to implicate Violet in Lovell's murder— and given how receptive Mr. Rhodes has been to the suggestion of her guilt—would he also try to force her to sign over her inheritance? Why not wait for her to hang for Lovell's murder?"

"The simplest answer," Langham said, turning to face her, "is that he can't wait for the wheels of justice to remove her for him. He needs the funds now."

"That's vicious even for someone like Lord Short," Poppy said with a scowl. "Not that it is difficult to believe. It still could be my stepfather taking advantage of Lovell's death for his own profit, however."

"Who else could it be?" Langham asked, wishing he could simply offer up the name of the killer so they could be done with this business once and for all.

"Any one of the people on the list we found in Lovell's bedchamber," Poppy reminded him. "We were already suspicious that the dates and amounts listed were related to Lovell's misdeeds, but my sister's revelation that Lovell blackmailed Lord Short for her hand makes the list highly suspicious. And if that's the case there are another half dozen possible suspects."

Now Langham's head was beginning to hurt.

"Have you had any luck deciphering the list?" he asked gently, not wanting to pressure her overmuch given the emotional whirlwind she'd endured last evening. "Perhaps we can work on it this morning."

Poppy grimaced. "I did try for a bit last night before I fell asleep, but the relief of finally having Violet somewhere safe must have exhausted me. I was asleep before I'd looked it over."

She slipped her hand into a hidden pocket of her gown and pulled out the folded sheet of paper. "I have it here. We can look at it after breakfast. Though I do think we should go speak to Lord Short again, as well. Especially now that we've spoken to Violet."

"Perhaps I should speak to him alone." Langham remembered how cruel and disrespectful the man had been to Poppy on their last visit to Rothwell Grange. "I can dangle the possibility that he can use his connection to my family as a way to find new victims. If I can spare you another encounter with the man, I am happy to do so."

To his surprise, Poppy placed her hand over his where it rested on the table. "You would do that for me? Even after I—that is to say, after my refusal of your—?"

He cut her off before she could finish. It was bad enough that she'd turned him down. He didn't want to hear her spell it out again, no matter how much he respected her decision.

"Of course I would," he said, turning his hand over to grasp hers. "I hope I at least made it clear to you last night that whatever might happen between us of a romantic nature, I count you as a dear friend. And as your friend, I would spare you every discomfort imaginable if it is in my power to do so."

He watched in bemusement as her kissable lips parted in surprise at his words.

"Thank you," she said softly. "It means a great deal to me to know you would do that for me."

He wanted to say there was nothing he wouldn't do for her, but didn't want to damage their fragile peace.

"There's something else I need to tell you," Poppy said into the quiet. "When I was talking to Violet last night, she made a slip while we were talking about the knife found near Lovell's body."

Quickly she recounted what she'd told Violet about the knife and her sister's verbal misstep about "Edward."

"You think she was talking about my cousin?" Langham asked, his mind racing.

"Who else named Edward would be able to give her information about the state Lovell's body was found in?"

"He never mentioned anything about talking to her," the duke said thoughtfully. "Though if there was any hint of impropriety between Ned and Violet, that would have given the authorities another reason to suspect her of killing him."

"Exactly," Poppy said. "I don't wish to cause trouble for your cousin, but—"

Before she could finish her thought, however, the butler, Jenkins, stepped into the breakfast room. "Your guests have arrived, Your Grace. I've put them in the red drawing room."

Langham thanked the man, then glanced at Poppy, feeling nervous not for the first time this week. He'd received word from Eversham first thing that morning that he and the others were arriving on the early train from London. At the time he'd written to the detective, Poppy had been reeling from the news that Violet was missing. He'd thought requesting that Eversham bring his wife and, if possible, Caro and Val with him for a visit was necessary, given just how much she needed her friends around her.

But that had been before his disaster of a proposal last night. Poppy might have greeted him this morning as if nothing untoward had happened between them, but he was not exactly looking forward to another row in the event that she disapproved of his high-handed decision to ignore her earlier request that he refrain from sending for Kate and Caro.

"More guests for the dowager's birthday celebration?" Poppy asked, clearly not looking forward to the new arrivals if that was the case.

"No," he said, rising. "I hope you will be pleased to learn the identity of our guests, though I suppose you will be the judge of that. I've arranged a surprise for you."

Damn it. He hadn't felt this nervous since he'd summoned the courage to ask Polly Lambkin down at the Pig and Whistle for a kiss when he was thirteen.

She looked startled, but her cornflower blue eyes were alight with excitement. "You have?"

He offered her his hand, and she took it, standing up from her chair.

"Allow me to show you," he said with a smile, hoping like the devil she'd be pleased.

When they reached the closed door to the red drawing room, he could hear the sound of voices on the other side.

"Please remember, however you might feel about this, I had your best interest at heart when I arranged for them to come," he said as he opened the door and allowed her to precede him into the brightly lit chamber.

As they walked in, four heads turned, but his eyes were on Poppy as she took in the sight of Lady Katherine Eversham, Caroline, Lady Wrackham, and their husbands, Detective Inspector Andrew Eversham and Valentine, Lord Wrackham.

He'd never seen her at a loss for words, but at the moment she was stunned into silence.

"Flora!" cried Caroline as she hurried forward, her hands outstretched. "My dear girl, why did you not tell us?"

The newly married Lady Wrackham was a petite brunette with a forthright manner that was not unlike Poppy's. And it was clear from the way she beamed at her friend that anger at Poppy's deception was the furthest thing from her mind.

"It's Poppy now, Caro," chided Kate as she followed close behind the new viscountess. "Though I vow I will have a difficult time remembering it. You've always seemed like a Flora to me."

Langham wanted to remain, just to ensure Poppy's reunion with her friends went well and she was indeed pleased with the surprise, but he'd barely had a chance to exchange a glance with her when he found himself being spirited from the room by Eversham and Wrackham.

"Come on, old fellow," said Valentine, Lord Wrackham, clapping him on the shoulder, "they won't be able to speak freely while we're about. Show me to your study. I suspect you've got some damn fine whisky, though it's early for it.

But I'm dashed if I'll allow you to ply me with tea like I'm the vicar's wife come to pay a call."

On Langham's other side, Eversham gave a snort. "Pay no attention to him, Langham. He's been damnably chipper since the wedding. It's annoying as all hell, but I suppose you'll be the same soon enough. On second thought, perhaps the whisky isn't a bad idea."

Regaining his equilibrium a bit, Langham led the men down the hall to his study. Once they were all seated before the fire with glasses of whisky—despite the early hour—the interrogation began.

"Really, Langham? Miss Deaver?" Val said with a look that seemed a cross between exasperation and chastisement. "I thought you hated each other."

"I thought the same of you and Caro when I first met you," Eversham said pointedly to the viscount. Then raising his glass to Langham, he said, "This is damn fine stuff."

"It's not what you're thinking." Feeling his face burn, Langham scowled at Val. "Do not make me deploy my quizzing glass on you, Wrackham."

Val snorted. "I'm immune to your affectations, Duke. And Eversham is a detective. It will take more than a glare from you to stop him asking questions."

"If it's not what we're thinking," Eversham repeated, "then how, precisely, is it? For it's quite obvious to me that the servants at least—and I suspect the guests and inhabitants as well—believe the two of you to be betrothed. Is that a falsehood?"

Langham drained his glass and then went to pour himself another. If he was going to be subjected to questioning from these two nodcocks, then he'd at least get a bit drunk before submitting to it, never mind how early in the day it was.

"The betrothal is not real. Though I would like it to be."

"You mean you actually wish to marry Miss Deaver?" Val asked, clearly fascinated by this turn of events.

"Her name is Poppy Delamere," Langham said curtly. "And yes, I do wish to marry her."

The silence that met his words was deafening.

He looked from one man to the other, noting their puzzlement and the look they exchanged a moment later.

"What?" he asked, feeling unaccountably alarmed.

"It's just that we're surprised," Eversham said carefully. "I'd never expected you to be so—"

He broke off, as if searching for the right word.

"Lovelorn," Val finished, not even making an attempt to hide his smirk.

"Oh, sod off." Langham should have known he shouldn't have invited Val. No one knew how to needle better than an old friend. "I'm not lovelorn. I am not convinced the situation is hopeless. I have a great deal of hope, actually."

"Do you, though?" asked Val, with a hand on his chin.

"I hate you," Langham said pointedly.

"You don't hate me." Val didn't appear to have taken offense. "You are quite fond of me. But what's more important is that you are quite fond of Miss Deav—er, Miss Delamere. Which is excellent news. It means you are not, as I previously thought, a hollow shell of a man."

"Perhaps," Eversham said in the voice that no doubt gave his underlings at Scotland Yard pause, "you had better tell us about the matter that caused you to send for me in the first place, Langham."

Grateful for the other man's prodding, Langham related everything that had happened from the time he met Poppy in Paddington Station until what Violet had told her last night—with the exception of the intimate interlude in the temple folly for obvious reasons.

"What the devil is going on in this village?" Val asked when he was finished. "I should have thought a single swindler would be the limit to one small area's criminal element, but Little Kidding would appear to also have a murderer, a dead maybe blackmailer, and a cult led by a chap who enjoys public nudity and eating raw meat that may or may not be the heart of the aforementioned murder victim."

"There does seem to be an overabundance of crime here," Eversham said, in a rare instance of stating the obvious. "But fortunately for you, I've experience with solving cases involving two of the three. And so far, it seems as if the naked chap and his friends have only committed criminal trespass, which doesn't seem as serious as murder or the fraudulent Amazon railway scheme."

"Now you understand why I sent for you," Langham said, unable to keep his relief from his voice. "I admit that when Poppy first told me about Violet's plight, I thought I'd be able to convince the magistrate to investigate further to find the real killer, but not only has that turned out to be more difficult than I imagined, but the crime itself has proved to be a thornier tangle than it at first seemed."

"It's hardly surprising given that you've not had much experience with such matters, so do not be too hard on yourself." Eversham drank the rest of his whisky and set down his glass. "Besides, when you sent your letter, I looked up Alistair Lovell and Lord Short at the Yard to see if we had any information on them. And given that they've committed crimes all over England it's no surprise I found quite a few complaints against them."

"You did?" Langham asked, feeling his spirits lift at the thought of proving Short's criminal nature. Now, if they could only tie his financial misdeeds to murder, then Poppy could truly count her sister safe from prosecution. "That's wonderful news!"

"I'll have to speak to Lord Short to assess whether I believe his explanation about the Amazon scheme, of course," the detective said, raising a hand as if to tell Langham not to be hasty. "But Lovell was the last person seen with the man who made the most serious complaint about the scheme before he was found dead under mysterious circumstances. And the fact that Poppy overheard Short talking about the scheme with Lovell ties him solidly to both crimes."

Thinking back to Adrian's story about his colleague, Langham asked, "What was the man's name?"

"Why?" Eversham asked, his eyes narrowing.

"Don't be such a grouse, Eversham," Val chastised his friend.

"Just tell me this," Langham said ignoring the men's byplay. "Was it a man from the Foreign Office named Henry Riggle?"

The detective sat up straight in his chair as if he'd been touched by a jolt of electricity. "How did you know that?"

Quickly, Langham repeated his brother's story about Riggle, the railroad scheme in the Amazon, and the subsequent murders of Riggle and Lord Twombley.

Eversham swore. "So they might be responsible for the murder of Lord Twombley as well? I came here thinking to investigate one murder, and now you've given me three."

"Until you confirmed that Riggle had made a complaint about Lovell and Short," Langham said with a shrug, "Poppy and I weren't sure that we could actually tie them to the other two murders. My brother is here, so you'll be able to speak to him if you need any more information about Riggle."

"We came just in time," Val said, slapping his hands on his thighs. "If I'd known Little Kidding was such a hotbed of criminality, I'd have come sooner."

"Yes," Langham said dryly, "because the only thing that's kept us from solving all these mysteries was your absence, Wrackham."

"It's possible," the viscount argued. "I have the sort of way about me that encourages mental acuity."

"You have the sort of way about you that encourages balderdash," Langham told him firmly.

Val only waved away his friend's harsh words. "You're just jealous because you know I'm right."

"What of the other problem vexing you?" Eversham asked, pointedly ignoring the back and forth between his friends. "You spoke of Miss Delamere turning down your proposal. Is there something we can do to assist with that matter? We are hardly as adept at dealing with such things as Kate and Caro are, but I believe Val and I have enough experience with matters of the heart that we could offer you some sound advice if required."

"Yes, Langham, let us help you," Val said with a surprisingly earnest expression. "God knows we have experience in dealing with headstrong ladies."

But as much as he'd like to take his friends up on their offer, Langham was not sure even the soundest advice in the world would make a difference when Poppy seemed so dead set against accepting his proposal.

"I appreciate the offer," he told the men sincerely. "But I think I will allow the matter to drop for a bit while we concentrate on clearing Poppy's sister of wrongdoing once and for all. Then, perhaps I will revisit the matter once Poppy and I are both in a calmer frame of mind."

Val clapped him on the shoulder. "If you change your

mind, you only need to ask. We both know what it's like to face rejection, so we're happy to commiserate as needed."

When Langham had invited them here, he'd thought only of helping Poppy, but he was grateful now for their presence for his own sake.

Perhaps Poppy wasn't the only one who'd needed to have friends about this week.

"I'm so sorry," Poppy said to Kate as she was swept into the other woman's arms for a fierce hug. "I should have told you my real identity from the very start. But I was so afraid my stepfather would find me that I dared not do it."

Her eyes stung with unshed tears as she spoke, remorse mixed up with relief as she reunited with her friend and mentor. She'd poured out the entire story of her ruse and Violet's situation once they were ensconced in a little-used sitting room where they could speak without being disturbed.

"There's nothing to apologize for," Kate chided her as Caro took her turn at hugging Poppy. "Your secret would have been safe with us, of course, but you wouldn't have known that at first. And by the time you'd come to trust us you likely felt as if too much time had passed."

"That was it exactly," Poppy said, grateful beyond measure that her friends understood her reasons for keeping them in the dark. "I do trust you both. Of course I do."

"Then why on earth didn't you tell us about your sister's plight before you left London?" Caroline asked, once they'd all been seated around a low table set with a tea tray. "We could have helped you."

"But it was your wedding day," Poppy protested. "I couldn't impose upon that. Besides, I had no way of knowing what I'd find here. I had only that short article in *The Gazette* to go by."

Kate pursed her lips then said, "But you turned to Langham of all people? The man is barely fit for polite company."

"Her fiancé, Kate," Caro tutted. "Do not forget that small detail. How on earth did that happen, Flor— ah, Poppy? I thought you abhorred the man."

"He's not what you think," Poppy said, feeling protective of Langham now that she knew him far better than she had in London. "He's been exceedingly kind to me, and I won't have you speak ill of him, Kate, no matter how much you might dislike him."

She added, "And before you go getting ideas about how things really are with us, I have to tell you that the betrothal is just a sham that we concocted on the journey here. He guessed that I would be reluctant to accept his help without giving him something in return, so he suggested that I pretend to be his betrothed this week. It protects him from the lures cast at him from the unmarried ladies at his grandmother's party, while also lending me the protection of his title while I work to clear Violet's name."

"A sham?" Caro asked, her shock evident on her heart-shaped face. "Are you sure? Because I saw quite clearly how the man looked at you when we first arrived, and that was not the look of a man pretending to be besotted."

Caro's words made Poppy's heart constrict, but she knew her friend had simply seen what she expected to see. "Believe me, I know just how he feels about me. There might be— well, desire between us, but he told me himself just last night that what he feels for me is friendship."

Poppy felt the full weight of Kate's gaze as she stared at her. "What did he tell you last night? And your use of the word 'desire' seems to indicate that there has been some demonstration of that between the two of you. Am I correct?"

And suddenly Poppy was telling them all about the bond she'd formed with Langham over the few days, from their time on the train up until this morning's conversation at breakfast before the party from London had arrived.

When she was finished, Caro shook her head. "You've managed to live the events of an entire season in the course of a few days, my dear. And that's just with regard to Langham. Add in your situation with your sister and the rest of the mysterious goings-on here, and I am shocked you're still able to speak at all."

"Or," Kate added with a thoughtful look at Poppy, "that you and Langham are still speaking. But you are. And considering how much the two of you disliked one another before, that is saying something. Like Caro, I'm not sure I believe the man I saw earlier is one who only feels friendship for you. I know we've spoken before of how clumsy men can be at times when it comes to showing their affection. Is it possible that his proposal to turn your betrothal from a false one into a genuine one was predicated on more than friendship and a desire to preserve your reputation?"

Thinking back to their conversation last night, Poppy tried to remember exactly what had been said. But she'd been so tired from the day's events—including the earth-shattering encounter in the folly—that she'd not even heard everything he'd said.

"Perhaps?" she said aloud. "I don't know. He didn't say anything about love. I know that much. And I simply knew that if I couldn't have the sort of happiness that the two of you have in your marriages, it would be better not to marry at all. So, I refused him. Was I wrong?"

"Oh Poppy, dear," said Kate, taking her hand. "No, not at all. Of course you must wait for love, if that is what you want. I can't imagine how hard it would be to marry where there is love only on one side. I simply think that you should allow yourself some time to get past the emotional turmoil of your sister's situation before you make a final decision."

"I've already said no," Poppy said with a pang of sadness. "I doubt he would be foolish enough to ask again."

At this both Caro and Kate laughed.

"Darling, he is a duke who is accustomed to getting exactly what he wants in this world," Caro said with a smile. "If he truly loves you and wishes to marry you, he will ask again."

Thinking back to the way he'd looked at her that morning, Poppy thought her friends might be right.

"Enough about frustrating gentlemen," Kate said with a wave of her hand, "let us talk about the murder that brought you to Little Kidding."

"Yes!" Caro said, her eyes lighting up at the mention of the murdered man. "You must tell us everything. You only revealed a few highlights earlier."

"Caro," Kate said in a dampening tone, "a man has been murdered."

"Yes," Caro agreed. "A very disagreeable man, whom our friend fled to London to escape. Not to mention that he was then foisted upon her poor sister, who is now accused of killing him. There can be no harm in relishing the details of the search for his killer thus far."

"I suppose when you put it like that..." Kate said grudgingly.

Poppy was so glad they were here. She'd needed them she realized now. How insightful of Langham to realize it. She'd thought when he first mentioned calling for Eversham—which would mean revealing her deception to Kate and Caro—that she wasn't ready to face them. But she should have known better than to think the two women would hold her duplicity against her. She should have told them about her sister's predicament from the first. Their presence here, now, was a balm she hadn't even known she needed.

"So, tell us everything," Kate said, echoing Caro's words.

Quickly, Poppy told them in more detail about what they'd learned of Lovell's murder, the Lucifer Society, and finally the Amazon railway scheme.

When she was finished, Caro whistled. It was wholly unladylike, and Poppy loved her all the more for it.

"I am now thoroughly cross with you for not telling us before you left London," she said with mock severity. "This story has everything. From murder to blackmail to scandalous goings-on in caves. The only thing missing is a ghostly monk roaming the halls of the abbey at night."

"There might be a ghostly monk," Poppy said thoughtfully, "but Langham hasn't mentioned one."

"Oh, it's no matter," Caro said with a wink. "The man has already made love to you in a folly. I think that beats out silly old ghost stories, don't you?"

"You'll have to forgive her, Poppy," said Kate with a quelling look in Caro's direction. "Her marriage has only given Caro license to make even more inappropriate comments than before. One would think that being the next Duchess of Thornfield would give her an incentive for gravitas, but that is not the case, I'm afraid."

"I'm sitting right here," Caro said crossly to Kate. Then

to Poppy she said, "I am sorry, my dear. I suppose it was poorly done of me to bring up your tryst with Langham, but you know what a romantic I am. I just know that man feels more for you than mere friendship. He was looking at you as if he would like to press you against the nearest wall and—"

"You may stop now, please, Caro," Poppy said, holding up a staying hand. Her face felt like it was on fire, and she was quite sure it was just as red. "I hope that you and Kate are correct in your assessment of the duke's feelings, but I am not quite so sanguine. But I will not give up hope. Which is more than I could say before you arrived this morning."

Caro had the good grace to look abashed. "I did not mean to make you feel bad, my dear."

"I know you did not," Poppy said, taking each of her friends by the hand. "And I love you both for your optimism, even when I find it difficult to find mine. Now," she said, straightening her shoulders, "let us turn our attention to the most pressing problem: clearing my sister's name. Until that happens, I cannot even begin to give my full attention to anything else."

"Agreed," Caro said, her expression turning serious. "And we will do what we can to help you."

"Which," Poppy said with a grateful smile, "is precisely what I was hoping you'd say."

Chapter Twenty-Three

That afternoon, Langham took Val and a few of the other gentlemen of the party out riding to tour some of the more interesting views on the estate.

While they were gone, Eversham had sought out Langham's brother, Adrian, to confirm his information from the Foreign Office regarding Lord Short's Amazon railroad scheme.

The riders had just returned and were shedding their greatcoats in the entry hall when Langham noticed Ned Jarvis standing just off to the side, obviously waiting for a lull in the conversation to catch his attention.

"What is it, Ned?" Langham asked, noting that his cousin's jaw was set and his normally merry eyes looked troubled. "Is there a problem with the estate?"

"No, Your Grace."

It was rare that the man addressed Langham by his honorific, which alerted the duke that whatever it was that was bothering Ned, it was serious.

"But I do need to speak with you," Ned concluded with a tense expression.

Perhaps noting the steward's discomfort, Val, who had been standing next to Langham, gave him a quick nod. "Thank you for the tour, old fellow. I'll just go see if I can find where Caro has got to."

When he was gone, Langham gestured to Ned with a hand toward the stairs. "Why don't we go up to my study?"

With a terse nod, Ned followed him toward the upper floors, and soon they were closeted in the book-lined room.

Langham had never seen his cousin looking so flustered, and he wondered if Ned was going to tell him he was leaving for another position. The other man had been steward of the estate since not long after Langham came into his majority, and he'd come to rely on him not only as a trusted employee but as a friend. If he were intending to leave the abbey, Langham would be sorry to lose him.

When Jarvis turned down the offer of a seat as well as a drink, Langham knew it was time to forge ahead and get the bad news out into the open.

"You'd better spit it out, old fellow," Langham said wryly. "I hope you aren't going to tell me you're leaving for another position, because I don't mind telling you it would break my heart. Though of course I would wish you the best."

Ned looked startled. "What?" Then, as if Langham's words had just sunk in, he shook his head. "No, no. I'm not offering my notice. Though once you've heard what I have to say you may demand I do so."

Puzzled, Langham wondered what else could be the issue. "Then, by God, sit down. Standing there like a schoolboy in the headmaster's office is just making us both more uncomfortable."

With a sheepish look, Jarvis reluctantly sat in the chair opposite Langham's massive desk, though his posture didn't relax any.

"I am glad to hear Miss Delamere's sister, Violet," Ned said in a tentative voice, "is recovering from her ordeal at the hands of her father and that the two sisters have been reunited."

"Yes, Miss Delamere is relieved to have her sister with her." He nodded, noting the nervousness in his cousin's demeanor. Recalling what Poppy had told him that morning about Violet's slip of the tongue, he guessed the reason. "But I think you are here for another reason relating to Mrs. Lovell?"

"There's no other way to say it," Jarvis began stiffly, "so I'll just come out with it. I am in love with Violet, that is, Mrs. Lovell. I know that she is under suspicion for the murder of her husband, but I intend to inform Rhodes and Stannings that I am the one who killed Alistair Lovell."

Langham stared in shock as he realized how off the mark he'd been about Ned's reason for speaking to him. Though he suspected he might do the same if he were in the other man's place, he still couldn't help but be aghast at the plan.

"And what has Violet to say to your plan?" he asked aloud. "She cannot be pleased at the idea of you taking her place on the scaffold."

"I have not informed her," Ned said with a scowl. "She may not like the idea, but I will not see her prosecuted for that bastard's murder."

"But did you actually kill him, Ned?" Langham asked harshly. "Because it would be damned foolish of you to hang for murder when neither one of you is guilty of killing the scoundrel. You'd condemn Violet to a life of misery simply because you were too impatient to wait for the real killer to be caught."

Jarvis made a sound of frustration. "You've seen how ruthless Lord Short is. He is the one who first put it in Rhodes's head that Violet was responsible. He just wants to get his hands on the fortune Lovell left to her on his death. A man who will implicate his own daughter in a murder will stop at nothing to get what he wants."

"We will not throw Violet to the wolves," Langham said. "You must know that, Ned. I could never let my fiancée's sister be prosecuted for murder. Indeed, Detective Inspector Eversham of Scotland Yard arrived this morning. We will find the real culprit. There is no need for you to fall on your sword. No matter how necessary it may seem right now."

Langham watched as his cousin took in his words. It took a moment but his expression finally changed from one of stubborn determination to skepticism.

"You truly believe Eversham will solve the murder?" Ned asked.

"Eversham's a friend. I know him well. It's what he does," Langham said reassuringly. "And he's brought along his wife, Lady Katherine, and her cohort, Lady Wrackham, both of whom are friends of Poppy's and quite familiar with conducting investigations."

"But they're ladies!" Ned protested. "Ladies do not solve crime."

"You'd better not let Poppy hear you say that," Langham said with a laugh. "She and her friends are quite adept at working out mysteries. She might insist that I dock your wages and toss you out on your ear. Not to mention it influencing her opinion on your relationship with her sister. Although I must say offering to hang in Violet's stead does give you a leg up."

Ned's ears began to redden. "Given who the magistrate is, I was convinced Violet would never get a fair hearing."

This brought Langham up short. "What do you mean? Stannings is a good man."

At his assertion, Jarvis looked uneasy again.

"I won't sack you for speaking ill of him, Ned," Langham said impatiently. "He's been a friend, but I trust you to tell me the truth. "

"It's just that Stannings was being blackmailed by Lovell," Jarvis said carefully. "And Violet overheard them arguing the day before Lovell was killed. Her husband was threatening to bring down the society, whatever that means, and Stannings said he'd see Lovell dead first."

Langham sat up straighter in his chair. Lovell must have been referring to the Lucifer Society. Could the naked man who'd led the group in the caves last night have been Stannings? It was difficult to imagine his old friend being involved in something so sordid. Yet Stannings was certainly familiar with the secret doors into the caves and St. Lucy's. "Why didn't you tell me this earlier?" he demanded. "Stannings can't preside over the investigation into the man's death when he himself had reason to kill him."

"I couldn't tell you without telling you about Violet and me," Jarvis said. "And at the time I couldn't be sure how you'd react to the news I'd been involved with your fiancée's sister."

It made some sense, but Langham was frustrated at the knowledge they'd been staring a viable suspect in the face this entire time but hadn't realized it.

While the gentlemen were off riding, the ladies of the house party had decided to embark upon a ramble to the far side of the lake, where they would enjoy a picnic tea.

As she walked with Kate and Caro, Poppy couldn't help but notice how much less intimidating the temple folly appeared in the light of day. It was difficult to imagine that beneath the graceful columns of the pretty building lay an underground network of meeting rooms used for the most nefarious of purposes.

Though the sun was warm, she gave a shudder at the memory of the gruesome ritual she and Langham had observed there.

"It is a little chilly this afternoon despite the sun," Kate said, pulling her own shawl more tightly around her. "These early summer afternoons can still offer a few surprises, can't they?"

"More likely she is recalling her romantic interlude in the folly with a certain handsome duke," Caro said with a wink as she threaded her arm through Poppy's. "Though I must tell you, my dear, that Ludwig is going to be terribly jealous. He has grown used to being the most important man in your life."

Ludwig was Caro's temperamental but lovable Siamese cat, whom Poppy had looked after for Caro from time to time.

"I imagine he is far more disturbed by the arrival of a new man in *your* life," Poppy quipped, even as she felt her cheeks flush at Caro's teasing.

"Oh, Ludwig and Val are great friends now," Caro said with a laugh. "You should see them together. It's really quite adorable. Though his valet still hasn't resigned himself to the reality of cat hair on his master's waistcoats. Poor man."

It was clear from Caro's tone that she wasn't in the least bit chagrined at the situation. Her affection for Ludwig was such that she would endure untold amounts of cat hair for him. And, she seemed to think, so should everyone else who came into his orbit.

"How are you getting on with Langham's family?" Kate asked as they continued on, following behind the dowager, who was flanked by two of her dearest friends. "You said that you've won over his sisters, but what of his grandmother?"

"I'm not altogether sure," Poppy said careful to keep her voice low so they wouldn't be overheard. "She seems to hold Langham in real affection, so I believe she will continue to champion us as long as the betrothal lasts, but we haven't had a chance to speak alone since my first day here." She had great admiration for the older lady, but she had to admit to finding her more than a little intimidating.

They'd reached the site where servants had laid out colorful blankets and had begun unpacking baskets laden with all sorts of delicious fruits, pies both sweet and savory, and other kinds of culinary delights.

"It's a pity the men didn't come with us," said Kate wryly. "I somehow doubt ten ladies will be able to do justice to this feast."

"Have no fear, Lady Katherine," said Genia from where she had seated herself on a corner of the blanket. "I believe the gentlemen mean to join us after they have had their tour of the estate. There is nothing like riding for working up an appetite."

"You must tell us about your column, Lady Wrackham," said Charlotte from beside her sister, indicating that Caro and Kate should sit by them. "Did you really meet Lady Katherine at a dinner party?"

Poppy was about to take her own seat beside her friends when the dowager's little dog, Percy, shot past, his short legs working as if the hounds of hell were in pursuit.

"Percy!" Miss Halliwell, the governess to the Carlyle children, whom Poppy had met the other morning on the terrace, came rushing forward, out of breath. "Come back here!"

"Miss Halliwell, Percy has run away," cried a small girl, with carefully styled ringlets and a petulant look about her. "Make him come back!"

Sure enough, as Poppy looked on, the child's bottom lip began to quiver and tears welled in her big brown eyes.

Poppy felt a pang of sympathy for the governess and went over to her. Percy's misbehavior was surely beyond her assigned duties.

"I'll go after him," she said, on impulse. She had a way with animals. Surely the little dog would come to her with a bit of coaxing.

The governess looked up from where she was kneeling beside the crying child. The expression on her face was one of unadulterated gratitude. "Oh, would you?"

"I will," she said with a smile. "Tell my friends where I've gone, please?"

"Of course," said Miss Halliwell. "I owe you a cake at the very least."

"I want cake," cried the little girl beside her. Poppy stifled a laugh. Miss Halliwell had her work cut out for her with that one.

"I'll be right back," Poppy told the other woman, before starting out in the direction in which Percy had disappeared.

Behind her, she heard Lord Adrian's voice saying in an astonished voice, "Jane? Jane Halliwell? What are you doing here?"

It took every ounce of discipline Poppy had to stop herself from rushing back to see just what was happening between Miss Halliwell and Lord Adrian, but that bit of drama would have to wait until she'd found the recalcitrant Percy.

When she'd last seen the little dog, he'd been heading for the folly, so she climbed toward it.

As she neared the marble edifice, she was surprised by how much larger it seemed when she wasn't approaching it on Langham's arm. Somehow, his presence had made the folly seem less imposing. On her own, she felt dwarfed by it, and not a little intimidated. Which was foolish, she chided herself. It was merely an empty space. The new iteration of the Lucifer Society was hardly performing rituals in the caves in broad daylight.

Even so, she was not eager to linger too close to the entrance, and she picked up her pace as she followed the outside wall of the folly.

Here, to her surprise, she saw that a stone monument of a fierce-looking St. Michael had been constructed to the right of the folly. Leaning in to read a plaque that had been placed at the statue's feet, she learned that it was a memorial to Michael Thaddeus Joshua James Fielding, Fourth Duke of Langham.

Something about the choice of Michael the Archangel to memorialize the man who had founded the Lucifer Society struck Poppy as particularly amusing. The archangel, after all, had been the one to cast Lucifer out of heaven. How Langham's great-grandfather would have loathed this. Which served the old reprobate right.

Just then, she spotted a brown and white flash of fur on the far side of the monument.

"Percy," she said in a singsong voice as she approached

where the little dog sat panting and watching her. "Nice Percy, sweet Percy, come to Auntie Poppy."

But as she neared the dog, he darted off again, stopping just far enough away to be out of reach.

Out of breath and losing patience, Poppy decided that the best way to capture the stubborn little animal was to let him come to her.

To that end, she took a seat on the stone base of the memorial and looked down across the grass toward the lake. A glance behind her showed that Percy was watching her. Hopefully it would only take another minute or so for curiosity to get the best of him.

Wishing she'd brought a book or some way to pass the time, she waited with growing impatience for Percy to give up his post and come to her.

Then, with a burst of elation, she remembered that she'd put the list they'd found in Lovell's bedchamber and a pencil in her reticule yesterday. Removing the page and the pencil from the cloth purse, she scanned the words, seven in all, that had been jotted down the page.

Xziobov
Givmgszn
Hgzmmrmth
Yirtsg
Triglm
Nliglm
Kirwv

Examining the letters in the list, she tried a couple of Caesar ciphers first—this was the code that Julius Caesar had used on his own correspondence and was created by shifting each letter of the alphabet a fixed number of letters to the right.

But this method yielded no results for long enough

that Poppy was convinced that she was following the wrong path.

Then, something struck her about the letters in the list. There were an unusually large number of letters that were uncommon, many of them found at the end of the alphabet. But three of the most common letters used in English were vowels—*a*, *e*, and *i*—all of which appeared near the beginning of the alphabet and yet didn't appear in this list at all or in the frequency one would assume.

Deciding that she might have hit on the solution, she tried substituting the alphabet from *a* to *z* with the alphabet from *z* to *a*. That is, *a* = *z*, *b* = *y* and so on.

And just like that, the words on the list began to make sense. They were all surnames. But it was the third surname on the list that made her gasp.

Stannings.

While it was entirely possible that Lovell had been keeping a list of debts, Poppy couldn't forget that the man had been a blackmailer. And the amount beside Stannings's name was by far the highest on the list. Could it be that the magistrate who was meant to be investigating Lovell's death was also one of his blackmail victims? If so, this called into question Stannings's ability to do his job with any degree of impartiality. For all they knew, the magistrate could have been the one to murder Lovell.

Even if Stannings wasn't the one who'd killed her brother-in-law, there were six other names here of potential suspects they should investigate.

She had to show Langham and Eversham the list— surely they'd finished their meetings and tours and had joined the picnic by now.

Percy would have to wait. She'd send one of the grooms after him as soon as she got back to the group.

Standing, she began to walk toward the path leading back to the picnickers. But she hadn't gone more than a few feet before she heard the little dog barking behind her.

With a sigh at the pup's timing, she turned back to see what he was yapping at but was startled to see Sir Geoffrey Stannings approaching from a path near the far side of the folly. Percy, as if recognizing that it would be dangerous to approach him, kept a safe distance away.

"Miss Delamere."

"Sir Geoffrey," she said, clasping a hand to her chest, "you surprised me. I didn't realize there was a path leading up the hill from this side of the folly."

"My apologies, Miss Delamere," the man said, bowing to her. "The way the paths up this hill are laid out is quite as labyrinthine as the caves that lie below them."

Reminding herself that his mention of the caves might be entirely innocent, she made an effort to keep her breathing calm.

"Were you looking for clues related to Mr. Lovell's murder up at St. Lucifer's?" she asked, keeping the subject to his work on the murder case, rather than alerting him that she now suspected he might have been being blackmailed by her brother-in-law.

"Clever girl," said Stannings with a wink. "That's exactly what I was doing."

Poppy didn't care for being called a girl. And certainly not by this man. But she schooled her features not to show it.

Instead she said, "Have you had any luck? It seems as if the site has been looked over so many times now by so many people that there would be nothing left to find."

"You might well think so, Miss Delamere," he said thoughtfully. "But you'd be surprised what can be discovered when one has a familiarity with the area. Why don't you come over here and tell me whether you think this might go some ways toward clearing your sister's name."

Poppy's instincts were telling her in every way not to trust Stannings. And remembering how one of Kate and Caro's earliest columns had warned vulnerable women to eschew good manners when they felt themselves to be in danger, she did just that.

Rather than moving closer to him, as he'd suggested, she turned to run in the opposite direction. Percy, who by this time had grown weary of barking at Stannings, ran after her.

But she hadn't counted on the fact that Stannings was faster, and she soon found herself being towed backward by the magistrate, one of his hands clapped over her mouth so that her shriek of outrage went unheard. In the scuffle, she felt his shirt rip beneath her grasp, and felt a grim note of satisfaction at the thought even as she watched Percy run toward the front of the folly and presumably down the hill.

Poppy hoped against hope that his return without her would be noticed.

"It's really too bad I've had to resort to this, Miss Delamere," said Stannings with a grunt as he caught one of her elbows in his ribs, "but it's only a matter of time before you and your lover realize it was me you saw in the cave last night."

And before she could reply, Poppy felt herself being pushed forward. The next thing she knew she was hurtling downward into nothingness.

Chapter Twenty-Four

When Langham went in search of Poppy, he was informed that she'd gone with the rest of the ladies to the picnic on the other side of the lake. Cursing, he remembered that the gentlemen had been meant to join them after their ride. His interview with Jarvis had pushed the outing from his mind.

He took the stairs two at a time, and when he reached the entry hall where the rest of the men were donning their outer clothes before they set out for the picnic, he pulled Val aside. "Stay here for a moment."

Then turning to Jenkins, he asked, "Have Eversham and my brother left for the picnic yet?"

"I don't believe so, Your Grace," Jenkins said with a frown. "Shall I send one of the footmen—"

Before the butler could finish the question, Eversham and Lord Adrian appeared at the top of the stairs.

With instincts no doubt honed by years of policework, Eversham's gaze sharpened at once. "What's amiss?" he asked as he and Adrian all but ran down the stairs to meet Langham and Val.

Deciding it would be best to keep their conversation from being overheard, Langham gestured for the others to join him in a small parlor off the entry hall.

Quickly, he told the men what he'd learned from Ned about Stannings.

"But you've known Stannings since you were a boy," Adrian said with a shake of his head. "He's one of the most respected members of this part of Buckinghamshire, not to mention England."

"Before our great-grandfather's involvement in the Lucifer Society became known," Langham reminded his brother, "he, too, was well respected."

"What could Lovell have been blackmailing the fellow over?" Eversham asked. "We know Lovell used his knowl-edge of Short's schemes in order to gain a wife, but if Stannings was cheated out of funds by Short, that would hardly be something to hold against the man being cheated."

Telling them that Lovell had mentioned "bringing down the whole society," Langham related what he and Poppy had seen last night in the cave.

Val whistled. "Someone has revived your ancestor's satanic club?"

"You aristocrats never cease to amaze me with the more and more outlandish ways you find to get into trouble." Eversham sounded disgusted.

Ignoring the detective's taunt, Langham said, "I need to find Poppy and tell her about Stannings. Whoever locked us in may have deduced that we were in the caves. If Stannings has heard about this, then he could have reason to hurt her."

"And you too, brother," Adrian said with a scowl. "I have no wish to become duke."

"I have no intention of allowing that to happen anytime soon," Langham assured his brother as he moved toward the doorway. To the others he said, "We need to get to the picnic. If I know Poppy and your wives, then they are taking the opportunity to do a little investigating. And if Stannings finds them, he might seize the opportunity to harm them."

"Lead on," Val said, "though we might better arm ourselves before we confront Stannings. If he's our man, he's already killed once. "

"The gun room is this way," Langham said, leading the men out to the hall.

Once they were equipped with the necessary weaponry, they set out.

When they reached the area where the picnic had been laid out, Langham was alarmed to see that neither Poppy nor Kate nor Caro were among the group.

"Where are Miss Delamere and her friends?" he asked his sister Charlotte, who was peeling an apple.

"Oh, they wandered off on the other side of the folly," she said with a wave in that direction. "Well, that's not entirely accurate. Poppy went chasing after Grandmama's little beast of a dog. You know what a devil Percy can be when he doesn't wish to be caught. Then Lady Katherine said something about it being a rather long time since she'd gone, and she and Lady Wrackham left their own unfinished plates here and disappeared after her. I do like your Poppy, but she and her friends are odd ones, make no mistake on it, Joshua."

Not bothering to reply, Langham raced off toward the folly, Adrian, Eversham, and Val not far behind. When he reached the far side of the folly, he saw Kate and Caro standing near a tree and staring down at the ground.

When they saw him, he saw Kate give a sigh of relief.

"Thank heavens you're here," she said, as Eversham strode toward her. But she held up a hand. "Don't come any farther. There's a trapdoor of some sort right here. I believe Poppy must have fallen down it, but Caro and I have no way of knowing for certain. We cannot see anything down there, it's so dark."

Langham remembered that there had been an entrance to the caves embedded in the ground near here. He and Stannings had climbed a rope ladder leading in and out of the tunnel beneath often as children.

"Have either of you seen anyone else wandering around up here?" he asked the two ladies. "A gentleman?" He described the man he'd known almost as well as he'd known himself when they were youths. It was hard to believe someone could change so much, but he supposed it had been some time since he really had any sort of meaningful conversation with the man. They'd both been busy with their own lives and, as sometimes happened, drifted apart.

"No," Caro said frowning. "No one. Who is it you suspect we might have seen?"

"The local magistrate, Sir Geoffrey," Val said, slipping an arm about his wife's waist. "Langham thinks he may have reason to harm Poppy."

"What?" Caro covered her mouth with her hand in shock.

Langham left it to the others to explain his suspicions about Stannings while he headed for the entrance to the folly. Once inside, he lit the lantern and quickly found the mechanism for the hidden door. And then, without a moment's hesitation, he stepped into the dimly lit stairway and began his descent to the caves below.

The fall wasn't quite so far as Poppy had feared, and when she landed on the hard ground of what she could now see was part of the network of caves, she saw that there was a rope ladder hanging down from the square of light in the ceiling above her. If her foot had got caught in it she might have broken her neck.

Which was, perhaps, not an unwanted outcome in Stannings's mind.

As it was, she'd twisted her ankle when she landed, and it hurt like the very devil.

Wincing, she tried to massage it a little as she watched the magistrate descend the ladder.

Stannings leapt nimbly from the last rung and then, with a deft pull, unhooked the ladder from where it was moored at the ceiling.

"I do apologize for that, Miss Delamere," he said, moving to light a lamp that hung from the wall behind her. "These old cave entrances can be treacherous. Even more so when you're tossed in, of course."

He chuckled wryly at his own cruel joke.

"It was you last night," Poppy said as she saw a golden necklace and pendant like the one she'd found in her sister's room hanging about the man's neck, now visible thanks to the tear she'd made in his shirt as they'd scuffled above ground. "Leading the ritual in the cave."

"Indeed," he said with a bow. "If I'd known we'd have an audience, I would have arranged for a more exciting performance. Though I suppose the party afterward was display enough for your poor innocent eyes. And if I know Langham, he used the opportunity to press his suit, so to speak." He laughed as if he'd made an amusing joke, and Poppy felt her insides roil with disgust.

"I had men keeping watch last night, and the one near

the folly saw the two of you disappear inside. The clever fellow thought it best to keep you in there for a bit so you couldn't summon anyone to break up our little gathering," Stannings continued. "Although poor Langham, he does so hate enclosed spaces. Never did get over that unfortunate incident in the tower. I had no idea it would follow him all these years later."

He chuckled mirthlessly at the memory, and Poppy went cold at the sound before a fiery anger overtook her.

"You know about his fear?" Poppy demanded. Then she realized the truth. "Of course you know. You were the one who locked him in the tower all those years ago."

"Very good, Miss Delamere," Stannings said, clapping his hands sarcastically. "But really, someone had to keep him from becoming full of his own importance. And yet he wasn't at all interested in the greatest legacy his great-grandfather left him, if you can believe it. I thought spending time alone in St. Lucifer's might change that. Instead, his time in the tower brought an outcome even better than I could ever have imagined."

Poppy's stomach dropped to think of the cruelty Langham had suffered as a boy, and suffered still, but she knew better than to let her emotions show.

Stannings clucked his tongue in disappointment. "It's really too bad the two of you won't be able to wed as you'd intended. Unfortunately, you'll be out of the picture before dear Langham will be able to do right by you. It's a shame. I thought the two of you made a handsome couple. If you and your interfering sister had just accepted my plan to have her take the blame for Lovell's murder, none of this would be happening. Though I suppose Lovell himself must accept some of the responsibility. He is the one who decided to blackmail me, after all."

So, it was clear at last. Lovell had attempted to coerce the wrong man and had paid the price for it. Poppy tried to summon some sympathy for her brother-in-law, but all she felt was disgust.

"That's enough chatter," Stannings said now, even though he was the only one who'd been talking. "Let's go. Up with you."

Poppy tried to stand, but when she put weight on her foot, the pain was excruciating and her ankle would not hold her.

Her cry of distress didn't move her captor, however. "Oh, do not pretend you've truly hurt yourself, Miss Delamere. That must be the oldest ruse in the maiden's handbook. Right next to the conveniently timed swoon. Now, get up before I am forced to hurt you in earnest."

"My ankle is truly injured, Sir Geoffrey," Poppy said, alarm coursing through her at what he might do to her if she could not follow his demands. "I landed on it when I fell."

"Of course you did, silly bitch," Stannings said with disgust. "Come on, then." He reached an arm down to help her to her feet, and despite her distrust of him, it was clear he'd believed her at last.

They hobbled along together for several feet, going deeper into the caves, before he halted.

"Can't you go any faster?" he groused. And before Poppy could object, he swung her into his arms. Unable to stop herself, she recoiled away from his body.

"Don't be such a simpering virgin," Stannings snapped. "I daresay your darling Langham has probably used you well enough."

At the mention of Langham, Poppy felt a surge of energy rush through her. She would get out of here alive.

Because she didn't care if he'd proposed to her out of some misguided sense of chivalry. His honor was, for better or worse, part of who he was. And faced with Stannings, who had no honor at all, she realized that it had been a straw she was clutching at in order to protect herself from the vulnerability it would take to tell Langham—Joshua— just how she truly felt about him. She loved him, and if— no, *when* she got away from this madman, she would tell him so.

Knowing she needed to distract Stannings if she was going to find a way to escape, she asked, "I suppose Lovell used your leadership of the Lucifer Society to blackmail you?"

"He was not the most intelligent of men, your brother-in-law," said Stannings with a nasty laugh.

They'd been following a circuitous path through the cave system until they reached a room not unlike the one where she and Langham had seen the Lucifer Society gathering the night before.

"Here we are," said Stannings with an almost gleeful tone. "The perfect location for our virgin sacrifice. Though we'll just keep the knowledge that you're probably no longer virginal between us."

He carried her to a raised dais, a thronelike chair sitting atop it. Setting the lantern down on the floor, he then raised her onto the chair and deposited her with a groan. "You're much heavier than you look, Miss Delamere. I'd say you might consider foregoing dessert for the next few weeks, but that won't be an issue, will it?"

Grateful to be away from him at last, Poppy glanced about the room as Stannings went around lighting the lanterns that hung from the walls.

"What is this place?" she asked, thinking that it looked

more cavernous than the room where last night's gathering had taken place.

"We use it for assemblies when the entire society is in attendance," Stannings said over his shoulder. "Last night we were just a small gathering. One day soon we'll have a large feast, just as Thaddeus did in the old days."

Poppy hated to think how many members the entire society encompassed. There was something disturbing about a large number of the county's most respected leaders agreeing to participate in such a spectacle.

She scanned the room for something—anything—that could be used as a weapon. Finding nothing, she surreptitiously ran her hand along the cushion beneath her. She'd just felt the edge of a hard object when she heard a voice she'd been terrified she'd never hear again.

"Sorry to interrupt your celebration, Stannings old fellow, but I'm afraid your guest of honor is leaving with me."

Chapter Twenty-Five

Langham held his pistol trained on Stannings, his arm steady as he watched his quarry startle at the interruption.

"What a spoilsport you are, Langham," the magistrate said, rising slowly from where he'd been crouched beside the throne, arranging tinder. "I vow old Thaddeus would be disappointed beyond measure at your cowardice. Even I am not going so far as he would have done. I daresay he'd have fucked the chit before setting fire to her. Where are my thanks for sparing your beloved that indignity?"

Langham had been prepared for Stannings to taunt him, but even so it took all of his self-control to keep from reacting. He needed to get Poppy away from this madman, and he couldn't do that if he let Stannings see the rage that was burning within him.

"You see, Stannings," he said conversationally, never lowering his weapon, "I do not measure my worth based on the opinions of a man who's been dead for a half century. I thought we'd agreed when we were sixteen that his society was little more than a weak man preying on his underlings in order to make himself feel strong. He was a pretender. Just like you."

"There's where you're wrong, Langham." Stannings's brown eyes were almost black with fury. "I am more powerful than he was. And I haven't had to pledge my soul to Satan in order to do it."

"Perhaps not. But you pledged yourself—or at least your money—to Alistair Lovell. And I'm sure Lord Short enjoyed having the local magistrate under his thumb," Langham said, hoping to draw a response from Stannings that would incriminate him as well as Lovell and Short. "It must have been quite a shock to be invited into their society, only to have them use it against you."

"Short is a fool. It was *my* idea to resurrect the Lucifer Society and lure these idiotic yokels into participating. From there it was easy to convince them to invest in Short's schemes. And if they suspected they'd been fleeced, it was easy enough to remind them that their involvement in the society would be delightful fodder for the press." Stannings was clearly reveling in his accomplishments, and Langham wished nothing more than to knock the smug expression from the man's face.

"He'd never bothered trying to keep his victims quiet when he'd conducted his schemes before," Poppy interjected, and Langham wasn't at all surprised to hear her voice was strong and steady.

"You have been away for some time, Miss Delamere," the magistrate sneered. "Your stepfather isn't as young as he once was. His wish is to remain in Little Kidding for the rest of his days."

Before Poppy could respond, Stannings lifted her to

her feet, and she cried out with what sounded like pain. As Langham watched, the viscount pulled her against him with his arm tight about her neck.

Langham had never wanted to kill a man, but at this very moment he could very well imagine using his bare hands to wring the life from Stannings. But as he watched, Poppy shook her head slightly, her gaze directed at his hands, which he hadn't even realized he'd clenched into fists.

"Look at you, Langham," jeered the magistrate. "One would think you actually loved the lady. You're an even bigger fool than I thought. No man of sense would ally himself to a wife for any other reason than wealth or status. And pretty Poppy can bring you neither."

"Let her go," Langham said, his voice hoarse with emotion as he watched Poppy struggle against Stannings's hold on her. "She's done nothing to you. If you want to kill someone, take me."

"Oh, I intend to," Stannings said with a cold smile. "Make no mistake about that."

Langham caught a glint of light at Poppy's side, just where her right hand was clasped tight against herself.

What the devil?

To his astonishment, he saw that she was gripping a long knife by the hilt. He might have known that his clever, clever Poppy would have found a weapon to save herself.

As long as Stannings didn't use the knife against her.

Thinking to distract the other man and buy Poppy some time to enact her plan, Langham called out to him. "You killed Lovell. Tell me how you managed it. You at least owe me that, in honor of our friendship all those years ago."

Stannings looked annoyed. "*Friendship*. What sort of friendship is it where one boy has the whole world laid out before him and the other is reminded at every turn how inferior he is? Friendship, bah."

"But you must surely have had a good reason for doing away with the man," Langham went on in another attempt to draw a confession out of Stannings. He'd admitted his involvement with Lovell and Short, but it was his confession to killing Lovell that would free Violet. "From everything I've learned, Lovell was a criminal. He was blackmailing several men in the village. Were you one of them?"

"Of course," Stannings said curtly. "But when Lovell tried his games on me, he didn't realize he'd crossed the wrong man. He'd already made the mistake of threatening his father-in-law. And there was that trouble with Lord Twombley and some flunky in the Foreign Office that he'd dispatched. He really was getting very full of himself."

While Stannings ranted, Langham saw on the periphery of his vision that Adrian, Val, and Eversham had begun creeping from the side tunnels and out along the edges of the main room toward the dais.

As they neared the center of the room, Poppy chose that moment to jam her knife into Stannings's side. From that angle she couldn't do much damage, but it was enough to startle him. When he cried out and instinctively let her go, she leapt from the dais to the floor.

Eversham and Val rushed forward and gripped a cursing Stannings by the arms. Adrian stood to the side, aiming a pistol at their captive.

"Love." Langham knelt down beside her and scooped her into his arms. "Are you hurt?"

"I twisted my ankle when he threw me down the trapdoor," she explained as she wrapped her arms around him. "That's all. He didn't harm me otherwise."

"Thank God," he whispered against her hair, more grateful than he'd ever been in his life to have her safe.

"I was afraid, Joshua," she said against his neck, her voice trembling in a way that made him wish he could give Stannings the thrashing he deserved. "I thought...I thought I was going to die before you were able to find me. And I wouldn't get the chance to tell you how much I love you."

She pulled back and looked at him, her cornflower blue eyes shiny with tears. "Because I do, you see. I love you. I know it's not convenient. You never mentioned anything about love when you proposed. Friendship, yes. But never—"

"I love you too," Langham said, leaning his forehead against hers. "I should have said so when I made that damned botched proposal, but I thought you were too sensible to think of marrying me because of something as sentimental as love. But dear God, Poppy, I feel so much more for you than mere friendship."

"Oh, I do too," she said leaning in to kiss him.

But before their lips could touch, Eversham broke in. "I hate to interrupt your tête-à-tête, but we wanted to let you know that we are taking Stannings away now."

Langham rose to his feet and then lifted Poppy into his arms. "We'll come along. Poppy's ankle needs to be seen by the physician."

Stannings, who had his hands bound behind his back with his own neckcloth, looked disgusted at the sight of them. "Who would have guessed that the great-grandson of the great Thaddeus Fielding, first master of the Lucifer Society, would turn out to be such a conventional bore."

"Darling," Langham said to Poppy, "do me a favor and untie my neckcloth."

Poppy gave him a questioning look but nevertheless reached up to unravel the cloth. When she was finished she asked, "Now what?"

"Hand it to my brother," Langham instructed. "I believe Stannings is in need of a gag."

"Gladly," Adrian said taking the tie from Poppy and stuffing it into a protesting Stannings's mouth.

But any silence they might have enjoyed with the villain gagged was interrupted by the arrival of Percy, who obviously held a grudge over the way Stannings had mistreated Poppy. Leaping at the magistrate, Percy sank his teeth into the man's trouser leg and refused to let go.

"Good boy, Percy," Poppy crooned from her perch in Langham's arms. "He deserves a beefsteak at least, Lord Adrian."

Finally managing to unclench the little dog's teeth from Stannings, who was shouting as well as one could with a gag in one's mouth, Adrian gave Percy a good rubdown.

"I'll make sure he gets one," he told Poppy before disappearing up the stairs to remove him from the cave.

"There," Langham said as he followed his brother toward the stairway. "Now, what were we talking about?"

"How you love me?" Poppy offered, nestling her head into the crook of his neck.

"Yes," he said, appreciating the feel of her in his arms. "I think it must have been the way your eyes flashed when..."

And as he carried her out of the cave and then the folly, he enumerated all the ways in which he'd been falling in love with her bit by bit since she'd run into him in Paddington Station.

Poppy, whom he had always been convinced was the cleverest of ladies, didn't utter a word of protest.

Chapter Twenty-Six

One month later

I t's still difficult for me to believe that only weeks ago we had no notion of who you really were and you hadn't even met the Duke of Langham yet," said Caro from where she'd tucked herself into one of the chairs surrounding the tea table in the Duchess of Langham's private sitting room.

"How do you think I feel?" the duchess asked, passing a plate of lemon biscuits to Kate, who sat on Caro's other side.

It had been two weeks since Poppy's wedding by special license to the Duke of Langham. In the storied St. George's, Hanover Square, no less. But, as Langham had agreed, to marry quietly as they both would have preferred would have given the gossips far too much to speculate over. Much better to do the thing out in the open, sending invitations to every last member of the *ton*, the idea being that the more transparently they behaved, the more the public would believe they had nothing to hide.

And, in truth, thought Poppy, the gossips already knew the worst there was to know about her.

Once Stannings was taken into custody for kidnapping Poppy, murdering Lovell, and the various other crimes he'd perpetrated with Lord Short, Eversham had managed to get the disgraced magistrate to disclose everything he knew about Lord Short's misdeeds. He'd even told the detective inspector about the murders Lovell had committed on Lord Short's behalf, including those of Henry Riggle of the Foreign Office and Lord Twombley, whom Lovell killed because Twombley had become suspicious about Short and Lovell's South American railroad scheme in the Amazon.

As a result, Lord Short was also taken into custody. But before he could be questioned, he'd hanged himself in his jail cell, robbing his victims of the chance to see him brought to justice.

"How are your mama and sister?" Kate asked Poppy, returning the plate to the table.

Poppy sobered. Though her mother had long ago lost any affection she might have felt for her husband, the sudden change in her circumstances and the shame of having his crimes known publicly had taken a toll on her. But to Poppy's relief, she'd agreed to make her home in London at Langham House. In truth, the house was so large that Lady Short could have hidden herself away in her suite of rooms and never had to see another person again for an entire year if she didn't wish it.

"Mama is doing a bit better," Poppy told her friends. "I think she's finally coming to realize that she can make her own decisions about what she wishes to do with her life. And I must admit, for me, it's been a relief to have both her and Violet near me after we were separated for so long."

Taking another biscuit—really she had to tell Mrs. Phipps, the cook, just how delicious they were—Poppy considered Violet's situation. "My sister will be going back to the abbey at the end of the week. She's been far too lonely for her dear Mr. Jarvis, and given how unhappy her marriage to Lovell was, I can hardly blame her."

"Nor can I," Caro said with a frown. "She deserves every bit of happiness that life has to offer her."

"I'm just delighted that Ned is a good man," Poppy said, grinning. "And he clearly adores my sister. That she'll be near enough that our children can grow up together is merely an added bonus."

Caro raised a brow. "Is there something you'd like to tell us, Your Grace?" she asked with a pointed look in the direction of Poppy's midsection.

Blushing, Poppy turned an aggrieved look toward Kate. "Can you not stop her from teasing me like this every time we are together?"

To Caro she said with a lift of her chin, "I have nothing to tell you, Lady Wrackham. Just as I did not the last four times you asked."

But Caro was unrepentant. "It's just that I know what it's like to be a newlywed. Why, there was hardly a day that went by that Val and I weren't f—"

"Caro!" Kate gasped, raising a hand to her bosom in mock horror. "Poor Poppy will stop inviting us to take tea with her."

"You didn't let me finish," Caro said with a pointed look. Turning to Poppy she said, "There was hardly a day that went by that Val and I weren't *finding* some way to be alone together."

"Yes, I'm sure that's what you were going to say," Poppy said with exasperation. "I hope you aren't so plainspoken in the presence of my darling feline nephew. Poor Ludwig is far too young for such earthy language."

Caro was spared from reply by the sound of a brisk knock on the door and the sight of the Duke of Langham's head poking around the corner. "I do not mean to disturb you ladies, but I wondered if I might borrow Poppy for a minute."

Once again Poppy felt her cheeks heat, only this time it was from the way his blue eyes caressed her.

Kate, perhaps seeing just how the newlyweds were gazing at one another, rose. "Never fear, Duke. Caro and I were just leaving. Weren't we, Lady Wrackham?" she asked before pulling her friend to her feet.

"We were?" Caro asked, grabbing up another biscuit from the tea table. Then, glancing over at Poppy, she must have seen the wisdom of Kate's decision. "We were," she agreed.

Before Kate could lead her away, however, Caro leaned down and kissed Poppy on the cheek. "I'm so pleased for you. Truly."

And then Kate and Caro were gone.

Once the door into the hallway was closed behind them, Langham leaned back against it and surveyed her lazily. "Did you enjoy the visit with your friends?" he asked, pushing off from the door.

"I did," Poppy said, removing the pins from her hair as she watched him approach. "But we can talk about them later."

"Can we?" he asked, unbuttoning his coat. "What shall we talk about instead?"

"I don't know." Her hair streaming over her shoulders, Poppy rose and met her husband on the far side of the room, where he stood in just his shirtsleeves. Running her arms up his chest and around his neck, she said thoughtfully, "I'll let you know if I think of something."

Slipping his arm beneath her knees, Joshua lifted her into his arms and walked toward the door leading into her bedchamber. "I have a better idea," he said.

"Don't keep me in suspense," Poppy said as he kicked the door shut behind them. "Do tell."

Without a word, he turned and let her slide down his body, then pressed her back against the door.

"You make a good point," she said as he took her mouth.

And it was quite a long while before they spoke again.

Acknowledgments

Every book is different. For some reason—maybe, you know, everything?—this was a tough one for me. So that means I am especially grateful for all the professionals, family, and friends who made it possible to produce this book.

Thanks to my truly extraordinary agent, Holly Root, who is always there when I'm in neurotic creative mode to talk me down with humor and grace. And who handles the data and numbers and everything that my lit major brain just cannot grok. I'm so lucky you took a chance on me lo these many years ago.

Thanks to my sharp-eyed and amazing editor, Amy Pierpont, who gets what I'm saying even when I don't. Your insightful suggestions and helpful critiques have made me a better writer. You rock, lady!

Thanks to the rest of the Forever team, including Sam Brody, who keeps me on track with deadlines and from making "Gen X in a Gen Z world" mistakes; my amazing former marketing and publicity guru Jodi Rosoff, who is very much missed; my current marketing and publicity guru Dana Cuadrado, who is probably the only person in the world capable of making me do Instagram videos; Senior Production Editor Carolyn Kurek, who makes the finished product happen; copy editor Lori Paximadis, who ensures my text is as error free as possible (all errors are my own); and finally all the sales team folks who I never get to meet who are out there flogging my books in the real world. Truly the Forever folks are the hardest working team in the book business (though I might be a little biased).

Thanks to the amazingly talented Sarah Congdon, who has outdone herself with every cover illustration.

Thanks to my writing friends, who keep me sane, and who understand this truly weird business in ways nobody else can: Cindy, Katie, Angela, Rachel, Gwen, and Lindsey. Love you guys!

My Twitter buddies, who laugh at my dumb jokes and are always there with an elegant riposte or a dirty joke when I need one, especially Limecello, my agency twin Megan B., Liz L., Tamara L., Carrie L., Emma B., Beverly K., Lorelei B., Adele B., Deneen S., Santa B., and probably dozens more I'm forgetting. We often refer to Twitter as a hell site, but I've managed to curate a pretty delightful group of friends there.

Sue, Nancy, Dee, Babe, Jessie, Vince, and all the cousins. Y'all might not all read my books because "it sounds just like" me, but you're pretty great cheerleaders anyway. Love you.

And last but not least, my always entertaining little pal Toast the cat. Who is at this moment tucked under my arm while I'm trying to type.

About the Author

Manda Collins grew up on a combination of Nancy Drew books and Jane Austen novels, and her own brand of historical romantic suspense is the result. A former academic librarian, she holds master's degrees in English and Library & Information Studies. She lives on the Gulf Coast with a squirrel-fighting cat and more books than are strictly necessary.

You can learn more at:
MandaCollins.com
Twitter @MandaCollins
Facebook.com/MandaCollinsAuthor
Instagram @MandaCollinsAuthor
Pinterest.com/MandaCollinsAut

Get swept off your feet by charming dukes and sharp-witted ladies in Forever's historical romances!

A SPINSTER'S GUIDE TO DANGER AND DUKES
by Manda Collins

Miss Poppy Delamare left her family to escape an odious betrothal, but when her sister is accused of murder, she cannot stay away. Even if she must travel with the arrogant Duke of Langham. To her surprise, he offers a mutually beneficial arrangement: a fake betrothal will both protect Poppy and her sister and deter Society misses from Langham. But as real feelings begin to grow, can they find truth and turn their engagement into reality—before Poppy becomes the next victim?

ALWAYS BE MY DUCHESS
by Amalie Howard

Because ballerina Geneviève Valery refused a patron's advances, she is hopelessly out of work. But then Lord Lysander Blackstone, the heartless Duke of Montcroix, makes Nève an offer she would be a fool to refuse. Montcroix's ruthlessness has jeopardized a new business deal, so if Nève acts as his fake fiancée and salvages his reputation, he'll give her fortune enough to start over. Only neither is prepared when very *real* feelings begin to grow between them…

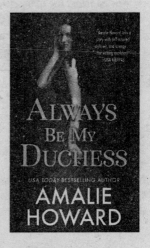

Connect with us at Facebook.com/ReadForeverPub

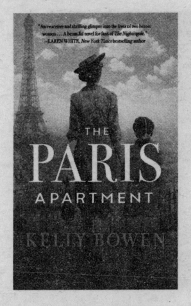

THE PARIS APARTMENT
by Kelly Bowen

2017, London: When Aurelia Leclaire inherits an opulent Paris apartment, she is shocked to discover her grandmother's secrets—including a treasure trove of famous art and couture gowns.

Paris, 1942: Glamorous Estelle Allard flourishes in a world separate from the hardships of war. But when the Nazis come for her friends, Estelle doesn't hesitate to help those she holds dear, no matter the cost.

Both Estelle and Lia must summon hidden courage as they alter history—and the future of their families—forever.

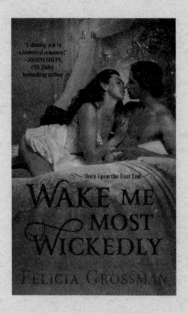

WAKE ME MOST WICKEDLY
by Felicia Grossman

To repay his half-brother, Solomon Weiss gladly pursues money and influence—until outcast Hannah Moses saves his life. He's irresistibly drawn to her beauty and wit, but Hannah tells him she's no savior. To care for her sister, she heartlessly hunts criminals for London's underbelly. Which makes Sol far too respectable for her. Only neither can resist their desires—until Hannah discovers a betrayal that will break Sol's heart. Can she convince Sol to trust her? Or will fear and doubt poison their love?